INDEBTED

KING BROTHERS BOOK TWO

LISA LANG BLAKENEY

WRITERGIRL PRESS

This Is Dedicated To My Dad, Walt, Who Should Never Read This Book But Who Has Always Encouraged My Love For Reading & Writing. Thanks Daddy!

BOOKS BY LISA

The Masterson Series

Masterson

Masterson Unleashed

Masterson In Love

Joseph Loves Juliette

The King Brothers Series

Claimed

Indebted

Broken

Promised

The Nighthawk Series

Gunslinger

Wolf

Diesel

The Valencia Mafia Series

Rum Runners

INTRODUCTION

There's something about Cutter King that reminds me of every bad relationship I've been in and every bad decision I've ever made…

He's desperately good looking, but he knows it. He's built sturdy and strong like a tank, but he's reckless. He looks like every woman's fantasy, yet for me he's a nightmare. Too bad I owe him big time. And now he's moved in next door to collect.

AUTHOR'S PROMISE: This is a full length, standalone novel, featuring a strong alpha with no cheating (and as always) a happily ever after. Be advised that due to strong language and yummy sex, this book is not intended for the easily offended or readers under 18.

ONE

CUTTER

Twelve Years Ago

I lift my knees higher and higher.

My feet move swiftly.

My breaths heave rapidly.

I move as fast as humanly possible, but the price of speed is that my feet hurt like hell. The inside seams of my Chucks are rubbing against my feet and ankles, and I'm going to have huge blisters by the end of the night. On top of all of that, I'm sweating like a country fair pig.

"We're going to get in on the other side!" my brother Camden yells at me with hurried breaths. "Move your ass."

Right this very second, the two of us are being chased by a pair of rent-a-cops. Stadium security. They caught us trying to sneak in to watch the first playoff game of the season. This series is a big deal to us and to the city, and we want the bragging rights to say that we were "there" for at least one playoff game for our hometown team.

We've been running from these two bozos for what seems like forever, because we're not trying to leave the stadium, we're actually still trying to find another way inside. We're counting on the strong probability that eventually these two fat fucks will give up running after us. They don't carry guns and they're not paid enough to put forth the effort. It's just going to take them a minute to realize it.

"Five more minutes and they're going to quit. They're already slowing down." My brother laughs as we continue to sprint around the corner of the massive building. "Let's split up, and I'll meet you inside at the spot."

I turn my head to take another look and notice that one of the men is severely out of breath. Holding his palm to his chest. His body hungry for oxygen. The other guard also notices his partner is in distress and slows down to assist. Camden was right. They're done.

I keep moving and try jiggling a few door handles until I reach a blue painted steel door that's open. It's probably a staff entrance, because it's close to something called the Omni Lounge. Some private area the ball players probably chill in after the game. I get a couple of looks from people walking by but not suspicious ones. That's when I know I'm finally safe. I'm smiling from ear to ear in triumph, not paying attention, when I run into something or rather someone.

"Ouch!"

I run right into her. The most beautiful girl in the entire stadium. The girl I'm going to marry (if I ever do something dumb like get married).

She's definitely my age if not a little younger. Her hair is pulled back into a shiny, jet black ponytail and it shimmies playfully against her honey colored flesh. She's wearing braces, and she's tall and sort of gangly, but her eyes are the shapes of almonds and they dance when she speaks. They brighten her entire face. In fact, they brighten this entire building.

"Watch where you're going, meathead," she says with what I suppose is her angry face. Eyes still sparkling but mouth really serious.

I'm not used to girls talking to me the way that she does. I'm tall for my age and not bad looking at all. Girls usually act goofy, lost for words, and giggle around me. Definitely not this.

"My bad." Is all I manage to respond with while staring at her glossy pink lips. Wondering what section of the city she lives in. Where she goes to school. If she has a boyfriend. If she's ever had a boyfriend.

"Eww, you're all sweaty." She points out the obvious with her face squished up.

I laugh out loud.

"What's so funny?" she asks. Perhaps afraid that I'm laughing at her. I'm not. I'm just amused by her spunk. Most girls find me intimidating. I'm really big for my age. She apparently could care less.

"What school do you go to?" I ask.

"Definitely not yours," she says.

"Can I get your phone number?"

"For what?"

"To call you."

"I'm too young to date."

"I just want to be friends," I lie.

"I don't need any more friends."

"You're hurting my feelings," I say giving her my biggest smile.

"I think you'll be okay." She smiles back.

That smile.

It's like sunshine.

I want to talk longer. I want to ask her a thousand questions. But before we can finish talking, two men walk over and move together to stand in front of her. Forming a human shield with serious "don't fuck with her" looks across their faces.

I've had my share of fights in school and with kids in the neighborhood, but I've never gone toe to toe with a grown man before. Not to mention two. I don't want to look like a pussy in front of her though, so my suicidal ass actually considers throwing my hands up for a moment until I hear my name being bellowed from behind me.

"Cut!"

My brother is flying around the corridor toward me at record breaking speed. At first, I think it's because he's still being chased, but then I quickly realize it's because he thinks I'm in trouble.

Crap.

Cam and I are practically carbon copies of each other. When we run, people notice. Something which isn't a good idea if the plan is to sneak in here and watch the game.

"It's cool." I try throwing my hand up to stop his approach, but it's a little too late. The two beefy dudes get into a defensive formation in response to Camden, and thanks to that we've gotten the attention of too many other people as well.

Including security.

"Is everything all right over here?"

"Dammit, Cutter," my brother mutters only loud enough for me to hear.

"What?" I whisper angrily. "You're the one who came barreling over here like someone had a gun to my head, big goober."

"Everything's fine, sir," I say in an attempt to salvage our evening, although I don't know what we're going to do if the guards ask to see our tickets. We don't have any. "My brother here misread the situation and thought I was in some sort of trouble, so he rushed over. Everything's all good."

One of the beefy dudes standing in front of my dream girl interjects.

"Actually, you both seem to be in some sort of rush. Your brother running through a crowd of people toward us like he was on the attack, and you almost knocking over this young lady rushing to wherever you were headed as well."

"There's no law against running is there?" I smile and say before Camden opens his big mouth, because if he does it's probably going to be something adversarial and then we'll really be up shit's creek.

Then *she* speaks.

"Oh my God, Percy, it's not a big deal. I'm fine. They didn't do anything. Can't we just go to our seats now?"

The stadium security guard's eyes enlarge. He seems to suddenly recognize the girl and now seems super concerned.

"Sorry to hold you up, miss. Please go take your seat. We can handle this."

I know *this* means we're about to be thrown out of here. Maybe even detained in the back office if he realizes that we don't have tickets.

I decide to look at her one more time. Commit her pretty face to memory. When I do she blushes and looks away. Before he died, our father taught us a lot about reading body language. He said it was a skill that would save our asses one day, but it's also a superpower I can use to read girls, and I like what her body is saying.

Cheers ring out in the stadium.

The starters on the home team are being introduced onto the stadium floor.

"Come on, Percy. Dad will kill me if he notices that I'm not in my seat."

She glances up at me one last time, whips her silkened ponytail around, and walks away. I continue to watch her as her narrow hips sway behind the two.

"What the hell was that?" my brother asks as we exit the stadium with a security escort and long faces. "Was she someone we were supposed to know? What was up with those two goons guarding her?"

"I'm not sure *what* that was."

"You should have just said excuse me to her and kept going to the meeting point."

"I know."

"Well I hope you realize that you've just blown our chance at watching a playoff game live. Now we've got to watch it at home like all the other suckers. I've never seen you act like that. She couldn't have been any older than fourteen."

"Probably."

He snaps his fingers in front of my face.

"I don't know what she said to you, but she must be one hell of a girl to get your undivided attention."

"I think she is."

"Well shake it off. It's not like you're ever going to see her again."

I have a feeling that I will though.

It's just a matter of time.

TWO

SLOAN

My heart, my liver, my lungs.

My heart, my liver, my lungs.

Every one of my internal organs seems to pulse in tandem with the beat of the song playing inside Lotus. An instrumental, bass heavy, dance song that is as familiar as apple pie on a Friday night in Philadelphia. The energy is so thick inside of the club tonight, that I could cut it with a knife and spread it on a piece of toast.

Endless bodies are winding and coiling around each other on the dance floor. Writhing to the beat in a sexual tango. A prelude of what's to come at the end of the night for some. It's quite a hypnotic experience. Even if you're just watching.

I'm a party girl by nature, but I come to this club specifically for the unique experience, the stunning ambience, and the beautiful people. Working the room of a place like Lotus gives me the most incredible high.

I usually go clubbing with a girlfriend or two, or sometimes with a group of coworkers, but I never stay with them all night. That's no way to meet a man. I'd rather fly solo. I think it was one of my mom's nutty friends who taught me that dating strategy.

I dance to be seen. I dance to sweat. Then I walk around on a complete euphoric high to the music and see who's inside. Stalking my prey much like a lethal predator. Hoping I spot someone worth dancing with, then perhaps exchanging phone numbers with, and maybe even sleeping with. But believe it or not, those kinds of men are very hard to find nowadays. Especially in this city. Talk about six degrees of separation.

I think I personally know or at least know someone that knows almost every single, professional, man between the ages of twenty-five to thirty-five in Philadelphia. It's a smaller pool of men than you would think. Tonight though, I'm not here for any of that. Tonight, I'm planting myself at the bar strictly for the alcohol. After the crappy day I've had at work, all I want to do is get blitzed, because my sales numbers are off.

Way off.

I ran my monthly sales statistics at work a ridiculous total of fourteen times, but the end result was still the same. Disappointing and well below last month's numbers.

Several years ago, I graduated with a degree from the prestigious Wharton School of Business at the University of Pennsylvania. Regretfully, I didn't get into Penn on my own merit, but because my father's fame and wealth bought me a spot. While I was able to keep my head above water academically, I'm actually amazed that I graduated in four years. I was mostly a partier or the type who would rather Netflix and chill—not study. After graduation, I stupidly thought that the school's reputation and the last name on my degree would be enough to land me a sweet position at a Fortune 500.

Boy was I naïve.

When it came time to secure a job after graduation, HR professionals didn't care that my dad was a basketball legend, all they cared about was my skillset–which wasn't that impressive. I was twenty-one years old, with no real job or solid intern experience, and my daddy was paying my rent. All I had was a fancy degree and a pretty smile. No one would hire me.

It was at that moment that I'd finally seen the light. I realized that I had been leaning on my family name like a crutch instead of a ladder. My dependency on my family was stunting my growth, and I didn't like who I had become. It was time to make a change. To stand on my own two feet. So I accepted the first decent job I could land, without my father's help, which was in the pharmaceutical industry. Specifically, pharmaceutical sales.

Drug companies are big in Philadelphia. I'm not exactly sure why, but a lot of big pharma companies have large offices or are headquartered here. I started working as an entry level sales representative for my company a couple months after graduating and have worked my way up to sales manager–leading a team of five. As jobs go, I haven't been working there that long, but I've been working there long enough to know that this low numbers thing isn't going to bode well for me.

When I first started out as a sales rep, it was easy, or at least it was easy for me. Selling pharmaceuticals (in my opinion) is all about being personable, looking your best, and building trust with physicians so that they feel comfortable ordering from me and not someone else. It also doesn't hurt that I get to sell the most popular drug on the market.

Men define their manhood based on their virility. Their dicks. If they can't get it up or keep it up, their whole world ends. It's my job to keep doctors up to their eyeballs in my company's generic brand of Viagra, so that they can prescribe it to their patients, recommend it to their friends, and to give it out like candy. In fact, I'm pretty sure that some of those men think I'm doing the Lord's work.

You'd be surprised about the types of men who want a prescription even if it's under the generic name of Silde-nafil. It's not just baby boomers suffering from erectile dysfunction who legitimately want to maintain healthy sex lives with their significant others. It's young guys too, and not because they medically need it. Some are single men who want the drug in order to be able to go all night, and the next night, and the next; and some are *not single* and want it so that they can keep up with the Mrs. as well as their chick on the side.

So the demand is there. That's actually the easy part. But now that I head my own team of sales reps, my job is much more complicated. It's all about making projections, meeting sales goals, and lots of team building. I'm not only responsible for my own results, but for the productivity of five other people as well. I'm a hard worker, and I want to climb the company ladder, but I'm learning the hard way that meeting productivity expectations isn't as easy as I hoped.

That's why I'm getting drunk.

"You're late tonight."

I turn around toward the stranger's voice and notice a man who looks unimpressively like many of the other men in here (average height, overworked, slightly buzzed) approaching me with a glass of wine in his hand. He's actu-ally my type in a sad sort of way. I tend to go for the corpo-rate shark types. The suit and tie. The man who doesn't look like he's ever put in a hard day of work with his hands. Not because I'm terribly attracted to them, but because I've decided that they are in my best interest.

I have my reasons for this, but if I had to sum it up, I

guess I would say that I choose men like him because that's what grown women are supposed to do. Pick men who actually look like adults, act like adults, and not like overgrown kids. I've had enough of that to last a lifetime.

I grew up as the daughter of Dan Pearson. My father was a bona fide superstar in his day. A point guard for the Philadelphia 76ers back in the early 1990s. Some say the most underrated basketball player to have ever played the position. I grew up in a privileged world. Private schools. Expensive gifts. Elaborate summer vacations. That was the nice part. The not so nice part of our life was the fact that my father's antics often overshadowed any talent he may have had; and they especially overshadowed any illusions one may have had about us having the perfect family. We didn't.

My father was considered a "bad boy" of the league. He hated structure and didn't think the rules applied to him. There was plenty of drinking, drugs, gambling and lots of women over the years. I think my father was a plaintiff in at least five different paternity suits, and while not all of them were legit, one actually did result in the birth of my younger sister, Dawn. So, while bad boys may look and sound good in theory, in real life they're all smoke and mirrors. Style and no substance. Immature. Headaches. I avoid them at all costs. I will not waste my time on them. No woman should, although I think that my best friend Elizabeth may be a lost cause at this point.

"I'm sorry, what did you say?"

I'm not sure that I heard him correctly. The music is really loud, and I may have misheard him. I could have sworn he just said that I was late arriving tonight.

"You like Pinot, right?" he asks as he tries handing me the glass.

Okay, now I'm not sure whether to be flattered or

freaked the fuck out. I give the head bartender, whom I know, Marco, a quick glance and he responds with a head nod. Letting me know it's safe to accept the glass from this perfect stranger. Men often buy me drinks here, but I only accept them if I know the man or if Marco has poured it himself and watched it the whole time.

"Umm, yes and thank you." I take a sip. It's delicious. Guess I'm starting tonight's "get blitzed" mission off with wine instead of the hard stuff. "Have we met before?"

"We have not, but only because I haven't had the chance to introduce myself to you. You're quite the popular girl at Lotus."

"Uh, I guess." Not really sure if that's a compliment or not.

"As I was saying before, I notice that you usually come around nine on Friday nights, but tonight you arrived a little late."

I raise my eyebrow at his creeper-like observation.

"And before you run for the hills, the only reason why I know that is because I come here at the same time too. Pretty much every Friday night I stay late at work, have a drink with a few of my boys, then we head over here. I always see you when you're headed inside. You're kind of hard to miss. You're a very beautiful woman."

I smile with some reserve. "So I take it you already know my name too."

He looks a bit taken off guard by my bluntness, but there's no need for us to beat around the bush. I can see where this is headed. I'm pretty sure he knows who I am because of who my father is, not because I'm such a "beautiful woman." Puh-lease.

"Of course. You're Sloan Pearson." He extends his palm for a handshake. "Nice to finally meet you. I'm Cord Prescott."

I don't shake Cord's hand but instead take another sip of my wine and give him a long hard glare. I don't really like that he's been watching me for however long he has. It's weird. While my gut reaction is to say "thanks for the drink, Cord, but this feels forced," I won't–because I'm starting to think that the only reason I haven't gotten laid in eons is solely because of me. Coming to a club just to get plastered is stupid. The whole point of this place is to meet other people, isn't it? Maybe I've judged Cord a little too harshly and too quickly. Perhaps that's my problem. I'm seriously jaded.

"Nice to meet you, Cord."

An almost smug smile spreads across Cord's face. *Bleck!* His arrogance is a huge turn off, but like all his other noticeable flaws, I dismiss it.

"Want to dance?"

I take a final gulp of my wine and set the glass down on the bar.

"Sure. Let me run to the ladies' room first though."

I'm either going to psych myself up, while I'm in the bathroom, to either dance with this guy and get to know him a little better or ditch him. I think I'm leaning toward the latter.

"I'll be right here. You want me to order you another glass of wine?"

"Are you trying to get me drunk, Cord?"

"Maybe." He winks.

Good grief.

"Don't bother," I say as I stand off my stool and smooth my skirt down. "I don't put out on the first date . . . or the second."

Cord grasps one of my arms. Not roughly but the contact is still unwanted.

"Not a problem," he says. His mouth practically salivating and not in a good way. "I can wait."

I don't mind the occasional one-night stand, it's the norm for a place like this, but a girl has to have standards, and right now I'm not too sure Cord will meet a single one of them. Sadly, at this point I feel like I'm just passing time. This guy seems like all the other duds I've met lately, and I'm bored already.

As I decide whether or not I'm going to ditch Cord, I scan the periphery of the room, wondering if I'll catch a glimpse of one of the club owners. There are three of them and they're like rock stars in here.

One is Elizabeth's fiancé and soon-to-be baby's daddy, Roman Masterson. Damn attractive but a real son of a bitch. While I can't deny that the two of them share something powerful, I wouldn't want any part of that type of love. I've always pictured my bestie with a soft-spoken, computer nerd, much like herself. Not Roman. He's too alpha. Too condescending. Too much.

Then there's Roman's best friend, Camden King. Now he actually is a computer nerd, or rather a computer hacker, but there's definitely nothing soft about him. He's just another overbearing jerk who's always sporting what I call the "alpha scowl" across his face. I tend to avoid him at all costs, because I never know what he's thinking behind those cold eyes of his. It always seems like he's talking about me.

And finally, there's Camden's brother, Cutter King. The one who's at the club the most. He's actually the worst one out of the three, because you don't tend to see his assholery coming. He smiles a lot. Laughs a lot. Flirts a lot. To the untrained eye he seems fun and easy going, but I know better. It's all an elaborate setup. A ruse. Because from everything that I know—he's not nice, he's not funny, and there's nothing easy about him except for the fact that he'll sleep with anything with a vagina.

The only reason why I look for him is out of habit. To gawk. I can't help myself. Roman and Camden tend to stay in the background, tucked hidden away in the club's office upstairs (when they're here) but Cutter doesn't.

He likes to stay among "his people." To hold court. It's a sight to see. Those women, or the "mindless minions" as I like to call them, are absolutely ridiculous when they're around him.

Eyelids fluttering.

Breasts heaving.

Mouths giggling.

All waiting for their self-appointed king to bestow his blessings of an eye wink, an ass grab, or a quick and dirty grind in the corner of the club.

I observe the lunacy from afar. It's best that way. In fact, anytime I come to Lotus, I try to stay completely out of Cutter's way. This is mostly because I don't want to actually have to be forced to speak to him. I made such an ass out of myself the last time I did, that I refuse to risk a repeat performance. He probably thinks I'm in complete lust with him, which I'm not, it's just that he uncharacteristically threw me off my game that night.

Admittedly—it was a train wreck.

THREE

SLOAN

Six Months Ago

Elizabeth's Aunt Juliette changed the venue for this year's Philadelphia-Montgomery Autism Awareness Gala, and by the looks of this place, it was a smart decision. In years past it's been hosted in the classically designed ballrooms of the some of the best hotels in Philadelphia including The Rittenhouse Hotel and my favorite–The Ritz Carlton, but this year it's being held in The Castle. An event space on the campus of a small, local university that's drop dead gorgeous and dramatically different.

With its expansive entryway, dark mahogany wood floors, oversized staircases, and exquisite crown molding– the space literally looks like an old-world castle inside. I have a thing for interior design, so I really like how Juliette used modern touches to complement the old-world architecture of the room.

I have a long history of coming to fundraising events like these. My parents were invited to a ton of them over the years and always brought me along. I didn't appreciate them much when I was young. I found them boring, pretentious, and I would've much rather spent my evenings drinking behind the bleachers with all the other over-privileged brats at my high school.

As I look around the sea of attending guests tonight, while there are some good looking, single, men here I wouldn't mind meeting, I realize that not much has changed since I was a kid. Same crowd. Same social climbers. Same agenda.

"Here to catch an investment banker tonight, Ms. Pearson?"

Scratch what I just said.

A lot has changed.

Now it seems as if they allow *anyone* into these events.

"Very witty," I say with a great deal of sarcasm to the dressed-up caveman seated next to me.

He grins like he thinks that I am actually amused by his degrading question, even though it's closer to the truth than I care to admit.

"Me. See. That. You. Found. Suit," I retort in the manner that Jane would speak to Tarzan.

Then he lets out a deep belly laugh that garners us a few glances from the other guests at our table.

"Let's dance, princess."

Ick, I think to myself. I hate that overused, unimaginative term of endearment.

"If you're going to address me, please use my name. It seems like you and your friend Roman have a problem with calling people by their God given names. Is that how they do things in your 'hood. Everyone gets a ridiculous nickname?"

"You were much nicer when we first met. Why can't you be that girl again?"

"I'm not even going to dignify that with a response. Now go away before people think we're here together. As if."

I motion for him to shoo with the back of my hand.

"Scoot. Shoo!"

The asshole laughs even harder.

I can't imagine what on earth I'm doing to encourage him. I sat on the edge of his chair for roughly ten seconds when we first met at Lotus. I was doing my flirty thing, not thinking much of it, and he's been giving me googly eyes ever since. Why I'm not inspiring that same type of adoration from the gazillion other men I've met over the last few weeks is anyone's guess.

"Fine," I say in frustration. "I'll move then."

As I motion to stand up, Cutter King grabs me around my waist with clear purpose. His eyes dancing. His grip strong. And he pulls me in toward his very large pecs. Then he stands up slowly. Making sure to slide his chest against my breasts as he rises to his full height.

He's tall. Really tall.

Muscular. Massive.

Brick hard and built like a caveman.

Strong enough to bash the head in of any intruder. Fast enough to catch any prey. And I'm not going to lie, big enough in all the right places to give me the fuck of a lifetime.

"Save that dance for me, princess."

Now I understand. Why Elizabeth always wears panties under her dress, and me going commando was a bad idea. Because what the hell is going to soak up all the wetness that the bass in Cutter's voice just produced between my legs?

"I need to excuse myself please."

And all I hear is Cutter King's arrogant, rumbling

laughter echoing behind me, as I hightail it from the table to find the nearest ladies' room.

After cleaning myself in the bathroom stall, I exit to find myself in the company of two other women at the sink area. I politely nod hello and begin washing my hands with several pumps of lime basil hand soap.

"This is quite an eclectic crowd," one woman says to the other.

"Yes, it is. I think I saw an Action News truck outside too. This event is probably going to get some eleven o'clock press coverage."

"That would be nice."

"And did you see that guy with Juliette's stepson?"

"The tall one?"

"They're both tall."

"I know who her stepson is. I'm talking about the one who looks like a Viking."

The first woman looks at me in the mirror and cracks a small smile. At first, I wonder if she knows that I was talking to said Viking just a few moments ago, but that isn't it. She just seems a little embarrassed by the content of their public conversation and is probably wondering if I'm judging them. I cordially return their smile, but continue with my primping process in an effort to act like I don't care ... as well as to eavesdrop.

"Yeah, him. I don't think I've seen him at this event before. I definitely would have remembered."

"Me too. He's gorgeous."

"And young."

"And did you see those tattoos? I think he has more than the stepson."

"I'd climb him like a tree."

They both start giggling like they're sixteen years old again.

Oh good grief.

"He's too young for us though."

"Yeah, he is, but it's all right to look," woman number one says giggling. Looking at me when she says it. "My husband looks at other women all the time."

I bite.

"I think it's totally fine to look," I add. "I'm sure the man you're referring to appreciated it."

"Oh, my goodness, do you think he saw us?"

"Don't worry. I'm sure a guy like the one (*asshole*) you're describing didn't give it a second thought. He's probably used to it. He may even enjoy it."

~

PRESENT DAY

It doesn't take long for me to spot him. Cutter is always the tallest man in the room. Covered in ink. Dressed much more casually than everyone else in a simple black tee, dark wash jeans, and a clean pair of black work boots. Standing powerfully at the end of the bar like he owns the place—which I guess is only right because he does. Towering over some Kardashian-built brunette who is staring at him like she desperately wants him to sire all of her offspring.

It's like watching a car accident on the freeway. I should really mind my business and keep it moving, but I can't help but stop and stare. That is until he turns his head and cuts his eyes clear across the dark room to meet mine. I immediately dart my eyes away and hold myself stock still. Only remembering a moment later to breathe. Angry with myself that I've been caught rubbernecking.

Remember who he is, Sloan.

A manwhore.

Remember who you are, Sloan.

A woman with a brain.

I raise my eyes back up. Meeting his head on. My plan is to stoically hold his stare until he turns away. My prediction is that it should only take a moment for him to become disinterested and turn back to his very attentive fangirl. Guys like Cutter have the attention span of a squirrel.

Hmm, he's still staring.

When one side of his mouth turns up into an absolutely hot, dirty, pornographic grin, I come to the conclusion almost immediately that my vagina is actually the real problem. The reason why I'll never have a half decent man in my life.

It wants bad things.

Tall, tatted, terrible things.

Things that make it wet.

I'm done with this stinking club. This is the last time I'm going to come here trolling for Mr. Wrong. I've got a weirdo waiting for me on the other side of the room who probably wants to hack me into teeny tiny pieces—and then there's *this guy*. Even more trouble. Taunting me with those perfect lips, those well-defined pecs, and that perfectly toned ass of his.

Gratefully, I'm distracted by a phone call from my teenaged sister. A call that I can barely hear over the loud music.

"Hey," I say in greeting while holding my opposite ear closed with my fingertip.

"Are you out partying?" she asks in an almost accusatory tone.

"Yes, I'm out, and I can hardly hear you in here. Are you all right?"

"Um, yeah, but I need to talk to you."

"Is it urgent?"

I ask the question, but I can already tell by her tone of

voice that she wants to talk to me immediately. Funny how everything with seventeen-year-old girls is a matter of life and death. I suppose I was the same way at her age.

"Just forget it."

"I'm not saying no. I just want to know if we can talk later. I can barely hear you, and I've been drinking a little."

"Later's fine."

"Good. Let's grab lunch. I'll call you with a time tomorrow. Is that cool?"

"Cool."

Before I can say goodbye, my sister already clicks me off the line. She's probably annoyed that I didn't make myself immediately available to her, but she's just going to have to deal with it. I do have a life.

Someone taps me from behind on my shoulder.

"I see you've lost your way."

I turn around and notice that it's the weird guy once again. He's standing behind me at another bar next to some other guy who seems to know him. They're both staring at me with the goofiest grins on their faces. I guess I was so distracted by Cutter, that I didn't realize that Cord had been walking right behind me the entire time.

"I thought you said you were going to wait for me over at the other bar?"

"I didn't want you to have to push your way through this crowd once you finished up in the ladies' room. It's getting packed in here. This way I'd be easy to spot."

He's right. It's definitely getting crowded, but I give him the side-eye anyway. Probably because he's a little too eager, a little too anxious, and mostly because every time I look at him all I see are flaws. His hands are small and soft. He doesn't look like he's worked hard a day in his life. His skin is pristine—no ink. In heels I can look him directly in the eyes, not up into them.

"You didn't have to do that," I say faking a polite smile.

"Sure I did. There's no way I'm going to blow my chance with Dan Pearson's daughter."

And that my friends was the sound of Cord hammering the final nail into his "no way in hell" is he going home with me coffin.

I'm definitely bailing on this loser.

And at this rate—on the entire male species.

FOUR

CUTTER

My eyes and attention are laser focused on a thick-necked, average looking loser, who drinks and talks too much. Although I've seen him around the club a couple of times before, I wouldn't describe him as someone memorable. He's just your average Joe. Trying to prove his manhood by grinding on the asses of grown women on the dance floor. Dry humping them like he's at some sort of high school dance. Desperately hoping that he can take them home for what is probably a lousy lay by the end of the night.

I usually don't pay men like him any mind. What any of these club losers do and who they hump is none of my business, and more importantly, dweebs like him pay the bills around here. They pay our inflated cover charge, they pay for the expensive bottle service from the bar, and they even order a plate or two of our overpriced signature spicy wings. Yet this guy just garnered himself some extra special attention from me.

I don't like the looks of him.

I don't like his style.

And I certainly don't like what I'm hearing coming out of his mouth.

Especially because he's talking shit about a woman. A woman who has been rambling around in my consciousness for no good reason at all and for much longer than I usually allow. Literally since the day we met.

"You tap that?" the dude's prematurely balding sidekick asks.

"Not yet. Soon though," the humper brazenly replies.

"I bet that's the sweetest piece of ass you're ever going to have the privilege of tasting."

"Privilege?" he responds incredulously. "She's definitely hot, but I wouldn't necessarily call fucking her a *privilege*."

His friend laughs at what he must know is a ridiculous statement.

"Sloan Pearson is practically Philadelphia royalty and the most gorgeous woman in this club tonight. There aren't too many men I know that wouldn't want a piece of that. Myself included."

"She's definitely sexy as hell, and her dad is a legend, but it's not like she's some sort of A-lister. Nobody even knows who she is. Plus, my family has money too. Trust me, the privilege will be all hers when I get inside of that."

A-lister?

Get inside of *that*?

What grown man talks the fuck like this.

"Your dad is in insurance, dude. He makes his money in the most boring way possible. Her father was the most famous ball player this city's ever seen outside of Julius Irving or Allen Iverson. Not to mention that off the court, his pimp game was legendary. He had some of the hottest women in Hollywood in his bed back in those days.

"You must admit, that it would definitely be the talk of the office if you brought her on your arm to the company fundraiser next month. Hell, it might help you get that promotion you've been lobbying for. Just the attention alone you'll get with her on your arm will make you look good, because the last woman you brought to dinner was kind of average, and *that* girl is definitely not average."

"True."

"Doesn't look like it's going to be hard for you though. I saw the way she was talking to you a minute ago. Seems like she's wet for you already."

"They all get wet for me, man."

My kick somebody's ass radar is going all kind of wonky right now. I could easily bitch slap this dude into next week for disrespecting the most beautiful woman in the room. In my club of all places.

"Ooh look, my favorite King brother is here! Can I buy you a drink, Cutter?"

Before I get to do a little house cleaning, I'm interrupted by an attractive redhead named Lynn, who comes to the club almost every weekend, laughs at anything that I say, and is a sure bet. We've partied together a couple of times and the evenings have always ended in an orgasm and a smile. Yet tonight the promise of a happy ending is the furthest thing from my mind. I'm more interested in having a persuasive conversation with two certain dickheads.

"I can't tonight, babe," I say apologetically. "Maybe next time. In the meantime, your first round is on me."

As if on cue, Lynn giggles, although I haven't said anything funny. I've long since come to the conclusion that it must be a nervous tic of hers.

"Are you working or something tonight?" she asks with disappointment.

"I'm always working, darlin'," I explain. "But buy me a scotch next time?"

I offer Lynn a flirty wink to end the conversation, and

then head back upstairs to take a call in the office. I'd rather stay on the main floor and deal with this jerk that Sloan has attracted into her orbit, but my brother Camden has evidently been on hold for five minutes.

"Why didn't you call me on my cell?" I ask without saying hello.

"I did. You never hear the damn thing when you're downstairs."

"Why aren't you here yet?"

"Why do you sound agitated?"

"No reason."

"I'm not coming. I'm staying home to get some preliminary work done on one of the Miami fixes."

I'm in a business partnership with Camden and our best friend Roman. While we own several businesses including a dance club and a restaurant, the bulk of our income comes from *fixing* problems for affluent clients. In other words, saving the asses of the wealthy people or companies who can afford to pay us. We've recently acquired a few new clients in Miami.

"Computer work?"

"Obviously."

My brother is a tech genius. If a fix requires any sort of complex computer research or hacking then he handles it.

"So why can't you do that here?"

"I'm dead in the middle of altering some dude's credit report, and I don't feel like stopping just to come by the club to check in if that's okay with your needy ass."

"What do you mean *my* needy ass? You're a part owner in the club last time I checked, asshole. If you enjoy sharing in the profits then you need to do your share of the work."

"Let's talk real talk, Cut. The club is your thing. Half the women lining up at the door every night are there to catch a glimpse of you. You are the face of Lotus now, like it or not. Roman and I are practically silent partners at this point."

"You're just proving my point."

"What point? That no one can run the club like you."

"No, my point that you and Roman are acting like silent fucking partners when you're not. That's not something we ever agreed to. When Joseph gave Lotus to Roman, we all agreed on a three-man partnership. You know I wouldn't have ever agreed to anything else."

I can't believe my brother's lame attempt to back pedal his way out of his responsibility to the club. I know the real reason why he hasn't been showing up. I share an assistant with my brother and Roman named Jade, but she's also my brother's girlfriend, and recently she's moved into the carriage house with us. I love the little snow pea to death, and I'm happy that she makes my brother happy, but their relationship has changed Camden in ways that I don't understand. Ways that have made me think twice about ever settling down with a woman.

"Is Jade at the house too?"

"Yeah she's hanging back with me for a little while."

"So, it's just me at the club tonight," I say with an icy attitude. "Again."

Jade usually works some nights at the club with me.

"I know you've been carrying some of the weight lately, but that's the beauty of a three-man partnership. We can't all share the load equally at all times. Sometimes there's going to be situations when one of us has to step up and the others fall back. Fortunately, we have that flexibility."

"That sounds like a really bullshit way of explaining why you two slackers never come to the club anymore or the tapas lounge for that matter."

"Would you chill out. I'm still handling business, Cut. I'm just doing it at home today."

"Monkey business."

"How many times have I been on the computer half of the night hacking into someone's personal life online, while you were at some titty bar watching women spin their asses around a pole. Let's not get into a pissing match about who works the hardest around here."

"That's different."

"It always is."

"My distractions are temporary and unimportant. They don't interfere with work. I can get up and leave at a moment's notice. Your distraction lives with us and seems to be the most important thing on your to-do list lately."

"I'm not going to tell you again, asshole. I am working. But speaking of distractions, you seem to have a few of your own. What about that bet we made a while back?"

"What bet?"

"Oh, now you're suffering from memory loss? The bet where you get in between the glamazon's legs for a thousand bucks plus breakfast cooked by *my* woman. Does any of that ring a bell?"

Glamazon is Roman's nickname for Sloan. Now all three of us have gotten into the habit of using it but rarely to her face. She'd definitely rip us all a new one.

"Obviously I was just messing with you that day. I wasn't remotely serious."

"Uh-huh."

"Jade would never have agreed to her part of the bet, and you wouldn't have allowed it even if she had. Someone is being a little stingy lately."

"You know the rules. We mutually agree to share a woman who's willing until one of us doesn't want to anymore."

"I get it. You don't want to share anymore. Fine."

"You'll understand one day."

"Kill me if that day comes."

"Hey, I just got a text from Rome. There's a job tonight. Room 2456 at The Four Seasons. It's Newman again. Newman's easy."

"Why can't you or Rome handle him?"

"You're the closest to the hotel and the situation is time sensitive. Marco can run things at Lotus until you get back. He knows the drill. I'll try and meet you at the hotel in about forty-five minutes or an hour. Not that you'll need me. You'll probably be finishing up by the time I get there."

"Fine," I reluctantly agree. It's honestly the last thing I feel like doing tonight, but it's work and I never turn down money. "I'll try to leave here in fifteen."

"Cool. So . . . let me ask you again. Are you still trying to tell me that you're not interested in Sloan at all?"

"It's funny how when some dudes get into relationships, they try and make their single friends feel like shit for not wanting the same thing. Well it's not going to work with me, big brother. Am I interested in the glamazon for one night? Hell, yes. Am I interested in forever? Hell, no. That's not me. I'm not a one-woman type of man. Never have been. Never will be. It's not fair to all the women of this fair city."

"It's not fair all right. God, you're full of yourself," he sneers. "Mom coddled you way too much."

"For good reason. I'm a King and the last of my kind. God made me this way in his infinite wisdom."

"I guess that's why he made me first then."

"Whatever, asshat."

"Is *she* there tonight?"

"Maybe."

"Poor, clueless Sloan." Camden chuckles. "I assume you've been sabotaging her love life tonight as per usual. Frightening away any gutless dude that comes sniffing around her in the club. The glamazon can't even get her womanly needs met, because you're so busy cock blocking."

"Shut up, Cam."

"I hate to break it to you, but the way you're acting reeks of the familiar scent of *wanting forever*." He chuckles again. "Not just one night."

"That's just me having a little fun." I attempt to blow him off. "Which has always been one of your biggest problems hasn't it? You hardly know the difference."

"Or maybe it's *you* who doesn't know the difference, because I don't think you're playing around at all. I think you're serious as shit about her."

"Okay, can we stop with all the relationship chat now, Dr. Phil? I've got a fix to get to by myself, and then probably will have a club cash register to close out after that—*by my fucking self*."

I can hear Camden's audacious laughter right before he hangs up the phone. He's so annoying. Just because I'm attracted—okay, deeply attracted—to Sloan doesn't mean that I want to put a ring on it. Why would I want to lay claim to a high maintenance, judgmental, party girl who barely says ten words to me? I don't. I'm just helping her out. Me eliminating some of these club douchebags from her life is not me being interested or wanting forever, it's just me doing what I do best.

Fixing shit.

～

FIVE

CUTTER

The club is on fire tonight. Fridays are turning into one of our busiest nights at Lotus. While I've been working on attracting a diverse clientele to the club, Fridays still belong to the suits—corporate men and women who come here after work ready to let loose. Even though it's dim and packed to the rafters tonight, when I hit the top of the stairs, nothing can stop me from spotting the dummies I've got less than fifteen minutes to handle. They're still at the bar and the glamazon is nowhere in sight.

Perfect.

"Let me have a word," I say finally approaching jerk number one with the big mouth.

Both of the posers back up a few paces once I approach.

"You talking to us?"

"No, just you."

"Is there a problem, man?"

They both give me a long confused look. Wondering who I am, what I want, and probably assessing how they plan on "handling" me if I turn out to be a problem. In all of ten seconds, I can tell by the new confidence in their stances that they're cautious but not particularly worried. I may be big, but there's two of them, so they think they're good.

Rookie mistake.

"Might be." I grin.

"What's your problem, dude?" the sidekick resembling a shorter version of Mr. Clean asks me.

"First of all, this is none of your business, Professor X, so you can step away. I've already made it clear that this is between me and Casanova here."

"I don't think I know you, dude. What's with the attitude?"

I stare down the poser's little bald headed friend until he does the right thing.

"Uh, I'm going to go take a whiz, Cord. Let you two straighten this out. I'll be right back."

Pussy.

"So, I think you might have me mistaken with someone else." Cord the poser starts timidly trying to talk himself out of whatever wrath he thinks I'm about to bring down on his ass.

Sometimes I forget that my size, my tats, and the way I carry myself intimidates most men. Most people really. That's because there's nothing average about me. So yes, I can be a scary motherfucker, but only when provoked. Most of the time I like to think that I'm a walk in the park.

"No, I'm pretty sure that I have the right jackass."

"Woe, dude, what are you so pissed about? I'm just here trying to have a good time."

I take a small step forward while simultaneously slipping my hand behind my back. Inside of my waistband and underneath my henley is where I keep Benny—my glock. Sometimes I like to touch the handle. Make sure it's there. Adjust it on occasion. I'm not reaching for it or anything. It's really just a habit. I like to play with something in my hands when I'm anxious, or angry, or excited. When I was two it was my stuffed dog. When I was four it was my GI Joe figurine. Then after tagging along on a few business runs with my father, it became a gun.

My father didn't talk much. He wasn't a big sharer. But I knew he was proud of the good shot I'd become when he gifted me my first handgun. A small Ruger revolver. I was way too young to have it, and he was probably a very bad father for giving it to me, but I cherished that gun.

Every day I cleaned it. Loaded it. Unloaded it. I had a special hiding place for it in my room, so that my mom wouldn't find it (she abhorred guns). And every time my dad took me and Camden on his "special runs" I'd carry it with me. Concealed like he taught me; but always reaching back for it. Making sure it was there. Just in case I needed it. Just in case one of my dad's runs went south. Which makes it all the more painful that the one day I left it at home, because my mom was watching me like a hawk that morning, was the day that my father was shot and killed.

Anyway, I'm guessing that the poser thinks I must be reaching for my piece or something, because a look of total terror passes over his face.

"What are you doing, man."

He places his drink on the bar top and starts backing away from me. He's getting worked up for nothing. I would never pull out in a club unless I absolutely had to, and I'd also never waste a bullet on someone like this no matter what he did. It would be too easy. There's no satisfaction in *easy*.

"Relax, Tinker Bell. Nobody's going to hurt you. I just want to tell you something, and I want to make sure that you hear me loud and clear."

"Sure, man, whatever. Speak your piece."

"A few minutes ago, you and your friend were talking about a young lady who's a friend of mine."

"Who . . . Sloan?"

"That's Miss Pearson to you."

"Miss Pearson," he parrots back in a forced but respectful tone.

"So, as I was saying, Miss Pearson is a friend of mine, and you were talking mighty disrespectfully about her. Being quite presumptuous about what you were going to *do* to her, and how that might benefit you at your sorry ass job. So I thought I should step in and make things super simple for you.

"You will *never* fuck Sloan Pearson. You will never kiss her, touch her, talk to her, or breathe the same air as her. If she's in this club, then you leave. If she walks by you on the street, then you better suck your breath in and hold it until she's ten feet away. She's a stranger to you. She doesn't exist. You understand what I'm saying, homeboy?"

You can always tell the guys who had to hold their own while growing up versus the ones who had everything handed to them on a silver platter. They're all the same. Say a couple of words to them and their faces crumple like they're ten-year-old kids being bullied on the playground.

This guy is definitely a powder puff. Soft as butter. It's not even fun to punk him, but it was necessary. I may not want Sloan for myself, but I can still do her this solid. We run in the same circles. Her best friend is marrying my best friend. I'm just eliminating some of the bad apples for her. At least the ones floating around in here. She should be thanking me. *You're welcome, glamazon.*

"Yeah, man, I . . . I understand."

"Good. Now is Sloan still here?"

I already know that she's long since ditched this guy. I

watched her sneak out through the delivery entrance less than ten minutes ago.

"Yeah, man, she went to the restroom or something."

"So where should you be going right now?"

"But my buddy is still—"

"Let me stop you right there, Cord. Do you think your friend is taking the longest piss ever or is it possible that he left you? Because I strongly believe that he selected door number two. Something you need to be doing as well. Leaving."

"I think there's been a misunderstanding. I was just shooting the shit with my friend earlier, because I'm drunk. I really like Sloan. I mm-mean Miss Pearson," he stutters. "I meant no disrespect."

"You meant no disrespect? Well guess what, I don't give a shit. Excuses are like assholes, Cord. Everybody's got one. Your membership to Lotus has been revoked. Get out now while you still can on two legs." I point toward the exit sign.

A look of sudden recognition passes over his face.

"Wait, are you the owner?" His eyes enlarge.

"Do I even need to answer that."

"No, Mr. King. My apologies. I'm leaving right now."

Cord quickly exits the premises without even the smallest glance back. Another sure sign that he wasn't worth Sloan's time. He gave in way too easily. If it were me, I would have fought much harder for much less.

A woman sitting at the bar by herself, who's been eavesdropping on our exchange the entire time, turns around and gives me the thumbs up sign.

"What's that for?" I ask amused.

"You're Cutter King, right?"

"I am."

I check the time on my cell. Honestly, I don't have time

for pleasantries. I should have left here for the hotel five minutes ago.

"I'm Aria. This is my third time at the club since joining two months ago." She holds her glass up then takes a sip. "I've heard a lot about you."

"Nice to meet you, Aria. How are you enjoying it here at Lotus?"

"Loving it so far. Listen, I know you're a busy man, but I just wanted to tell you that I happened to overhear what that jerk was saying, and you definitely did the right thing for your friend by sending him on his way."

Now this is a smart woman.

"It's nice to see that someone appreciates my superpowers," I say throwing on a little appreciative charm.

Aria responds with a chuckle which only confirms my conclusion that I must have the unmistakable ability to say almost anything and make every woman I meet laugh.

Every woman but Sloan.

"You should tell her what an ass that guy was. You probably saved her from wasting a month of her life going on some really bad dates with him. She owes you a debt of gratitude."

"That's exactly what I've been saying." I nod in agreement. "I'm helping her out and probably a whole lot of other women too."

"You are," she agrees. "I should know. I'm one of those women who went on about six weeks worth of bad dates with a man that nobody warned me about."

Exactly what I thought.

"So *the king* is actually performing a public service."

"I'm sorry, the *who is?*"

SIX

CUTTER

It's not even midnight yet and the room reeks of fear and blood. I'm sitting in the corner of a Four Seasons hotel suite, spinning my slimline glock round and round atop of a red mahogany desk with my pointer finger. Watching someone I once respected, with tears streaming down his face, crumble like a house of cards.

Today's disappointment to mankind is the district attorney of Philadelphia, Cliff Newman. Today I've learned that he's just your average politician. A liar. Crooked as a three-dollar bill. Nothing special. A complete greedy fuck up, with a God complex, who regularly cheats on his wife to feed his fragile ego; but this time his dick has gotten him into some serious trouble.

The beaten, bloodied, woman sprawled across the bed next to him is some poor soul who worked in the communications department of his office, and probably thought she was in love with him. Now she's dead and all this guy seems to be able to do is talk about himself.

"My life is ruined. My life is over."

He keeps looping the self-pitying and slurred words

over and over in heaving sobs. Holding his head in his hands, feeling sorry for himself, as if someone committed some heinous act against him.

"Selfish bastard," I mutter under my breath.

And even though I'm pissed that this is the third time my brother Camden has conveniently canceled showing up to a job with me, I think I'm starting to understand part of why something *keeps coming up* for him. Other than Jade that is.

It's probably safe to say that we're both growing tired of helping self-serving assholes like Cliff Newman. They're always wealthy, indulged, narcissists who create problems for themselves again and again, never learning from their mistakes, and then hiring us to make those problems go away for them. Over and over.

The shit is getting old.

At the very least, this waste of human life deserves life in prison for savagely beating this woman to death. Why should I save his ass? Why should he get away with this crime unscathed? Why should this woman's family never know what happened to their daughter, their sister, or their aunt?

Because you're getting paid a lot of money to do it, dummy. Don't get all sanctimonious about it now.

Yes, I've done my share of dirt, but I've never killed a woman. Never had to. In fact, I've never even put my hands on a woman unless it was to make her come for me. So yeah, maybe I can be a little sanctimonious tonight, because this is some fucked-up shit. What if she was one of the women in Newman's family? Brains splattered all over a hotel bedspread.

"Oh, for God's sake, shut up," I bark. Tired of his drug induced whining. "You think your life is ruined? This woman didn't even live to see thirty thanks to you."

District Attorney Clifford Newman. A man I've seen countless times looking and talking tough as nails about crime on the evening news, is now looking up at me like a little boy who wants his mommy to kiss and make it better.

Pitiful face.

Puppy dog eyes.

Pussy.

"Don't you think I know that? You think I meant to do this? It was an accident. I swear! It was a goddamn accident." He starts sobbing again.

"So enlighten me." I continue spinning my gun around with my finger on the desk. A habit of mine that just happens to be a handy intimidation technique. "How do you accidentally beat a one-hundred-twenty-pound woman to death?"

"We argued," he says as if those simple two words should explain it all. "Things got heated."

"She's butt ass naked. Did things get heated *after* you fucked her, or did you fuck her *after* things got heated? 'Cause that's just weird, man."

"I didn't realize the money I'm paying you included a police-styled interrogation, and I don't see why the details matter at this point. Just help me fix it!" Newman screeches as spittle flies out of the corner of his mouth.

I immediately stop spinning Benny around.

My right eyelid starts twitching.

The batshit crazy timber of Newman's voice makes my hackles rise, and when my hackles rise, my right eye twitches, and when my eye twitches, I tend to shoot shit.

I prop my right elbow casually up on the desk, with my gun in hand, and aim it directly at the asshole's forehead. Now this I can do. I may not be able to hurt a woman, but I sure as shit can kill a man at point blank range, and go out for a burger and fries ten minutes later like nothing ever happened. I know it's fucked-up, but it's just the way I'm built. Yet no matter how much immediate satisfaction shooting him would give me right now, that's not what I'm supposed to be doing here.

It's my role in the three-man business partnership I'm a part of to smooth things over. Talk people into things they normally wouldn't do. Use my power of persuasion to settle disputes and fix sticky situations. Why? Because I usually have the temperament for it. Unlike Camden and Roman, I'm usually a pretty easy-going guy to deal with, until I'm not, and bitch ass Clifford the DA is definitely pushing all of my "I am not" buttons.

"I don't fucking work for you," I say with a bite to my voice that lets him know I'm at the end of my patience.

"Wait, I'm sorry. I didn't mean it like that."

I'll admit that I'm uncharacteristically pissed about this fix. I've seen people do some terrible things in this world. You can't be in this business and not have the stomach for violence, but something about this one is different. Maybe it's because my brother bailed on me *again* and I'm angry. Maybe it's because I'd rather be drinking at the club or lying in between a pair of a woman's legs instead of doing this tonight. Or maybe it's because the overall nature of our job is changing. Each fix we take on seems to be more violent than the last. Increasingly pointless. Less satisfying.

"Listen, *Clifford,* I know you're upset, but raising your voice at your only ticket out of a life in maximum security isn't a good idea. You're the district attorney. You know better than anyone that those boys upstate are going to fuck your asshole ten ways from Sunday if you get sent there for murdering a defenseless woman. Do you like wearing eye shadow and lipstick? Because I bet you'll be somebody's bitch in less than twenty-four hours when you get there. So, I highly suggest that you lower your voice and change your tone if you want my help. If not then I've got a drink and a pair of nice tits waiting for me across town."

Funny how all I can see inside of my head are flashes of Sloan's rack in fucking technicolor the moment I say the word tits out loud. Yeah, I'm definitely losing it.

"You're right, you're right. I'm sorry. It's just that I'm in way over my head. Tell me what to do," Newman pleads. "I'll do whatever you tell me to do."

Still holding the gun, I decide to finally stop letting my growing disgust for this man get in the way of business. The DA is a douche and a dummy, but I've never let those characteristics get in the way of business before, so I decide to get to work. Time is ticking and every minute counts. The first order of business is to take a long look around the room to assess the damage and more importantly the cleanup. Especially because there's only me here to do it.

The trouble with five-star hotels is not getting in and out of the rooms, but the fact that cameras are everywhere. My job is to make it look like nothing ever happened in this room, and like they were never here, when there is probably footage of this dickhead and the girl from the minute they hit the front lobby of the hotel. The trick will be finding the right person to pay off to get rid of all of that footage and getting this room clean. But first things first . . .

"I want to be paid double for this clusterfuck."

"Double?"

"Yes, double."

As if he has any choice.

"I didn't pay that much last time."

"You didn't kill anybody last time either."

"Kill accidentally," he corrects me.

"Tomato, tomahto."

"I don't have that much money liquid to pay you."

"So get it."

"I'm just a civil servant. I don't make a huge salary, plus I'm totally mortgaged to the hilt. I don't think I can get that type of money."

"Then I guess we don't have anything else to discuss." I start getting up to leave. "Your best bet is to call the police and plead to second degree. I'm sure in your line of work you know a good lawyer."

Cliff runs over toward me in a panic. His hands up in a pleading formation.

"Wait–I have something else you might want as payment," he says while gripping the front of my shirt in his fists. Funny how the mention of a plea sobers him right up.

"Goddamn it, Clifford, you're getting that girl's blood all over me."

I try quickly wiping off the blood, but actually only end up smearing it farther into the fibers of my shirt.

"I'm sorry." He backs up. Wiping his runny nose with the back of his hand. "But I swear I have something you may want that's worth more than money."

"What could you possibly have that would interest me other than money?" I ask while continuing to inspect the smeared fingerprints on my sweater. I really should keep some spare all-black sweats in my trunk like Roman does. It hides blood stains much better.

"Information. I ran a background check on all three of you when I first hired you guys."

My ears pop up at the mention of a background check. My brother has been very thorough in cleaning up our digital footprint. If there's something we don't want people to find, Camden has and still can make it go away with a few clicks of a mouse. So while I'm not exactly worried, I don't like that the district fucking attorney has been snooping into our business.

"And?"

"And there's someone in your file you may find interesting."

"You're trying my patience, Clifford. Someone like who?"

"Another family member."

"Be more specific." I place my hand behind my back on Benny's handle again. "Quickly."

SEVEN

CUTTER

"Our investigators found another biological sibling," Newman finally spits out. "A brother."

If there's one thing that I've never been good at, it's concealing the fact that I'll do anything for my brother, Camden. Family means everything to me, especially because I have so little of it. Our father was murdered. Our mother is gone too. We may have a couple of cousins somewhere out west, but I've never met them, so as far as I'm concerned there's just me and Cam. I don't like that Newman is trying to play me by using what he thinks is my one vulnerability.

I start fingering the handle of Benny inside of my waistband, as I sneer at his statement, because I honestly would love to shoot him in the kneecaps right now. He's lying and I hate liars. It's just so unnecessary and it always causes problems.

"I don't like people giving me the runaround, Newman. I thought you knew that about me. So good luck upstate, because I only have one brother, and you've met him."

"I'm not lying. There's definitely another King brother,

and I have a file on him. A very thick and interesting file. The information is yours if you help me tonight at the usual price."

"Where's this supposed brother been all my life?"

"It's in the file."

"Who's child is he?" I say what I'm asking myself out loud, but I can only assume that any mystery kid out there would be my father's. I can't imagine my mom, the saint that she was, would have hidden some sort of love child from us.

"It's in the file." Newman grins thinking that he's got me on the hook now.

I pull Benny halfway out of my waistband.

"I *could* just have Cam break into your hard drive and steal the fucking file. That is what he does for a living."

Newman watches my hand closely but doesn't waver.

"He could try."

I smirk to myself. Maybe this guy does have a bit of balls left.

"So how long have you had this file of yours?"

"Since the first time I hired the three of you."

"You've been sitting on this information for over a year?"

"Yes, but in my defense, that's what my office does. We search and save information for the day that we need it. Today seems to be that day."

Newman is somewhat convincing, but it could be because he'd say just about anything to save his ass right now.

"This is my final offer," I say firmly. "I'll fix this mess for you tonight for the regular price *plus* an extra thirty percent on top *and* the file. Otherwise I'm walking."

"Thirty percent? That's kind of high. I'm giving you the file which I'm sure is worth more to you than money."

"You sound like an idiot. There's nothing more important than money," I lie. "Thirty percent is a whole lot better than my original offer. If I were you I'd take it."

"This isn't how we usually negotiate payment. Camden and Roman–"

"Let me clarify things, you're right it isn't; but Camden and Roman aren't here and there's a dead woman over there on the bed. So that's the price."

"Do they know you're robbing me like this?" he asks while rubbing his temples as if he's having a migraine.

"You've gotta be shitting me right now. You think I'm the one robbing you?"

"You're just randomly making up prices," he continues to complain.

"I'm not sure how many ways I need to say this, but there's a woman in this hotel room whose body is growing colder by the minute. Head bashed in. Brains on the pillow. So you tell me. How much is your life worth to you, Clifford?"

He looks back over at the woman and tightens his lips.

"Ten more seconds and the price goes back up to double," I warn. Fed up with negotiating.

"Okay, okay. I agree to your terms."

As if there was any other choice.

"Good decision. I need the money wired and the file in my inbox by nine a.m. sharp."

Newman turns around and looks at the woman once more with a defeated look on his face. He's still coming down off of his high, and the gravity of his actions seem to be finally registering inside of his drug scrambled brain.

"I'm not sure that I can get that amount of money together that early."

"Send the file in the morning, and I'll give you until the end of the business day to wire the money."

"Okay."

"And if this long-lost brother story of yours is a load of bullshit that you're feeding me, then I'm coming for you, Newman. You feel me?"

"Yes, I understand completely."

He doesn't take his eyes off of the corpse when he responds to my question. I'm afraid that he may be slowly unraveling, and the last thing I need is for this dirtbag to lose his shit.

"Newman, hey!" I snap my fingers loudly in his face. "Are you with me right now?"

"Yes," he says somberly.

"Good. So the first problem is that you're covered in this woman's blood and now I am too. You'll need to strip, put all the clothes in this pillowcase, and go into the bathroom and take a shower. A long hot one. Scrub the shit out of yourself. Especially under your nails. Don't keep going over your skin with the bloodied cloths, or you'll just rub the blood back into your skin. Use every washcloth and hand towel in that bathroom and plenty of soap."

He nods his head with what I hope is some semblance of understanding.

"When did you check into the hotel?" I ask as I pull my sweater off and turn it inside out.

"Umm, I think about ninety minutes ago."

"You think or you know?"

"I . . . know."

"How many people did you talk to when you checked in?"

He thinks hard. "Two women at the front desk, and some other staff who greeted me as I made my way through the lobby. Maybe about six staff people in all."

"You're a married public figure who decides to carry on an affair at a five-star hotel, but then you go ahead and speak to everyone in the damn lobby? That's what's wrong with the politicians in this city. You all think that you're untouchable."

Newman is silent for a moment. Hopefully pondering his stupidity.

"I guess I didn't put that much thought to it."

"That's pretty obvious."

"Um, there's one more thing."

"What else."

"I can't go home."

This night just gets better by the minute.

"What the hell are you talking about? You need to go home and slide in bed with your wife, so that you have a solid alibi for tonight."

"I can't."

"Why not."

"My wife thinks I'm out of town."

"For how long?"

"A few days."

I should have stuck to charging him double.

"Surprise her. She'll love it."

"She'll know something's up. She's already suspicious about the affair."

"Fine, I'll put you up somewhere for a couple of days, but you're going to owe me for this headache. Lodging wasn't part of the deal."

"Agreed."

After we finalize our arrangement, a few tears start to fall down Newman's face. *Good fucking grief.* I'm going to kill my brother for making me deal with this nut job alone. I just want to finish this and go get shit-faced at the titty bar. Ever since Cam and Roman fell in love with their women, I've been the one doing all of the dirty work lately. This is exactly why I want out. I send my brother an angry text.

Me: I hope you have a good reason for blowing off work.
Camden: Absolutely.
Me: You better not be fucking Jade right now.
Camden: lol:)
Me: Why are you laughing? Did you actually ditch work to get your dick wet?
Camden: How can I help you, brother.

I can hear the annoyed undertone of his text. Full of Camdenesque attitude as if what I said about getting his dick wet was disrespectful. Okay, so maybe it was. *Getting your dick wet* are words we use to describe sleeping with whores, not with girlfriends or wives, but he knows that I didn't really mean it that way. Jade is not a whore. She's our assistant, my friend, and his woman. I more than respect her. It's just that now that he's become so possessive of the little minx, he's entirely too touchy about everything I say. He needs to relax and be a little patient. It's going to take some getting used to the fact that the two of them are together. Really together. Like monogamous together. And living in our house as a couple.

In the beginning of their relationship things were fun. In the beginning, he used to share. My brother and I have always shared women ever since we were teenagers. Now we don't. I guess change in any relationship is inevitable, but that doesn't mean I've got to like it.

Me: This thing tonight is not easy like you promised. It's a *situation*.
Camden: I'm sure you've got it handled.
Me: I know I can handle it, but it's really a two-man job.

It doesn't happen often but the words *situation* and *two-*

man job have always been code between us that there's a violent situation to deal with.

Camden: You've got this. I'm not worried.

Me: What happened to the mantra you've been preaching since Dad died? About not making mistakes.

Camden: Are you going to make a mistake?

Me: No, you condescending asshole, but best believe that I'm going to kick your ass when I'm finished with this shit storm tonight.

Camden: Good luck with that, little brother. Gotta go. Duty calls.

Me: You're so pussy whipped.

Camden: Indeed:)

I don't even bother telling Cam about how I've managed to arrange for us to get paid extra for this job or more importantly about the possibility of us having a long-lost brother. I decide the news of both can wait until I know for sure whether Newman's intel is real, because how could we have possibly missed something as huge as having another brother? I'm pretty sure we couldn't have, but I'm willing to allow this thing to play out however it does.

"You're not in the shower yet?"

I try gaining Newman's attention, since all he seems to be preoccupied with as of now is sitting on the edge of the bed and gawking at the gory scene he's responsible for. This guy's head is all over the place. He seemed fine when he was negotiating the price of this fix, but now I think he may falling into shock.

"Should I cover her up?" He gingerly touches the dead woman's leg. "She feels cold."

The woman's limbs are somewhat contorted and her chocolate brown eyes are wide open but the color of her pupils are dulling. I'm no CSI expert, but I can pretty much surmise what went down in this hotel room tonight after assessing the scene.

The two of them probably came here to get high, and they came here to fuck, and my guess is they did it often. But tonight they argued about something. Something that took him completely by surprise and enraged him. Maybe she told him that she couldn't do the whole clandestine thing anymore. Maybe she threatened him by saying she'd tell the wife or tell the press.

Whatever it was, the look on her dead face and the scratches on Newman's face tells me that she was fighting for her life until the very end. Now that the scotch and OxyContin that he has probably been inhaling all night is wearing off, he seems to be feeling some semblance of remorse and sadness. Almost as if he had genuine feelings for her. Too bad that it's too little too late.

"Hey, hey. Eyes on me. We don't have time for regrets. She's cold because she's dead, and there's nothing you can do about that now. So do what I told you and get in the shower. It's your ass on the line. I'm going to run out and get some supplies that I'll need for cleanup, and I'll also grab you some fresh clothes so that you can walk out of here easily. And one more thing . . ."

"Yeah?"

"Try not to touch her body again if you can help yourself," I say sarcastically.

"How long will you be?" he asks as a look of dread settles across his face.

This is exactly why you need a partner at a fix. It's risky leaving clients at a scene by themselves. They might make a mistake or freak the fuck out. Newman is scared, but in order for this fix to work, I've got to make him feel like I've got total control over this thing and over him.

"Look at me, Newman. I've got this. I can do this all day and night in my sleep. I'm going to get you out of here, I'm going to get her out of here, and I'm going to make it like this never happened. That's what you're paying me the big bucks for. Now where's your cell."

"Okay, umm, let me find it."

He starts to scramble around the side of the bed looking for his phone, and finally finds it underneath the other side of the bed. The side she's on. The screen is seriously cracked and the tempered glass looks like an intricate spider web. He must have thrown it at her and it hit the wall or something. What a dick.

"I'll take that."

"What for?"

"You can't call anyone, so I'm taking away the temptation. In fact, I meant to ask if you called anyone besides me after this happened?"

"No one."

"You're sure? I need to know."

"Yes—you can check my outgoing calls."

I take a look at the cracked screen, click on the home button, and then raise my eyes up.

"Really?" I show him the screen. "Because whose number did you call approximately thirty-five minutes ago."

"I d-d-don't know," Newman stutters as his eyes drop to the ground. "I don't recognize the number."

"You better figure it out." I act like I'm reaching back for my gun.

"I was high earlier," he blurts out.

"That's already been established. The question on the table is who did you call?"

No sooner do I ask then there's a heavy rap at the door. I draw my weapon and point it straight toward the middle of Newman's head. I'm betting that whoever he called is the person on the other side of the door. Making this a bigger mess than it already is.

With my free hand I bring my pointer finger to my lips, motioning for Newman to keep quiet, as I take a look through the peek hole. There's a rather rotund man, at least three hundred pounds, dressed in a tight-fitting navy blue suit looking rather stoic and extra official.

I wait for a moment to see if he'll leave.

"I'm here, Cliff," he says through the door. "Open up."

I look over at Newman. The stranger called him by name, and it's obvious that Newman recognizes the voice as well, because his eyes are as big as saucers and he's stock still. I motion silently for him to walk into the bathroom, but he won't move.

"Walk," I whisper angrily under my breath.

Once we're in the bathroom, Newman sits on the toilet seat and drops his head in his hands. I tap him twice on the side of his head with my gun and give him my "what the fuck" look.

"I forgot that I called him."

"Called who?"

There's increased knocking at the door. Shit, this guy's not leaving.

"I panicked."

"Understandable in this situation," I say through gritted teeth, "but I need to know who's on the other side of that door before I can handle it, Newman."

"He's . . . FBI."

I knew he looked official.

"What are you talking about."

"He's my sister's husband."

"Is he cool? Will he protect you?"

"He's on the management track at the bureau, so he's

completely by the book. I doubt that he's just going to let this go."

"So why the hell would you call your by the book brother-in-law to a murder scene? Are you insane? Did you buy your law degree off of the Internet? You're the district attorney. You're supposed to be smart."

There are another few hard knocks at the door, and then Newman's cell starts ringing. This guy won't quit.

"I think I can get rid of him."

"You think or you know, Newman, because you look petrified right now."

"I'm remembering bits and pieces. I think I may have left Rick a short message about needing his help." He firmly pushes into his temples with pads of his fingers. "Dammit, I didn't actually think he'd come. We're not even that close."

The knocking has stopped which I hope means the fed has given up, but what it probably means is that he's left to get security to grant him access into the room. I could go now, and leave Newman on his own, but that's bad business. Newman is a client, and a contract is a contract. Risk is part of the deal. So I re-evaluate the scenario.

There's a dead body on the bed.

Newman is covered in blood.

My prints are all over the room.

It looks incriminating for the both of us, so I make the only decision that I can live with.

"You're going to have to get rid of him. There's no other way for this to play out without anyone getting hurt. You aren't paying me enough to assault a federal agent, and that's what I'd have to do if he comes inside this room."

"I don't want anyone else getting hurt. Especially Rick. My sister would never speak to me again. Tell me what to do."

But it's too late.

Someone is sliding a key card into the lock.

And that's when it hits me. I forgot to engage the safety latch on the door.

The door bursts open to angry commands.

"On the ground now! Hands behind your head!"

I slowly lower myself to my knees. Hands clasped behind my head. All I can see through my peripheral vision is the barrel of a gun pointed at me, and the very wide orthotic shoe belonging to a man I can only assume is Rick. There's no one else with him, not even hotel security, which is a good thing.

"Is that a dead woman on the bed, Cliffy?" he asks Newman.

"It was an accident."

"Did he do this or did you do it?"

"Calm down, Rick," Newman says nervously. "It was an accident."

"I am calm, but you need to start talking, man, because this looks really bad."

"I know and I'll explain, but first let my friend get up. He's here to help."

"Help you do what?"

"Fix this."

"Fix this?" Rick begins walking around me. Sizing me up. Judging me as most official tightly wound guys like him usually do. Cops, feds, and other official types see my size, my tats, and the way I handle myself as a threat. It's always been like that. It probably will always be that way.

"Nah, I don't think so," he objects. "Not until I get a better understanding of what happened tonight."

Exactly like I thought.

"I'm standing up now, Rick," I say coolly. Sick of kneeling.

"Stay right where you are."

My eye is twitching.

"I had nothing to do with the girl getting hurt," I explain calmly.

"Stay right where you goddamn are!"

"Get your man, Newman," I warn but decide to acquiesce by staying low to the floor for now.

"Rick, please," Newman pleads. "He's only trying to help."

"No fucking way. Both you and him can stay right the hell where you are until you explain what went on in this hotel room."

I sigh to myself. This isn't going to end well for Federal Agent Rick. I hate involving innocent people in my fixes, but there's only so long that I'm going to tolerate a gun in my face. I don't mind a good bar fight, but there's something about a gun in my face that I fucking hate.

While still crouched low, I make my move to end this. I extend my right leg and spin around on the ball of my left foot. Swiping the fed behind the knees and forcing them to buckle. Unfortunately, I don't use enough power, or the guy is heavier than I thought, because he doesn't fall like timber. Instead he catches his balance and takes a hard swing at me which lands right against the back of my head.

Then we start fighting.

We're going blow for blow for about twenty seconds, while Newman cowers over in the corner. It's an unfair matchup, because I'm actually really good with my hands, so I try holding back. I don't want to kill the dude. I just want to tire him out a little. That is until Rick lands a lucky right-hand jab above my left eye and slices it open.

Blood quickly starts to drip down my face.

I wipe my cheek and stare at my bloody fingertips.

Now I'm mad.

When I see my opening, I take two of my fingers and

jab them straight into the fed's windpipe. His hands quickly claw at his throat, and when he gasps for air, I pull out Benny and aim it right at his fat head.

"It's not fun having a gun pointed at you is it," I say snidely as he continues heaving.

"Listen, jackass, you better–" He tries speaking but can't finish his sentence.

"Still talking shit, huh?"

Whap!

I knock him out with the butt of my gun, before he can finish his idle threats. I've had enough of playing nice with Federal Agent Rick.

"What have you done?" Newman cries out. Probably afraid that his brother-in-law is dead.

"New plan. We've got roughly ten to ten minutes to get ghost. I already have a cleanup crew coming here to take care of the body, and I've got a car coming that's going to take you to a safe house. There's no phone there. No Internet. Just a TV, a bed, and a kitchenette. Don't do anything but sit in there and watch some *Law & Order* reruns or go to sleep. We'll figure out how you're going to make the wire and file transfers later. Understood?"

"But–"

"Am I fucking understood?"

"Yes, but what about Rick?" Newman asks reluctantly. His eyes fill with panic. "Is he going to be okay?"

"Don't worry about Rick," I assure him. "I've got this."

~

"So how much do you need?"

"Five hundred."

My mouth is agape. Sometimes I forget just how cavalier seventeen-year-old girls can be, but then again, why am I surprised? It's my baby sister. This is what she does.

The day got away from me, so I ended up meeting Dawn for a late dinner instead of lunch at a restaurant that's walking distance from my office.

"What do you need it for?"

"For prom."

"For prom? Ask Dad for it."

"Daddy doesn't have it."

"Dad doesn't have five hundred dollars? I seriously doubt that. What's more likely is that you've already asked him and he said no, or you haven't even bothered asking him at all. Why ask him when I'm around, right?"

My sister, Dawn, stares me down with a mixture of disdain and the totally judgmental look of an entitled teenager. She thinks because I'm dressed in designer clothes, and that I have an expensive handbag fetish, that I should willingly serve as her own personal ATM machine. As if I owe her something. As if I don't work my ass off every day for the things I have. We're close to nine years apart, and sometimes I think her generation is totally a lost cause, and she's their poster child.

Sometimes, though, I think I understand her.

She's angry.

She was the love child of my philandering father and his "soul mate" of the year. Dawn's mother Marsha. Unfortunately I was the one who ended up growing up with my father in the house (because my parents were married and still are), and all she got were infrequent phone calls and birthday money in the mail. So of course she's angry about that.

What she doesn't understand, or maybe the better word is believe, is that living with our father was no day at the beach either. In many ways she probably dodged a bullet, because I'm pretty sure being raised by him has ruined any chance I have of ever being in a normal relationship with a man.

"I couldn't ask Daddy for the money."

"Why?"

"He's away in Boston on business and evidently cell phones don't work in Boston," she says sarcastically.

"So you're saying that Dad didn't return any of your calls? Did you leave him a message?"

"The first thirty times I did."

"Really, Dawn? Thirty times."

"Okay, maybe not that much, but I definitely called him like three or four times and left a message."

I send my father a quick text. My father's cell phone is practically attached to his hip and always has been. It's out of character for him not to respond. Hopefully he'll see my message, because he knows how to handle Dawn and her drama a lot better than the rest of us.

"Well maybe he didn't call you back because he knows all you want is money. That's all you ever call him for anyway."

"And so what if I do? He probably owes me thousands of dollars in back child support. How does someone who has made millions of dollars in his lifetime never have any money?"

Funny how I often ask myself the same thing.

"Listen I have things to do tonight," I say in the middle of a forced yawn. "I don't have time to discuss everything that's wrong with our father. That could take all night. I just need to know what you need this money for before I give it to you."

Dawn's eyes start to dart all around the room in an obvious attempt to avoid eye contact with me. I am quite familiar with this aversion tactic. Except when I did it, I was only seven years old.

"This isn't about prom is it. Jesus Christ, Dawn, are you pregnant or something?"

"Uh, no and why is that the first thing you assume about me?"

I openly sigh.

"Can you please stop trying to act like you're some sort of vestal virgin. You and I both know that there is always a possibility that you could be pregnant. Not using birth control and ditching the gynecologist appointment that your mother made for you last month widens the likelihood of that."

I already know that Dawn is having sex and isn't on any birth control. Her mother has called me several times crying and begging for me to use my so-called "sisterly influence" to get her to stop spreading her legs. As if anyone could stop a hormonal teenager from getting their rocks off.

Marsha's got a lot of nerve anyway. My father's one-time mistress has little room to judge anyone about their sexuality. She slept with a married man (my dad) for over a year, then sued him publicly for paternity when she was barely twenty-two years old herself, but I guess you see things differently when it's your kid.

"I told you that I'm not putting synthetic hormones into my body only to make the pharmaceutical companies rich when I get cancer twenty years later."

A not so subtle jab at what I do for a living.

"Fine—you don't want to use birth control pills? Well last time I checked, there's no capitalist conspiracy around the sale and use of condoms."

"I'm allergic to them."

"You sound ridiculous. Did your boyfriend tell you that, so you wouldn't ask him to use a condom? Latex allergies aren't even that common."

"I'm *not* pregnant, okay. Let's stop talking about my sex life."

I wish she'd just spit whatever *it* is out then. I'm obviously going to help her no matter what she tells me. I always do. I'd just like to know the details before I do. The last thing I feel like doing is pulling teeth to get the answers though.

"I need to get going so—"

I pull out my Tokyo Tea colored matte lip creme and apply it liberally to my lips. Checking my reflection in the butter knife on the table. It's the only pop of color I allow myself on my otherwise nude makeup look.

"Okay, you win. I'm in a smidgeon of trouble. I'm on the after-prom committee at my school. It was my subcommittee's job to buy lights to decorate the room. Stuff like string lights and strobe lighting. The budget was five hundred dollars."

"And?"

"I didn't need to buy the lights right away, so I loaned the money temporarily to someone. I thought I'd have it back by now, but they're short. They don't have the whole five, and I couldn't buy the lights. Now the prom chair wants to see what I've bought and my receipts for the lights by the next meeting, or she wants the cash back so she can do it herself. The little control freak that she is."

"The committee gave you cash?"

Idiots.

"Uh, yeah. We held a couple of candy bar fundraisers to raise the money, and that's what you get when you sell candy—a whole lot of singles."

"So you loaned a *friend* money that didn't belong to you?"

"Yes." She rolls her eyes. Apparently tired of my interrogation. "It wouldn't have been an issue if my friend had stuck to the agreement. I thought I'd have the money back a long time ago."

"Who is this *friend*?"

"Relax, Wonder Woman. I don't need you to go beat him up for me. I just need you to temporarily loan me the money while I work it out."

"So it's a *him*."

That answers that question. It's got to be the guy she's dating. David, Darren, Damien . . . something like that. It has to be that loser.

"Give me your phone."

I grab Dawn's cell phone off of the table without waiting for her consent and start scrolling through her text messages until I land on the loser's name. It's definitely Damien, because there are a lot of ridiculous heart emoji's next to his name. Something about that irritates me even more, so I change my mind about sending him a nasty text, and decide to call him instead. I press down on the number under his contact, put him on speaker, and wait patiently while it rings.

"What are you doing, Sloan?! Please, give me–"

I swat her hand away.

"Hey, babe–"

"Hello, Damien," I say brightly. "This is Dawn's sister Sloan. Heard of me?"

"Oh, sure. The sister. What's up?"

"What's up is I need you to give my sister back that five hundred dollars she lent you. Today would be fantastic."

"I don't have it, and I ain't going to have it," Damien scoffs. "It was a gift from Dawn, not a loan, and if you really want me to keep it a hundred percent real–what Dawn and I give each other is really none of your business."

The nerve of this degenerate.

"Well guess what? Let me *keep it real* with you as well. My seventeen-year-old sister doesn't have that kind of money to gift to anyone. So you *will* give it back, or I'll be pressing charges first thing Monday morning."

"Press what charges? I didn't steal any money from her."

"Not for theft, idiot. For statutory rape. Trust me, judges love to send jerks like you to jail for a year on a statutory charge. You're too old to be messing around with a girl in high school."

"Cunt," I hear him mutter under his breath. Clear as day.

"What did you just say?" I ask in an appalled voice. My ears are burning. God, I hate that word "Did you just call me . . . a cunt?"

I can barely say the word without gagging.

"Yeah, I said it."

"Just get the money, jackass."

And then I hang up.

After ending the call, I notice that Dawn is staring at me with watery eyes. If she starts full-out crying I swear I'm going to toss a glass of water in her face. All she cares about is *the way* I talked to her boyfriend and not the fact that the user basically stole five hundred dollars from her . . . and called me names!

"What?" I say in a clipped tone.

"I can't believe you did that!"

"I did and you're welcome."

"You've just ruined my entire life, and that's all you have to say?!"

"Ruined your entire life? Don't you think that you're being a little overly dramatic?"

"Of course you'd say that. You haven't had a boyfriend since . . . never. And just for your information, Damien is twenty-one, not forty! That statutory rape threat was really below the belt. We're only four years apart, and we're in love with each other."

"You love a boy who just called your sister a cunt? That's what we're doing now? Falling in love with disrespectful assholes who steal from you? That's just wonderful. I'm so proud."

After we both finish our meals in awkward silence, I stand up and check my reflection again using my camera app. I've spent enough time cleaning up the latest Pearson family mess, and I'm ready to go. I place a couple of twenties on the table before I leave.

"Dinner and an Uber ride home are on me. When do you meet again with the committee?"

"Tuesday," she replies as a tear rolls down her face.

I pretend not to see it. My sister often uses crying as a manipulation strategy. Not really sure where she learned that tried and true technique. Marsha isn't a crier and neither is our side of the family.

"That gives your guy plenty of time to raise the money. I'm sure he can sell a few nickel bags or something over the weekend and get you the cash."

"My boyfriend does not sell marijuana!"

"Uh-huh." As if I believe that. He sounded high on the phone just now. "Anyway, if you don't have the money in your hands by Sunday night, call me."

Hope lights up her eyes. "And you'll give it to me?"

"No, I'm going to go over to his house with a freakin' baseball bat and get it myself."

My sister wipes her eyes and then gives me a deflated look.

"Don't."

"Get the money from him and I won't have to."

"I don't mean beating him up, because I know you'd never actually do that. I mean don't talk about him like that, because I really love him, Sloan. I just wish you'd be a little nicer. I'm not sure why but it seems like you already decided to hate him the moment I told you about him."

"Because you don't listen. Haven't I told you a thousand times? Stop going for the bad boys. The fake gangsters with hard bodies. The dumb ones with the souped up cars and tattoos on their necks. The ones who are always broke and full of excuses. Having a father and a fistful of fake uncles just like him wasn't enough for you? Find yourself a nice, soft in the middle, nerd. One that thinks that you're the best thing since sliced bread. A guy that knows the true meaning of respect. A guy who wouldn't dare call your sister the *c* word."

"So you want me to bang the type of boring guys you do all the time is what you're basically advising," she spits out caustically.

Ugh, the mouth on this girl.

"Exactly, little grasshopper." I pat the top of her head in a patronizing manner as I leave, even though I'd rather give her hair a good yank.

"But what kind of advice is that? It never works out for you," she says snidely.

"Yeah well, my guys don't steal from me. Call me if you end up needing my assistance, baby sis," I say on my way out.

"Forget I even asked."

"Trust me, I wish I could."

~

NINE

SLOAN

Not two minutes after stepping outside of the restaurant does a skinny, stringy-haired boy approach me with an ugly frown across his face. The kind that looks permanently etched there. I know immediately who it is. The damn bum made it here in record time.

"Are you that Sloan bitch?"

There he goes again with the name calling. And does this creeper have a tracker on my sister's phone? How did he know where to find us so quickly?

I stare at him quizzically. Trying to figure out what my sister sees in this ameba. I don't get it.

"That's me."

"You had a lot of shit to say on the phone a few minutes ago. Why don't you say it now that I'm here?"

"If you need me to repeat myself, I have no problem with that," I say in the most condescending voice I can muster. "Give my sister her money back, because she did not give it to you, she lent it to you. And especially because it wasn't even her money to lend."

"How about this is none of your business. Dawn can fight her own battles."

"So, you're admitting that this has become a battle. You're admitting that you're not going to willingly pay back the money you owe her?"

"If or when I pay her back has nothing to do with you. So I'm warning you for the last time to stay out of it."

He finishes his cautionary statement with an air of finality then sticks his greasy forehead to the restaurant's large glass pane window. I assume to look for my sister but primarily to dismiss me.

"Or what?" I ask bravely or stupidly depending on how you want to look at the situation.

He turns back around, surprised and apparently irritated that I've challenged him. It's obvious that he has a problem with women. A major one. Maybe his mother didn't hold him enough when he was a baby or something, because I see nothing but pure hatred in his eyes.

"What did you say?"

"I said *or what*," I repeat not backing down. "What exactly are you going to do if I don't stay out of it?"

"This, bitch."

The only time I've ever been hit in the face was in the middle of an underground game of fifth grade recess dodgeball. We weren't supposed to be playing dodgeball at all, according to the new school "acceptable game play" rules. But a group of the school's fifth grade renegades didn't like to follow rules (myself included), and unfortunately, I paid the price.

Little Joey McFallon was doing his best to get out of the way of the ball and accidentally elbowed me in the eye. Hard. I thought I saw a few stars then, but my sister's deadbeat boyfriend punching me in the eye—hurts ten times worse.

"Ouchhhh!!!"

I hate the feel of Philadelphia concrete.

Especially when it's against the side of my face.

Cold. Bumpy. Hard. Unforgiving.

I can hear the devil spawn's laughter bouncing around in the air above my head. Apparently proud of what he's done.

"Told you to mind your business."

I know that I've got to get up, even though I'd rather stay curled up in a ball on the ground. When he hit me, I didn't just fall down–I slid. So the part of my face that skidded against the sidewalk feels like it's been ripped to shreds. Everything hurts. I don't want to move. But this guy is a maniac, and I can't let him anywhere near my sister again. So I keep trying to move. To get up. It's difficult though, because not only is my face on fire, but one side of my hip is bruised. I must have hurt it on impact.

Then the laughing suddenly stops.

And I hear three rapid sounds.

Bap. Bap. Bap.

They sound like kicks or jabs into a person's stomach or chest. I'm not quite sure which. Definitely something squishy. Then Damien drops to the ground next to me. His face close to mine. His arms around his middle. His eyes rolling up inside of his head.

What on earth?

I try getting up off the ground one more time. Disoriented. Not really sure what's going on with me or around me. Every hair on the back of the neck leaps to attention.

"Don't move, princess."

Holy. Hell.

I know that voice.

Cutter *effin'* King gently slides his hands and forearms underneath my body. Effortlessly lifting me up and curling my body into his. When the side of my face accidentally rubs against his jacket I wince in pain. It feels like a cheese grater shredded my face, but it smells divine. Like leather and musk.

"You have the worst fucking taste in men," he practically growls.

Anger rolling off of him in waves.

"He's my sister's boyfriend," I try explaining. Then I panic. "Wait, my sister. I've got to get to her. She's still in there."

"Taking you to get patched up, princess."

"But my sister—"

Damien is still on the ground, grimacing in pain, but coherent enough.

"You better watch your back, bitch," he threatens me followed by a small groan.

Still firmly holding me, Cutter looks down at him and offers a few menacing words.

"Stay away from this woman and her sister. You touch them, you talk to them, and I'll be back. And trust me, it'll be ten times worse. You feel me?"

Damien doesn't respond. I'm not sure that he can. I'm not even sure if he should. Cutter kicks him once again in the ribs and this time Damien responds with a yelp. Watching the jerk grimace in pain gives me mixed feelings of both glee and guilt. It's the strangest dichotomy.

"Answer me, dickhead. I said do you feel me?"

"Yesss," he hisses but looks right at me with the deadest eyes I've ever seen.

A chill runs down my spine.

Cutter turns back to me and asks, "We good now?"

"No, I told you my little sister is in there. Would you just leave if it were your brother inside?"

I may not know everything about the King brothers, but

from what I've been told, they would probably kill for each other. He has to understand that I can't just leave Dawn inside while this maniac is still out here.

"Fine," he says after sucking his teeth.

"She's only seventeen," I add for good measure.

"Understood. Let's get her and go."

Now that the adrenaline rush I felt earlier is starting to subside, I notice that Cutter's normally beautiful face is a frightening sight. I'm not sure why, but one side of it is completely covered in blood. He looks absolutely lethal.

"Your face," I say. "Did he hurt you?"

"Don't insult me, princess. That piece of shit didn't touch me. *This* here is something else."

"You should go to the hospital," I say. "That looks really bad."

"Nah, babe, you should see the other guy."

He attempts to make light of his injury, but this time the flirty smile I've seen on his face about a dozen times doesn't reach his eyes. I get the feeling that the other guy actually does look worse. A lot worse.

"I hate that I have to do this, because if this were any other day I would patch you up myself, but I've got a few things tonight that just won't wait. I'm in the middle of work. So I'm going to go in there, get your sister, and then drop you two off at Jefferson."

Jefferson Medical is one of the best hospitals in the city and is walking distance from here. It's probably a good idea for me to be seen, but it's Cutter who probably needs to see a doctor more than me.

"I think you're the one who needs the stitches," I say although he chooses to ignore me.

Cutter walks into the restaurant effortlessly with me still completely held in his arms. Bloodied. Battered.

Bruised. He's still angry. I'm still stunned. I'm sure we both look a sight.

"Can you put me down now? I think I'm fine to walk."

"You may have a head injury."

"You're making a scene."

"The answer is no."

Cutter carries me through the restaurant, weaving us through the maze of white tablecloths, as if I weigh nothing which as much as I'd like to wish was the case–just isn't. I'll never forget how a guy I was seeing last year tried to lift me in the shower during sex, and when he couldn't hold me, asked me to ease up on the chips. I kicked his ass out, but it was still mortifying.

"Point her out," Cutter orders quietly.

"There she is."

Dawn runs over to us.

"Oh my God, what happened?" she asks frantically. Looking at me. Then Cutter. "What happened to my sister?" she shrieks at him.

"We're taking your sister to the ER. I believe it was your *boyfriend* who just punched her in the face."

"What?" she asks incredulously as if one of us could actually make this stuff up.

"I said your lowlife boyfriend hit your sister like she was a goddamn man. Now are you going to the ER with her or not?"

The whole restaurant is staring at us.

"I um–"

"Let's go if you're going. Got things to do, little girl," he says as he strides back toward the exit with me still in his arms. "And when we get outside, you better walk by that piece of trash like you don't even see him."

Dawn looks at me for a moment, stands, grabs her things, and follows us solemnly out of the restaurant. Typically I would not have let that slide. Normally I wouldn't have let someone talk to my sister like that. Especially a man.

But my eye is swollen shut, my face is on fire, and watching Cutter King silence my sassy, seventeen-year-old sister was probably the hottest thing I've seen in a long time.

Wait a minute, I think I actually may have a concussion.

TEN

SLOAN

"**S**top laughing."

"I can't."

"Try harder."

"I'm sorry, but it's just too funny. I should stop though, because when I laugh hard like this I either get nauseous or the sudden urge to urinate. At this rate, I just may throw up all over myself or pee my pants."

"You and this pregnancy are getting grosser by the minute. It's amazing to me that the dark knight still wants to have sex with you."

"You'll never have to worry about that happening. Roman always wants to have sex with me."

"Oh good grief."

Elizabeth continues to laugh. Even though I'm pretending that I'm annoyed with her, I enjoy hearing my friend laugh like this. I'm reluctant to admit it, but she's never sounded happier than she does now, and I suppose that her soon-to-be husband has a lot to do with that.

"I can't believe that you find it *so* funny that I was assaulted."

"No, drama queen, I'm not laughing about you being hurt. I'm laughing because it's hysterical that out of all the people in this city that Cutter King happened to be the one passing by that night. I mean what are the chances? I love it."

I've spent the last ten minutes in my underwear, underneath the covers, retelling Elizabeth the entire story of what happened with my sister and her brute of a boyfriend. Of course the only thing she wants to dwell on is the part about Cutter swooping in to save the day.

"I suppose it is a little ironic."

"Or serendipity."

"Oh brother."

"I've been watching you two since you both met at Lotus. There's an undeniable attraction between the two of you that someone would have to be blind not to see. It's just a matter of time before you call me panicking that you had a few too many lemon drops and now your naked, looking out of Cutter's bedroom window on a sunny Saturday morning."

"You're in the wrong profession. You should have been a romance novelist, not a freaking coder. And I don't drink lemon drops anymore for your information."

"What would be so awful about one night with him?"

"There's a slew of reasons. For one, I might catch something."

Elizabeth laughs. "I know what it must look like. All the women that chase after him, especially those girls at the club. It makes you think that there's no way that he isn't sleeping with a different woman every night, but believe it or not, Cutter is not a whore. He likes to look, like every man on earth, but I don't think he lays down with just anyone."

"Can we change the subject, because this one is dead and stinking in the water. The best he and I are ever going to be are strictly friends. Supporting our mutual friends as they marry and have a baby. Nothing more."

"Fine, crazy girl. Whatever you say. So tell me . . . how's your face looking?"

"Horrible," I admit while staring at my purple bruises in a handheld mirror. "There's no way I can take sales calls looking like this. They won't want to buy drugs from me, they'll want to prescribe them."

"You better come up with some sort of stay busy plan, because you're going to go stir crazy sitting in the house all day. Maybe you could help me decorate the nursery."

"I'm not coming out of the house looking like this. I've decided to drown my sorrows in bad carbs and bad television. We've got plenty of time to decorate my godchild's nursery. You know I'm going to hook it up."

"Are you going to press charges against Dawn's boyfriend? You probably should."

"No, I think the scrawny jerk is way more afraid of caveman Cutter than he is of any jail cell I could put him in."

"Really?!"

"Yeah, I'm pretty sure that the caveman scared him straight. Plus, he physically assaulted Damien too. If I report Damien to the police, it's going to open a whole other can of worms."

"True."

"I hate to say it, and I'll never admit it to anyone outside of this phone call, but I think that I'm going to owe Cutter big time for this. Dawn's boyfriend had crazy in his eyes. He probably would have hit me again if Cutter hadn't stepped in."

"So I'm wondering if this whole thing may have changed your bad opinion of our Mr. King?"

"Bitsy, be serious. While I am soooo grateful that he was

there to help, the guy came to my aid already drenched in blood. I don't even know if it was his blood or someone else's. Of course Dawn's boyfriend was scared of him. So was I. Any sane person would have been."

"You couldn't have been *that* afraid. You let him carry you around like you two were shooting a scene in *An Officer And A Gentleman*."

Before I can retort with a snarky comeback, there's a heavy knock at my door. A man's knock. It has to be my neighbor Kyle from down the hall. He saw me earlier and stopped to ask me why I had bandages on my face, and if I heard any news about the quiet lady who was evicted out of the apartment next to him. He's a bit of a gossiper.

"Let me call you back, Bitsy. It's my neighbor."

Kyle's seen me at my worst, so I think nothing about throwing on the closest thing to me (a ratty, old, oversized Penn sweatshirt) and grabbing the door.

"Hey, Kyle–" I say as I open the door.

But it's not Kyle.

Instead I find Cutter King standing at my front door looking pretty much like he did last night. While his face is not covered in blood like it was before, it's obvious that his wound hasn't been properly cleaned. I can clearly see the long gash above his eye which looks like the blood was simply wiped off and temporarily covered with Vaseline.

"Who the fuck is Kyle?" he asks in a no nonsense, authoritative voice.

"None of your business."

"Humor me."

"My neighbor," I respond woodenly.

"That's the way you answer the door for Kyle The Neighbor?"

I look down at myself. I love this throwback sweatshirt from my college days. It's big, and worn in, and while my favorite sweatshirt is long enough to almost hit past my knees, I have nothing on underneath it but a pair of lacy boy shorts. I didn't think much about it before, because I have no romantic interest in Kyle, but maybe I should have put something else on before answering the door.

"He's like a brother to me," I explain.

"I seriously doubt that's the way Kyle sees it."

I pull at the hem of my shirt.

"Are you going to continue to stand in my doorway, or would you like to come in?"

Cutter finally smiles and walks through the door like he owns the place. His thick soled boots sound thunderous walking across my wood floors. I consider for a moment asking him to take them off, so he won't scuff my newly buffed living room, but he might interpret that as an invitation to stay. Which it isn't. I only let him in for the sake of being polite.

He takes a seat in the center of my couch. Spreading his tremendously muscular thighs widely apart. Hands clasped behind his head until he notices a hand-carved wooden statue of a woman on my side table. A keepsake from my last trip to the Caribbean. He picks it up. Rotating it around in his hands. Examining it in a way that I imagine he appraises a woman's actual body. With great interest and deliberate care.

I inadvertently clear my throat. "Wait here for a second. I'm just going to change."

"Please don't put on any pants on my account," he says coolly. "What's good for the neighbor to see is fine by me."

"Me putting pants on has nothing to do with you. I'm just a little cold. Something is going on with my thermostat."

"Uh-huh."

I walk into my bedroom and look for a pair of clean sweatpants. Mr. chatterbox continues to talk to me while

I'm in there. His booming voice reverberating against the walls of my apartment.

"Why did you think it was *Kyle* at the door?"

"We're not sure but we think the woman who lived next door to him was evicted. I thought that was him coming down to talk about it. We're just a little concerned about her."

"You mean a little nosy."

"Same thing."

"I see they took good care of you at the ER."

While it took forever to be seen, my wounds were definitely well irrigated and bandaged.

"They did."

"Did they give you good pain meds?"

"Yep."

"You know you shouldn't take those with alcohol."

He must have noticed the opened bottle of Cabernet I left on the kitchen counter.

"I'm aware."

I find a pair of clean navy blue leggings in my bottom dresser drawer. They actually match perfectly with my sweatshirt.

"And how's your sister?"

"I haven't talked to her."

"Are you angry with a seventeen-year-old kid?"

"You were pissed at her too."

"Yeah, but she isn't my sister."

I return to the living room.

"Obviously I'm still worried about her. That boy has some kind of hold over Dawn, and I'm not sure if she sees that it's toxic."

"He's probably convinced her that you had that punch coming."

"You think so?"

"Yeah, I've known dirtbags like him my whole life. Don't worry about it though. I'm pretty sure he understands who he's fucking with now. I bet right now he's deciding on whether or not your sister is even worth the trouble. I guarantee you he'll decide by the end of the week that she's not."

I'm quite familiar with the King brothers' reputation, and I'm a little worried that his words seem like a threat. While I know Dawn's boyfriend shouldn't be allowed to just walk around violently hitting women in their faces, I'm worried about my sister more. The last thing I need is for Cutter to do something to that kid that would push Dawn further away from the family and right into his arms.

"Don't touch a hair on that kid's head," I order.

"Did I say I was going to hurt him?" he asks obviously offended by what I've said.

"Get up."

"Now you're kicking me out?" he asks incredulously.

"Get up and sit down over at the dining table."

He raises one of his eyebrows suggestively and flashes one of his twenty-four-carat smiles.

"Oh yeah? Why? Are we going to do something fun on it?" he asks as he sits at the table.

I turn my lips up and don't answer him. Then I wash my hands after retrieving the first aid kit from one of the drawers in my kitchen, pull out the antiseptic spray and a fresh gauze pad, and diligently begin spraying his cut and dabbing it gently with the clean gauze. Repeating each step methodically until I've cleaned all of the dried blood off of the gash.

He watches me closely and quietly the entire time. The only sounds in the room are the inhaling and exhaling of breaths.

He follows my fingers.

Then observes my neck as I swallow.

Then he ogles my breasts as they secretly pebble underneath my shirt.

His inspection of me is unsettling, but I continue my work in a diligent manner. Knowing that this is the only way that I can thank him properly. At least the only way that my conscience will allow.

"You know you never mentioned how your face got like this."

"You're right, I didn't."

He doesn't want to talk about it, but I continue to prod anyway.

"Was it work related?"

"What is it exactly do you think I do for a living?"

"You own the club."

"Yeah."

"You own that restaurant in Manayunk."

"I do."

"And you help wealthy people fix their problems."

He nods silently in agreement to that.

"But I'm sure that sometimes that problem solving stuff gets messy."

"Sometimes," he says gruffly. Obviously annoyed with the direction of our conversation.

To finish I pull out a tube of Neosporin and spread some of the ointment across his cut. Although Cutter doesn't flinch at all, I imagine that a cut this deep must hurt something awful, so I start to blow gently on the wound. Hoping that it will provide some relief. Realizing almost immediately that I probably shouldn't have done that.

"Dammit, princess."

He starts shifting in his chair.

"Shh." I quiet him. "Stay still."

I'm pretty sure I already know what he's thinking. What

he's feeling. The sexual tension between us is palpable. It's been this way since the first day we met.

After finishing with the ointment, I look through my assortment of differently sized Band-Aids in my kit and decide on a couple of Mickey Mouse ones for his gash. He'll probably hate them which is entirely the point. They'll look hysterical on his gargantuan body.

"These are going to look great on you." I giggle.

Cutter surprises me by sliding one of his massive palms behind one of my thighs to pull me closer. His touch immediately initiates a gush between my legs.

My body is a backstabbing turncoat.

"I'm not a Mickey Mouse fan," he grumbles in protest.

"What are you talking about. Everybody likes Mickey Mouse, and these will help you get lots of attention in the club. The girls will be falling all over themselves trying to make sure that you're okay."

"They will, huh."

I can feel his warm breath on my neck.

It smells like a peppermint Tic Tac.

He slides another hand behind my other leg.

"What are you doing?" I whisper.

"Nothing. What are you doing," he says in a deep voice that makes me tremble. Close to my ear. Being careful to avoid the side of my face covered in gauze.

"Cutter–" I say unconvincingly.

"When that kid hit you in the face and I saw you fall on the sidewalk, I wanted to put his ass in the ground."

"Thank you, but–"

"Can I have a kiss?"

His provocative question dangerously tickles my neck.

I can't talk.

My only response is to offer him an inaudible head nod no.

"No?" he chuckles softly. Pressing his lips into my skin.

"No," I manage to eek out.

"What's his name then? Can you at least give me that?" he asks as he takes a good whiff of my hair.

"What?" I ask feeling a little loopy.

"I was so fucking furious that night, I forgot to ask you," he explains. "I'm going to need the kid's name."

I close my eyes as he just barely places his lips along my collarbone.

"If he even breathes in your direction again, it will be the last breath he takes."

Then my eyes pop back open.

Cutter's words splash over me like an icy cold jug of water.

Just when I thought I was patching up my own personal wounded hero, I'm quickly reminded that Cutter King is and will always be a menace to society. He's nobody's hero. He's a dangerous thug for hire, and I don't want to be responsible for unleashing his brand of crazy onto anyone. Even trash like Dawn's boyfriend.

"Don't touch a hair on that kid's head, Cutter."

He laughs into my neck.

"You said that already."

"I mean it."

"Or what? What are you going to do if I touch him?"

"Or . . . or . . . I don't know what. Just leave him alone. Pretend like it never happened. Like you didn't see anything."

"As if I could ever do that."

He gingerly touches the edges of my bandages.

"When did the doctor say these could come off?"

"Where is this coming from?" I yank my head away from his touch. "You and I aren't even friends. Why do you care about what happens to me so much?"

"That's a valid question."

Cutter takes both hands and pulls my knees forward. Lifting then sliding my butt completely onto his lap. As I fall forward I have no choice but to grab ahold of his shoulders. Shoulders so strong that they feel like they could carry the weight of the world on them if they needed to.

"First of all, I would defend any woman who was sucker punched by a man. Friend or no friend. And secondly, your best friend is about to marry my best friend. In my book that means you're like family now, and a King always takes care of what's his."

"Like family? That's a big leap," I say while foolishly trying to push against his shoulders and wiggle out of his hold. "I'm not yours."

"Not yet."

"Not ever."

"You should stop fighting this." He grins flashing a couple of teeth. "You're going to regret those words later when we're holding each other post orgasm, and then it's going to be all awkward for you."

I almost slip up and laugh.

I've got to admit, the guy is hilarious.

"Are you going to make a pass at me every time we see each other?"

"Probably."

"It's such a waste of his majesty's energy," I tease.

He laughs out loud.

"Nice to see you finally recognizing my royal lineage, as well as accepting the fact that we'll be seeing each other again . . . and again. I think I'm growing on you."

He pulls me in tighter. Staring at me hard. Without even blinking. Gripping the sides of my hips and my ass. The position enables me to feel how hard he's growing through his jeans. Like a stiff steel rod. A *very* thick, steel rod. It's way more information than I needed to know. I suppose I imagined that he was pretty large down below, but to have proof, to actually *feel* the proof is a whole other matter. I panic and push on his wound with the heel of my hand, hoping he'll wince, then loosen up his hold on me. It works.

"Christ! Are you trying to hurt me on purpose?"

"I'm trying to get you to stop manhandling me."

"All you had to do was ask nicely."

"I'm not a nice girl."

He smirks, then drops his hands away from my hips in a dramatic fashion, allowing me to maneuver myself off of his lap.

"You're a confusing girl."

"You're confused about the fact that I don't want to sit on your lap?"

"You were all over me when we first met."

"You have quite a knack for embellishing, *your majesty.* That did not happen. I was cordial. Pleasant. I was *not* all over you."

"I'm not imagining it," he says with a clipped tone. "You're just fighting this for whatever reason."

"Fighting what exactly? Sleeping with you?"

"Obviously."

"Are you implying that it's obvious that I want to sleep with you?"

"One thing I know is a woman's body, and yours definitely responds to me every time I'm within ten feet of it. I'm confident that if I had asked nicely, I could have talked you right out of that pretty dress today."

"Unbelievable." I shake my head in astonishment. Annoyed with his presumptuousness but mostly angry at myself. "I'm sure my behavior just now confused you, but please understand that I didn't just let you kiss my neck because of some strong attraction toward you. It's because you've caught me in a weak moment."

"Weak for me."

"I know this may be a difficult concept for you to grasp, but I'm just not interested in sleeping with you. It would be a waste of time. For both of us."

"No, seriously."

"Oh my God, you're so irritating. I am serious!"

"Seriously stubborn," he scoffs. "I'm attractive, I'm rich, and a damn nice guy. What's not to like?"

"Plenty."

"Are you afraid of just how good it could be between us? Is that the real issue?"

"No, I'm *afraid* that you need major psychological counseling. There is no issue. I'm just not interested. Do you *comprendo* yet?" I ask in my version of a bad Spanish accent.

"Oh, there's definitely an issue." He chuckles.

"Believe it or not, not every woman is charmed by you."

He cocks his head to the side, in a quizzical manner, as if what I've just said is an impossibility.

"No, you're definitely attracted to me. It's something else. Every time I try getting close to you, you run from me like you're frightened."

Because I am.

"So then I guess the real question is why do you keep trying to get close to me?" I retort.

He sits for a moment, as if he's contemplating my question, when really all he's doing is eye fucking me as usual. It's actually disturbing how I'm starting to get used to it. Expect it. Dare I say . . . enjoy it.

"Well?" I say.

"Oh, I thought that was a rhetorical question," he says after a few deep chuckles.

I grab a bottle of water from the fridge, pop an eight-hundred-milligram pain killer, then pick up my cell to start checking texts.

"Is there anything else I can get you before you leave?" I ask him nonchalantly. Hoping he'll take the hint and scram.

"I feel like I just got here."

"You came here to check on me and I'm fine. I cleaned your cut for you, and so you're fine, although I highly recommend that you get some stitches. Our business is finished."

"Did I overstay my welcome?"

I stand with my arms crossed. Staring at him silently with turned up lips.

"Oh, I'm sorry," I finally say after a long pause. "I thought *that* was a rhetorical question."

Cutter belly laughs and there's something about it that I admittedly like. This time his laugh makes the smile on his face actually reach his eyes in the most genuine way. It's not the kind of fake smile he gives his minions at the club. This one is different. Softer. Almost kid-like.

"That's fine," he says. "I've got some business to take care of anyway. Make sure that you take a day or two off of work, stay in bed, and I'll be back to check on you soon."

"I'll be fine. If I need anything—"

"Elizabeth can't run errands for you, she's way too pregnant, and that sister of yours doesn't seem too dependable."

"If you'd let me get a word in edgewise, you'd know that I wasn't going to bother Elizabeth at all. I was just going to say that if it's important, my neighbor will get me what I need. Anything else I can just order online. So don't concern yourself."

Cutter's voice immediately drops two octaves.

"I don't know who the fuck *Kyle* is. So like I said, I'll be back. I'll even cook you dinner. I can grill the hell out of a steak."

I sigh to myself. I meant one of my other neighbors, not

Kyle, but it'll probably just be easier to agree with the caveman, so that he'll finally just go.

"Fine."

He gets up to leave.

"Remember, no work for a few days. Just rest. Your face will heal faster."

"I heard you the first time, *Grandma*."

"That's the king to you."

"Yada. Yada."

"Later, princess," he says on his way out the door.

"And the name is Sloan!" I yell down the hallway as I watch *his majesty's* body quivering with raucous laughter.

ELEVEN

CUTTER

"Things have to change," I say to my brother after slamming down a plastic cereal bowl on the kitchen island and pouring myself a bowl of Raisin Bran–the only edible thing left in our kitchen. Apparently, his girlfriend doesn't think we should eat eggs and bacon for breakfast anymore.

Jade's the devil.

"I know, Cut." Camden chuckles. "Jade's on a vegan kick lately. I'll talk to her about it when she gets home. She's at the gym right now. And where the hell do you buy Mickey Mouse Band-Aids?"

"No, I'm serious, and hand me the fucking milk if that even is milk."

My brother knows perfectly well that my bad attitude has nothing to do with breakfast. We haven't talked or seen much of each other in the last few days, and if I didn't know better I'd swear that he's been purposely ducking me. Probably a smart idea on his part. The way I've been feeling lately, I would have definitely taken a swing at him.

"It's cashew milk and I promise I won't leave you hanging like that again."

"That's not good enough. I want to talk about a restructuring. The fuck is cashew milk?"

"Restructuring what?" He stops to ask while staring hesitantly at a putrid green colored smoothie in the same blender that I use to make my infamous old-fashioned vanilla shakes. He's totally cross contaminating the blender. I'm never using that thing again.

"Lately I've been doing the work of three men and getting paid for one," I gripe.

"Not true."

"True as shit."

"Not fucking true."

"True as all hell! You both are so busy getting your dicks led around by your women that you're forgetting that we have a business to run." I open the fridge and stare blankly inside of it. "Do we have one thing left in this house to eat that had parents?!"

"If you'd get your own girl, you wouldn't be so wrapped up inside of your feelings like this."

"I get a different girl *of my own* every single night, and then I send them right back home where they belong."

Camden's body stiffens. "Do you have some sort of a *problem* with my woman living here?"

"I'm not sure that you've noticed lately, since I've been cleaning up this Newman mess for the last few days, but do you see what my normally pretty face looks like? What I have is a *problem* that one side of it is black and blue and sliced open. What I have is a *problem* that I had to fight, knock out, tie up, and move a fat ass federal agent out of a hotel and into the trunk of my brand-new Mercedes Benz by my fucking self. What I have is a *problem* that a gun was pointed at my head by said fed. What I have is a *problem* that Newman was not an easy fix like you said he would be. In fact that fix required me to pull off some James Bond-esque shit. So the answer to your question is no. My *problem* isn't with Jade or the fact that she lives here with us. My *problem* is with you!"

Camden doesn't even blink at the fact that I'm raising my voice, and continues to calmly stuff a handful of spinach into the blender with the rest of his goo. I don't know why I bother yelling at him. He rarely gives a damn.

"Obviously Newman didn't tell me that he fucked around and killed a woman. If I had known that, I would have dropped everything and been there to assist. You know that."

"You should have been there regardless. It's *our* business. A joint partnership. I don't work for you or Roman. I'm not your employee. Just because I'm laid back doesn't mean I'm easy."

Camden exhales deeply. "One thing that you're definitely not is easy, Cut, and I've never once thought of you as anything less than my partner. Ever. You're my brother and my best friend, but you're beating a dead horse at this point. I don't know what more you fucking want. I've already said I'm sorry, and that it won't happen again. I'm not going to apologize twice."

"No? Well that works out then, loverboy, because I'd really rather not hear your half-assed apology again. I want a restructuring."

He runs the blender again for a moment and then stops.

"Explain."

"I'm leaving."

"What do you mean?"

"Leaving town. I'm sure that fat fed is gunning for me ever since he woke up in the trunk of a car, somewhere in New Jersey, with a lump on the back of his head. I figure

I'm going to need to get out of dodge for a while. While I'm gone, I think the three of us need to figure out a better working arrangement."

"The fed isn't going to be a problem. Roman's on it. You don't have to leave town."

"You're not understanding what I'm saying. I want to go. I need to go."

My brother stares at me and his posture stiffens for a moment. It's the first honest reaction I've gotten out of him today. Then he pours and takes a swig of the disgusting green goop he's made, grimaces, and asks me a question.

"Is this your way of punishing me, little brother?"

I sit down with my soggy cereal and start talking with a spoonful of it in my mouth.

"I think that vegan smoothie Jade makes you drink every day is punishment enough. So no, I'm not trying to punish you. I just need a break."

"A break from me."

"From everything. I'm being pulled too thin right now. The club. The restaurant. The fixes."

"So you need a vacation." He takes a long final swig of his smoothie and plunks the cup down on the counter. "Done."

"That's not exactly what I meant, Cam."

"I heard you loud and clear. You need some time off. Done."

I shake my head to myself. It's my brother's one short-coming. Sometimes he only hears what he wants to hear. It would be pointless to argue him down. So I just let it go.

I get a call from one of "my" kids from the old neighborhood. A boy named Johnson who I pay sometimes to gather a little intel for me. I'm hoping he can tell me a little something about the dude who hit Sloan.

"Let me take this," I say to Camden then I answer my cell. "Hey, Johnson."

"Hey, man."

"What's up? You find out anything?"

"So he's not from around the neighborhood."

"I know that already. I would have recognized him. I told you that he looked tweaked. Did you check with some of the corner boys? See if he buys from anyone. Sells for anyone."

"I put a call out. Based on your description nothing came up yet. I've got eyes everywhere though."

"Then what are you calling me for?" I say raising my voice.

"You told me to keep you updated."

"Call me when you've actually got something."

I end the call abruptly.

Frustrated with Johnson.

Pissed at Camden.

Wondering how Sloan's doing. What she's doing.

"You probably can't find him, because he's not on anyone's radar. He's just some random kid who thinks he's a tough guy. Did you go on the girl's social media to look for him?" Camden asks.

"I know how to do my job and yours. Obviously, I already did that. She has nothing up about him. No pictures. No posts. In fact she hasn't posted anything at all in about six weeks."

"That's weird for a seventeen-year-old kid."

Yeah, it is.

"On another note, during my *time off*, I'm going to work on a little research project that you may be interested in."

"What is it?"

"I got something else from Newman other than three wasted days of my life."

"I hope we got paid."

"We did. It's in the account. An extra thirty percent by the way, and you're welcome, but I'm talking about something else. He sent me a file of an investigation that he did on the three of us, and get this—it supposedly includes information about some long-lost brother you and I have. He was probably just feeding me some bull to ensure that I'd take care of the body, but just in case he wasn't—"

Camden goes stock still, and I swear he starts turning the color of the green crap he just drank.

"I'm not understanding your reaction," I say suspiciously. Wondering why he's so quiet. "Tell me you don't already know something about this."

He exhales painfully. "Maybe a little something."

"A little like . . . we actually do have a brother and you failed to mention that shit?"

"I didn't think there was any truth to it."

"Truth to what?"

"Something that Joseph said in passing when we were in the middle of a heated discussion. I thought he only said it to get a rise out of me. I didn't think for one second that it could actually be real."

Joseph Masterson is Roman's father, our former boss, and most times a domineering asshole. It's totally plausible that he was trying to get under Cam's skin, but he usually does that with hard truths. Not lies.

"When did the two of you have this heated discussion?"

"At least two years ago."

Two fucking years ago?!

I'm so angry right now that I can't see straight. My brother blatantly broke several of the King brother rules. Rules that the hypocrite himself has spent half of our lives enforcing.

1. Family comes first

2. We do not lie to each other.

3. We do not keep secrets from one another.

4. We do not fight about money.

5. We do not fight over women.

I pick up the closest thing to me, which is my mushy bowl of Raisin Bran, and sling the entire thing across the room at Camden's head.

He ducks just in time.

Bran flakes and cashew milk drip down the wall directly behind him.

The big fucker has always had quick reflexes.

"The only reason why you're getting away with that—" He points his finger at the wall then at me. "Is because you already got your ass kicked once this week."

My eye starts to twitch. If ever I have felt close to wanting to pummel my brother into next month, it's at this moment, but I might really hurt him if I did that. We're not kids anymore. We're grown men. We don't need to fight. That would be disastrous.

What we need is space.

If I wasn't sure about it before, I am crystal clear about that right now.

"I'll be out of here by the end of the week."

"Do what you gotta do," Camden says in his bitter *I don't give a shit* voice, as if I'm the one being unreasonable.

No remorse.

No apology.

So I pack my two large black duffels and walk out on my brother for the very first time in our lives. If the one brother I've loved all my life treats me like this, I've decided that I'm definitely in no rush to meet another.

~

TWELVE

CUTTER

"Hey, man, it's me again."

My phone rings through the Bluetooth acti-vated sound system in my car. I've basically been driving around the city in a fog for an hour trying to calm myself down. Worried like an imbecile about things like who's going to schedule the waitress shifts at the tapas lounge or who's going to make sure that Marco remembers to put in those extra orders of vodka at the club. Then realizing that it's not my problem anymore. Somebody else is going to have to step up while I sit on my ass for a while. Maybe then Camden and Roman will realize how they've made the mistake of taking my kindness for weakness.

"What's up, Johnson."

"I think I've got something."

"What."

"A flag went up at your lady's job."

I pull the car over.

"Explain."

"A kid fitting your guy's description just applied for a mailroom position in her building."

"Did you get a name?"

"No, my contact saw the guy go in for an interview. No names yet."

"What businesses are in the building?"

"Only the drug company. They own the whole thing."

Fuck me.

"He's doing a piss poor job of it, but he's fucking stalking her."

"We won't know for sure that it's him, boss, until we get the name. Probably half of the mailroom there fits his description. Give me another day or so. My guy's uncle works in the IT department there. He has to try and pull the human resource records without leaving a footprint. In the meantime, you keep trying to get some info on him too."

"Who's hiring who, Johnson?"

"Sorry, boss. I'm not telling you what to do. Obviously, you're still working your magic on your end. Just want to make sure we get this scumbag for you."

I'm just giving Johnson shit because I'm mad at myself. What kind of fixer can't find a twenty-one-year-old kid.

"Gotta take another call. We'll catch up later."

It's Roman.

"What's up," I answer flatly. Already assuming that I know what this call is about. Roman doesn't do chitchat.

"I talked to Camden."

Of course he did. That little snitch.

"I hear that you're taking some time off."

"That's right."

"I know what happened at the hotel, and I feel fucked-up about it, Cut. Normally I would have been there, but Elizabeth was having something called Braxton-Hicks contractions that night."

"Uh-huh."

"We thought she was having the baby early. She was

scared out of her mind. I was shitting bricks. Wasn't going to leave her by herself, brother."

"I'm not trying to be an asshole, Rome, but that wasn't the only night you and Cam both left me hanging. I understand that there's going to be a lot of things that come up now that you're getting married and are about to have a baby, but me carrying all of the weight isn't the solution. We need another plan if this is going to be a true partnership moving forward. Otherwise it feels more like *my* business instead of our business.

"You serious?"

"Fuck yeah I'm serious."

I hear muffled voices in the background. He's apparently distracted by something or someone around him. Probably Elizabeth as usual.

"Listen, brother, we can talk about the inequality of how we're dividing up work later. Just trust that we'll fix this. Right now I'm calling about something else, and then I've gotta go."

The blow off as expected.

"What."

"It's the glamazon."

"What about her?"

"I heard about the black eye."

My chest tightens. I can tell by the tone of his voice that he's going to say some shit I don't want to hear.

"And?"

"*And* I called you because it's no secret that you've been scaring away dudes at the club who even think about looking at her two seconds too long. Not totally sure I understand why, but understand this, Cut—she doesn't belong to you. You haven't made a claim. I'm not even sure that's what you're planning to do. So I wanted to make sure you understood that she's my woman's best friend, and I'll take care of it. It's nothing. The scrawny kid that bags my groceries at the mini mart could deal with this asshole. So don't worry. He won't hit her again."

"Do you know who he is?"

"Not yet."

"Do you know where he is?"

"Not yet but like I told you, I'll handle it."

"Do you seriously think you can just call me up and order me to stay out of this? You're not her father or her brother. In fact, from everything I've observed, she doesn't even like your ass."

"Well from what I hear, she doesn't like you very much either."

"Listen, asshole–"

"I didn't call to argue, Cut. Just stay out of my way."

"You arrogant mother–!"

"Bye, Cut."

Click

I rake my hand across my head several times in frustration. This day is going to complete shit. Until the best idea I've had in a long time pops into my head. I'm going to beat Roman at his own swinging his big dick around game.

"HOW DID you know about the opening in our downtown property, Mr. King? We haven't even posted it publicly yet."

"Oh you know how it is, Ms. Toddson," I say flashing a smile. "News of prime rental vacancies spreads fast in this town."

"I guess it does." She grins. "And please call me Maria."

"Maria then."

Maria Toddson is a middle-aged realtor with an oversized wedding ring on her finger, and deep crow's feet, who was probably hot as hell in her heyday. She's not the best realtor in the city by a long shot, but she's the one I need for this specific listing.

"I have no problem showing you the apartment, Mr. King, but based on your credit profile you may be more interested in a vacancy in one of our luxury buildings. I've got a beautiful penthouse coming up in a month on Spruce. It's totally your style."

"No thanks, Maria. I want that specific apartment, on that floor, in that building, and as soon as possible. Can you make that happen?"

"If that's what you want, then that's what we'll do. I'll grab the paperwork right now, but just so we're clear, the minimum commitment is a twelve-month lease in that space."

Aww, that's cute. She's trying to play hardball.

"This is just a temporary arrangement, Maria. I don't want to be pinned down to a year commitment. Let's just do a month-to-month."

"Hmm—then if you don't mind, I really think I should show you another space. The owner wants at least a twelve-month commitment on the rental. I promised him that."

I already did my homework before approaching Maria about this rental. The building is under distress and is in the first leg of the foreclosure process. The owner has a bit of time to turn things around before the bank takes back the property, but he's not handling it well. I'm guessing he probably has nothing but month-to-month renters in the building who are paying rent rates from ten years ago.

"Does it really have to be this space?"

"Yes."

"I don't usually say this to clients, but I feel like you're totally down to earth."

"I like to think that I am."

"So then I'll be honest with you. I have to be careful with this particular rental. I took a chance the first time and rented the space to someone who couldn't afford it, and now my boss is giving me a hard time, because we had to spend money to evict her. So while it's obvious that you can afford it, I don't want you to take it if you know you're just going to leave mid-lease. I'd have to find another renter six months from now, and I just can't risk having any more drama."

I didn't become this wealthy at this age by making stupid decisions. Normally I would wait and try to buy a piece of real estate like this once the property reached the point of a short sale. That's when you can grab a property at a dirt cheap price and immediately make a profit. Yep, I'm about to make a stupid decision, but I can afford it and most of all—I'm highly motivated.

"Do you think the owner would consider selling?"

"You want to buy the unit instead of rent it?"

"No, Maria. I want to buy the whole building not just the apartment. A cash offer. Would that settle things?"

Her eyes widen.

"Really? I mean if I was going to be totally forthright, Mr. King, I'd tell you that my boss would probably jump at the right offer."

"Get me in the room with the owner today, and I'll make sure that part of the agreement includes that you get a five percent commission."

She tries to contain how excited she is.

"You're positive? The entire building?"

"Positive."

"Awesome! I'll get him on the phone right now." We shake hands to make it official. "Welcome to the neighborhood, Mr. King."

~

FOR THE LAST FIVE YEARS, I've lived in the carriage house that my brother and I bought together. It was our first substantial real estate purchase since leaving our mother's tiny row house in the old neighborhood. We made sure to buy a place that was spacious, with high ceilings, to accommodate our large statures. A home that's modern, professionally decorated, and is regularly cleaned by a diligent crew of women who know exactly how we like things. So, even though I'm not moved in yet, I can already see that this new place is going to be a little different than what I'm used to.

It was important that I get this particular apartment. A modest corner unit with exposed brick in the living room, two decent sized bedrooms and a great view. I decided the easiest way would to get it would be to cut out the middle man. To accomplish that, I am now the brand-new owner of a seven floor, twenty-eight-unit, Center City, rental property.

And best of all . . .

I don't have to listen to Camden and Jade having sex half of the night.

I can stock the fridge with whatever carnivorous snacks I want.

And I'm going to be within walking distance of my latest fix . . . or rather my fixation.

Her.

THIRTEEN

SLOAN

"Morning, Ms. Pearson."

"Good morning, Mr. Stokes."

Our sales division head, John Stokes, walks out of the elevator with his bike and complete cycling gear on. I admire that he's sixty-four years old and still rides his bike five miles to and from work every day, but he's also the last person I feel like seeing right now. Frankly, he's my boss's boss. I didn't even think the man knew my name.

"So how are you adjusting to managing your own team?"

According to my pitiful sales numbers, not so well.

"I'm really enjoying the challenge, sir. Thanks for asking." I smile painfully.

"How long have you been a manager in the department?"

"A couple of months. Not that long."

"Hmm . . ." He holds his chin as if he's in deep thought. "I spent a bit of time going over your numbers over the weekend, and while you're doing a decent enough job, I think there's definitely room for improvement."

Could my luck get any worse? The division head picks

my numbers to review out of all the teams in our department.

"You're a hundred percent right, Mr. Stokes, but I'm not worried," I say with feigned confidence. "My team is young. Give us some time, and we'll get the numbers up."

"Cocky, huh? I like that."

"Not cocky . . . just confident, Mr. Stokes."

"Even better." He smiles. "So Sloan, may I call you Sloan?"

"Of course."

"You show a lot of promise, but unfortunately we are a numbers driven department and potential doesn't make the stockholders happy. Results do. So I'd like to check in with you personally around the end of the quarter. See where your numbers are. Then we'll know how to proceed from there."

"Sure, that sounds fair."

"You took the day off yesterday, right?"

Wow, he's definitely paying attention.

"Because of this," I say referring to my face.

"May I ask what happened?"

While my scars are healing nicely, I still basically look like the bride of Frankenstein. People at work are trying to be polite about it, but I know they're talking about me. Especially because I haven't told anyone the truth about how it happened. In my opinion, it's really nobody's business.

"Freak accident."

"I see. Well, Sloan, I'm not going to beat around the bush. I'm thinking that I'd really like to see you match the numbers that Regan Pullson's team is bringing in by next quarter."

A wave of nausea hits my stomach. He has to realize that he's asking me to perform an almost impossible feat.

Regan's territory is larger and more established than mine. Two facts that she never lets me forget.

"Um, okay," I say while holding back angry tears. "I'll work on that."

"Make sure to book yourself on my schedule with Martha."

"Will do, sir. Looking forward to it."

Mr. Stokes turns to walk toward his office when he stops to speak to me once more.

"And one more thing, Sloan."

"Yes?"

"I didn't see your name confirmed for the advanced sales training program."

Crap.

Every manager in the company has been strongly encouraged to enroll in the company's advanced sales training program. An invitation-only program which is offered once a year and is held in a different city every year. Our company is global, so sales managers from all over the world attend. It's expected for me to enroll since I've newly been made a sales manager, and it's actually a privilege to be invited, but I dread the entire thing. Sitting in an auditorium and listening to panels of men speak on how innovation in pharmaceutical production is changing the world all day is not my idea of a good time.

"I actually planned on confirming with Fern this week."

Fern is my immediate supervisor and the person in charge of confirming my enrollment. I hadn't confirmed my participation with her yet, because I had a personal conflict with the date. The conflict being I didn't want to do the shit. I'm sure she couldn't wait to share my procrastination with Mr. Stokes, because although she puts up a good façade, it's obvious that she, as well as another woman in this division, namely Regan, do not have my back.

"The training is always a good time, and you'll definitely learn a lot. I'm a keynote speaker on one of the goal setting panels this year. It'll be nice to have a few members of my team in the class."

I'm not entirely sure what's happening, but the fact that the head of the sales department knows that my numbers suck, calls me out on them, and is double-checking to make sure that I attend the sales program tells me everything I need to know. I have to go if I want to keep my job. But I'm going to hate every minute of it.

"Sounds awesome, Mr. Stokes. I'll be there."

~

"THERE'S a man in the lobby who I guarantee you just made me ovulate. If I'm pregnant by next month, you all will know the date of conception and who the father is."

I almost spit out my cup of coffee from chuckling at the comments of our office receptionist, Gidget. She's a relatively new hire. Young and spunky, a little thick in the thighs, and someone I'm starting to have a serious girl crush on. She basically has no filter, and that's rare to find in the very corporate—boring—world of pharmaceuticals.

"Who is he?" I ask. Always curious about whatever gossip she has to share for the day. Desperately wanting to think about anything but my own personal drama.

"What are you two hens clucking about now?"

Enter the company's resident hair flipper and ass kisser, Regan Pullson. Also known as the biggest passive aggressive bitch in the office and the woman who Mr. Stokes just threw in my face. Reagan and I have been at odds with each other since basically the first moment we met. There's just something about me that she doesn't like, and now that we both head our own team of sales reps it's getting even worse. Everything is a competition with her.

"I haven't had enough coffee for her this morning," I mutter under my breath as Gidget chuckles at my comments. I knew almost immediately that Gidget and I would get along famously when she was hired. She totally gets me. "If she flips her hair one more effin' time."

"I was telling Sloan here about the giant wet dream in the lobby," Gidget says to Regan. "He's so hot that I'm about to go to the bathroom and use the hand dryer to dry my thong out."

I belly laugh again.

This girl's a hoot.

"Honestly." Regan rolls her eyes and turns her lips up with distaste. "You're so inappropriate, Gidget."

"I try, thank you very much."

Gidget curtsies facetiously.

"Why are you even back here talking about him anyway? Isn't it your job to find out *why* he's here and who he's here to see?"

"That's exactly why I am back here." Gidget grins and turns to point directly at me. "He's here to see you, Sloan."

"Me?" I respond incredulously.

"Yep, he specifically asked for you, and I just need to say this. If you're not seeing this guy romantically, then please tell him that I'm ready and available to have his babies. His big, strong, Viking babies. Tell him I'll be sure to raise them in the ways of his Viking gods."

I can't help but laugh out loud this time.

Gidget is certifiable.

"Well now I have to take a look," Regan says. Which is not surprising. Now that she knows that the mystery man has asked specifically for me, all of a sudden, she *needs* to know who he is and what he looks like. As if it's a problem that a hot looking guy is asking for me instead of her. That's why I take great pleasure in the look on her face when she returns from the lobby.

A look of a woman who just swallowed crow.

"He's definitely here for you," she says dismissively.

"And what's that supposed to mean?" I say. "Who does he work for?" I ask standing up and meticulously freshening up my red lip gloss in the reflection of my computer. It's the only bit of makeup I can actually apply considering that I have a large, ugly, gauze pad on one side of my face and a bluish eye.

"I don't think by the looks of him that he works for anyone *the three of us* know," Regan says as she walks away. "He's definitely not in pharmaceuticals. Not legal ones anyway."

I can't imagine the kind of person matching Regan's description who'd be here to see me. But as I get closer to the lobby, I smell *my guest* before I see him and realization sets in.

I know him.

My visitor is wearing a distinct woodsy, but clean musk and leather scent that smells expensive and unique only to him. And once I make my way around the corner of the hallway into the lobby, and verify who it is, I almost choke on my own saliva.

He's massive, muscular, and standing against the wall in all black, stubble covering his strong jaw, his midnight kissed hair shorn low, with his tatted forearms crossed in front of him. It's only been a few days since I last saw him, but he's grown hotter if that's even possible. Even I have to admit, that if I didn't already know him, I'd climb him like a pole right in this entryway.

But I do know him.

And there's something about Cutter King that reminds

me of every bad relationship I've been in and every bad decision I've ever made.

He's desperately good looking, but he knows it.

He's built sturdy and strong like a tank, but he's reckless.

He looks like every woman's fantasy, but for me he's a nightmare.

In the real world Cutter King is dangerous, arrogant, and entirely too smug. All excellent reasons why I'm not remotely interested in exploring anything physical with him; not to mention the fact that he alludes to getting inside of my panties almost every time I'm within six feet of him.

Pervert.

"Is everything okay with Elizabeth?" Is my passive aggressive way of asking him what the heck he's doing at my place of business unannounced and uninvited.

"The baby's still in her belly as far as I know."

"So then why are you standing in the middle of my lobby?"

We now have an audience. At this point I should shove a bucket of buttered popcorn in Gidget's lap and a bag of Twizzlers in Regan's, because all four of their eyes are fixed on the two of us. Moving back and forth between us like a game of ping-pong.

"I came by to check in on you, like I said I would, but guess who wasn't home in bed like a good girl?"

"What are you talking about?" I ask defiantly.

Cutter gives me a stern stare.

"You know what I'm talking about. You're here at work when I specifically told you to take a few days off. Good thing for you I knew where to find you."

Gidget giggles under her breath, and I'm quickly reminded that people are listening. People who are probably interpreting this conversation in the completely wrong way.

"Can you go into my office for a moment, Mr. King? Third door on the left. I'll be there in a moment."

"Of course, Miss Pearson," he says as he shamelessly winks at both Gidget and Regan before walking toward my office. "I'll be waiting patiently."

~

FOURTEEN

SLOAN

I stand with my back flat against the wall a few feet down from my office door. I need a moment to collect myself. My one good cheek is flushed. My panties damp. Apparently, all Cutter needs to do is make a pop-up appearance in my life and my hormones go into overdrive. I become combative, flustered, and freaking horny which is a dangerous and potent brew. Of course the reason I feel this way could totally be because I haven't gotten laid in a really long time. In fact, I'm sure that's what's going on. So that's an easy fix.

I need to make myself a good old-fashioned dick appointment.

I take a few steps farther down the hallway toward the west elevator and start scrolling through the contact list on my cell phone, looking for an oldie but goodie. Someone that I can have a no strings attached night of carnal pleasure with, somebody that I'm still on good terms with, *and* a guy that will make me forget all about how ridiculously attracted I am to the man sitting in my office.

Crap, that's a tall order.

I text Elizabeth instead.

Me: Talk me off the ledge.

Elizabeth: Well good morning to you too.

Me: I'm about to jump.

Elizabeth: What are you talking about?

Me: Wait a minute, I'm going to call you instead.

"Hello?"

"I need to get laid."

"Excuse me?"

"Some dick. The pipe. A little cock."

"I'm sorry but I only have a vagina."

"And *he's* here."

"Who's where? What are you talking about? You sound like you've had five espresso shots too many."

"I'm literally hiding out in the hallway at work, because Cutter King is sitting in my office taking up the entire room with his . . . freakin' dominant Viking energy."

"Holy crap, he's popping up everywhere," she says. Her voice still husky with sleep. "And you like him."

"No, I don't like him and wake up. What CEO in America sleeps past ten a.m."

"A pregnant one. And yes you do like him. I haven't seen you act this flustered over a guy since Brandon Miller in Greek Mythology sophomore year."

I can hear Roman's muffled voice saying something snarky in the background. Figures he's listening. It's guaranteed that every time I talk to Elizabeth, her fiancé is somewhere in the vicinity. Lurking. Just like freakin' Batman.

"What is the dark knight saying? Doesn't he ever work?"

"Nothing just—"

There's some rustling in the background as if they're scuffling for the phone, and then all of a sudden, I can't hear Elizabeth. The phone's been muted. Then after that, I hear her voice fussing in the background and Roman's voice on the line.

"Did you tell Cutter the douchebag's name?" he practically snarls through the phone.

"Good morning to you too, sunshine."

"I'm handling it. Don't tell Cutter shit."

I feel a small twinge of disappointment. Cutter's not here to actually see me. He wants to find Dawn's boyfriend and probably finish what he started.

"Listen, Roman, I appreciate the fact that you all want to protect me. I seriously do. But I had unofficial body-guards protecting me when I was a kid and their "preventa-tive measures" to keep me safe never ended well. I don't want any of your good intentions to ultimately create more bad blood between me and my sister. So for me that means dropping this whole thing and leaving her boyfriend alone."

"Not a good choice."

"It may not be, but it's *my* choice."

"Then don't bother the mother of my baby with any shit in regard to him. If he bothers you from this point on, then you go somewhere else for a listening ear or a helping hand. She doesn't need that stress."

"Did you listen to anything that I just said. Why do you have to be so nasty?"

"I'm just looking out for my family. You should under-stand that."

I'm trying very hard to find something likable about Bitsy's man, but as usual he makes it extremely difficult.

"I would never do anything to jeopardize *my* best friend's pregnancy, and I certainly don't need you to tell me that."

"Then I guess we're good."

After the dark knight hands Elizabeth back the phone, she attempts getting off of the phone as quickly as she can, and now I feel like dog crap. She hates when the two of us disagree.

"Hey, I'm wiped. Can I call you back later? I didn't get any sleep last night, because the baby decided to do somersaults until two a.m. I'll call you once I've totally woken up."

"Bitsy, I'm–"

"Listen to me, Sloan." She sighs with exasperation. "There's a big, sweet, man in your office who stopped by because he gives a damn. End of story. So pull up your big girl panties, go back in there, and talk to him. This anxiety ridden side of you is not attractive."

Click

"What . . . Helllllo?"

Gah! She hung up on me.

Pregnant women are such bitches.

I go back to my office, and Cutter is exactly where I left him. Sitting at my desk playing Tetris on his phone. I stand at the doorway and take a moment to observe him for a moment.

The confident way his strong, large body lounges at my desk. The broad width and careful slope of his shoulders. Everything about him oozes confidence, and strength, and sex. In fact I'd bet that he probably just had sex an hour before he came here. He reeks of it, and now (thank you very much) I've just pissed myself off.

I enter the room and slam the door behind me.

"Well hello again, beautiful." He greets me brightly.

"What exactly are you doing?" I say with my hands firmly on my hips.

"Looking at some dangerous curves wrapped up in a pretty blue dress. Turquoise, right? The color suits you."

"I want you to stop dropping by my house and my job without an invitation. And stop flirting with my coworkers."

"You call *that* back there with them flirting or what the two of us are doing right now."

He stands up and takes a step toward me, which inevitably makes the room feel smaller. Yet I stand my ground.

"*We're* not doing anything, and you winked at two women you don't even know while visiting another. Uninvited by the way. So yes, I believe that's called flirting."

"I didn't know you were the jealous type, princess. Me likey." He flashes one of those ridiculous panty melting grins of his.

"Listen, caveman King, I have work to do. You know that thing that some of us do during daylight hours. And just FYI, I'd have to actually care in order to be jealous. But I'll tell you what I actually do care about and that's keeping gainful employment. So I'm going to need you to leave now."

"Not until we talk."

"About what?"

"Have you heard from your sister?"

"Once," I lie.

Actually I haven't heard a thing from Dawn, although admittedly I haven't reached out to her either. I've been pretty angry with her over the last few days, and I've been depending on the fact that if she was really in any sort of trouble, Marsha would have called me about it already. But I'm the older sister, and should be the bigger person, so I plan on checking on her soon.

"Did you know she hasn't been on any social media in a while?"

"No I didn't, and should I even bother asking how it is you know that?"

"That's strange for a teenager don't you think?"

I guess it is.

"Did she say anything about the boyfriend when you talked to her?"

Now I feel like a really bad sister.

"I don't want to talk about this right now."

"Why?"

"Again, genius—" I wave around my hands in the air. "Because I'm at work."

"So when do want to talk about it? Remember, I owe you dinner."

"I don't want to talk about it at all, especially with you. I got into a disagreement with my kid sister's boyfriend. So what? Shit happens. And while I appreciate the help that you gave me that night, I need you to let this go, Cutter. Please. It's my business. Not yours. Not Roman's."

Cutter walks behind me, purposefully sits back down at my desk, spreads his massive legs, and leans completely back in my chair. Making a show of it. Making it clear that he's not going anywhere until he's ready.

"Who said anything about Roman." He says tight-jawed.

"He seems to be almost as interested as you in finding the kid, but I wish you two would drop it. You're making a mountain out of a molehill. I just want to forget that it ever happened."

"I can't drop it. If he's not out of your sister's life, that means he's not out of your life. You needed my help once and you may need it again."

It's exhausting being attracted to such a relentless pain in the ass.

"Seriously, Cutter, get out of my chair."

He ignores my demand and instead squints his eyes carefully at me, examining every inch of my face, like he's looking specifically for something.

"You're not sleeping."

"What—"

"Your eyes. They usually light up like Christmas morning, but today they're dull and dark. My guess is that you haven't been getting any sleep, because you're stressing about this. Probably stressing about other shit too. That's why I'm here. I'm going to fix all of that. Want to see that light back."

How unfortunate that his assessment of me is spot on. I haven't had a good night's rest in days, yet I'm marveled by the sweet sentiment behind his words. It's almost as if he actually cares, but obviously he doesn't. He's just really good at knowing what to say to women.

"Aren't you supposed to be some sort of ladies' man?"

He shrugs his shoulders unrepentantly. "That's what they tell me."

"Well here's a tip. What you just said about me looking like crap is not the best thing to say to a woman."

"I didn't say you looked like crap. I said stressed."

"Still not good."

"I don't lie, princess. If you look stressed, then I'll tell you that you do. Not to be a dick, but to let you know that someone notices. Someone gives a shit. But how about this, the rest of you looks fucking phenomenal. In fact I bet I could help you relax a little right now, if you let me slip my hand inside the slit of that dress and—"

"Quiet." I silence him while inadvertently squeezing my thighs together. The lower half of me clenching at just the thought of his hand coming anywhere close to between my legs. "Stop talking to me like I'm one of your minions at the club."

"Minions?" He chuckles at the word. "Explain."

"You know who I'm talking about. The girls who wait for you and follow you around Lotus like female dogs in heat."

"That's a very specific description." He laughs. "I didn't think you noticed me at all at Lotus. You never say hello."

"You and your minions are a little hard to miss."

"So you think I'm talking to you the way I talk to them?"

"Exactly."

"And how is that?"

"Inappropriately. Indecently. Arrogantly. Presumptuously. Egotistically. Shall I go on?"

"Maybe they like how I talk to them."

"Maybe they do, and that's fine for them, but not for me. You want us to be friends? You said I'm practically like family now that Elizabeth and Roman are getting married. Then treat me like a friend. Treat me like family. Not like some sort of sexual challenge to be surmounted."

I chastise him with the most sanctimonious speech I can come up with off the top of my head, but at the same time can't help but be transfixed as Cutter sexily licks the corner of his mouth with the tip of his tongue.

Dammit, he has the most interesting mouth. There's a small dent that leads from his nose to his top lip. A scar that the eye can't help but be drawn to. A mark that adds to his sexy. I want to kiss it.

"So basically, you're saying that you want me to keep it strictly business."

"Now you're catching on, your highness."

"Then give me the name of the kid, and I'll be on my merry fucking way."

"That's not happening."

He leans even farther back in the chair with an insufferable smirk across his face.

"Then I guess I'll just have to sit and wait until you change your mind."

I plunk down in my new ergonomic chair opposite Cutter. A small perk of my new office and position with the company. We both watch each other very carefully. Much like two stealth-like cats sizing each other up. I slide myself closer to the desk, place my palms flat on the desk, and look him square in his hypnotic whiskey colored irises.

"What is your fucking deal?"

His smile grows wider as Gidget knocks lightly on the door then pokes her head in to interrupt us. "Umm, excuse me."

"Yes, Gidget!" I inadvertently bark at her.

"Sorry, Sloan. I just wanted to know if your guest here needs anything. Coffee? A bottled water?"

A blow job perhaps?

I just shake my head as Gidget shamelessly gawks at Cutter. He must have the biggest ego on the planet the way women drool and lose all of their common sense when he's around. The way she's acting she's headed to minion land herself.

"Uh, he's leaving in a minute, so he won't be needing anything."

"*He* can speak for himself," Cutter says while flashing Gidget all of his pearly whites. "Water please, darlin'."

I swear some sort of unidentifiable sound comes out of Gidget's body that resembles a cross between a squeal, a snort, and a chortle. I laugh to myself as I hang my head in shame for my entire gender.

"Sure thing," she manages to eek out.

"Close the door please, Gidget," I plead. Then I whip my head back around toward him. "Stop it."

"Aww, why don't you admit that you're a little bit jealous? The only way this *thing* between us is going to work is if we're both brutally honest with each other."

"Oh my God." I have to laugh to keep from screaming. "There is no thing."

His eyes rake down my body.

"Not yet."

"It's such a complete and utter waste of your time to flirt with me."

"There's no such thing as time wasted when I'm around you. I love every minute of it."

Where is Gidget with that water.

"Let me be frank. I have a type and you're not it."

"Someone once told me that I was everyone's type."

"Well someone lied to you."

I look down at my hands when I say that, because I tend to look away when I'm lying straight through my teeth.

"Sloan . . . look at me."

I lift my head slowly. Unsure of whether or not he's seen through my ruse.

"What's his name?" He stares gently into my eyes. "I'm not going to threaten him. I'm not going to hurt him. Just give me the name, and I'm out of here."

"Why do you want to find him so badly?" I ask anxiously. "If I give you the name, then what are you going to do?"

"Don't worry," he assures me with a small smile. "I'm not whoever or whatever terrible thing you think I am, and I guarantee you that I can be very charming with assholes. Much more charming than Roman will be. I just want to have another small chat with him, minus the kicking him in his ribs part, to make sure that the two of us are on the same page. That's it."

"I haven't heard a peep out of him, and I don't think Dawn has either. I don't think you even need to bother. Like I said—"

"Sloan, I kicked him in the ribs. Hard. He probably can't talk or at least doesn't want to right now. A punk kid like him is probably filled with rage and embarrassment over what I did, that I did it publicly, and the fact that I did it for you. I just want to make sure that I dot my i's and cross my t's. Calm him down a little."

"Okay, but I'm trusting you."

Something I don't do too often.

"Understood."

"His name is . . . Damien Hardwick."

"Do you know where he lives?"

"Now you're pushing it."

"What's the point of the name if I can't find him."

"I thought finding people was your specialty."

"You're cute."

He taps my nose.

"Is that right."

"I think you know how cute you are, Ms. Pearson."

There's a knock at the door, and oh my God, it's Gidget again.

"Hi there." She flashes nothing but teeth and gums. "Sorry to interrupt again, but I'm back with your water, Mister—"

"Right . . . the water," I mumble to myself.

"The name's King, darlin'. Don't forget it."

Gidget starts to blush and while it was funny earlier, it isn't as funny now. It's starting to grate my nerves.

"Here you go, Mr. King. Is there anything else I can get for you?"

She makes sure to place an emphasis on the word anything.

"No, this is great."

Cutter twists open the plastic cap and chugs down the entire bottle in a few long swallows as we both shamelessly watch. I'm not really sure how he can make something as simple as drinking a bottle of spring water look totally pornographic but he does.

After Gidget leaves to no doubt dry her thong out in the

bathroom, Cutter and I finish up our conversation. Now it's his turn to lean forward on the desk and for the first time, I notice a tattoo on his left hand. I'm not sure how I've missed it in the past. An intricate king's crown that spans the width of his hand. Each tip of the crown inked on each of his fingers up to the first knuckle. I'm staring right at it when he asks me the most unusual question.

"Do you believe in love, princess?"

I almost laugh at the ludicrousness of the question.

"What?"

"It's a simple question."

"You ask everybody questions like that?"

"It's just a question. Not a proposition."

"Fine. No, I don't think I do."

"Why?"

"Probably because I've never seen a good example of it."

My parents have a terrible marriage.

"I knew it."

He taps his palms on top of the desk, then stands up like he just made some sort of great discovery.

"You knew what?"

"That you're totally my type."

Cutter walks around to the other side of my desk. Because I'm still sitting, I can't help but turn around in my chair to see what he's going to do next. He's so tall that my head is dangerously close to his crotch.

I reactively take a small breath and hold it.

Still holding.

He takes a hold of my chin with his thumb and pointer finger and raises my head up, holding it steady and meeting my gaze.

"I don't believe in love either," he continues. "It makes things much simpler when both parties have no grand illusions of anything more happening."

"Well, aren't we both the saddest," I say not quite loud enough for him to understand me completely.

"You know you look fucking beautiful in this position. Low to the ground. Chin up. Eyes on me. I'd love to kiss you right now."

I nearly choke on my own saliva as he bends down dangerously low to reach my mouth. He stops just a few millimeters from my lips, perhaps waiting to see if I'll protest, but I don't—so he continues on.

His mouth is warm and hesitant at first. Testing me. Teasing me. Making me raise my head and adjust my neck just a little higher to make contact. Making me work for it. It's such a fucking turn on.

His hand slides into my hair, cradling the uninjured side of my face, as his tongue slowly begins to move and curl inside of my mouth. He controls the tempo of the kiss. It isn't rushed. It's exploratory. In fact it's almost reverent. Like he's cherishing each and every moment. It's the most incredible kiss I've ever had in my life. And all I can think about, is that if he kisses like this, what else he must be able to do. To my body and worst of all . . . to my heart.

I break the connection between us. Forcefully pushing my chair back with my butt and standing. I've made a big mistake allowing that kiss to happen.

"I'm leaving," I say totally flustered.

"This is your office," he says as his chest rumbles with an almost sinister laughter. "Where are you going?"

"To call security," I deadpan as I try to gain back my composure.

"Did you know your sarcastic sense of humor is one of the things I really like about you? You remind me a lot of myself."

"So my theory is right then."

"And what's that?" he asks while wiping some of my lip gloss off of his bottom lip.

"That ultimately you'd like to fuck yourself."

That comment makes Cutter laugh out loud with such a rich, resonant, rumble that the entire floor must be shaking, and the fact that I am responsible for it is something I oddly find gratifying.

"I'll see you later," he says before I make my exit.

I don't know if he intended that as a threat or a promise, but he says the casual farewell in a way that makes me think he knows something that I don't.

"And why on earth would we see each other later? I've seen enough of you for a lifetime."

He stands to leave.

"I'll be stopping by to check on one of my new investments tonight."

New investment?

"What in the ham sandwich are you talking about, and what does that have to do with me?"

"I'm your new landlord."

"You're my what?!"

Oh. Hell. No.

FIFTEEN

SLOAN

"You're laughing at me again."

"I know. I'm sorry—"

Elizabeth can't even finish her sentence as she laughs even louder. I don't understand it. She's never laughed this much the entire time I've known her nerdy ass. She's lucky that she's growing a little baby Roman inside of that tummy of hers, because I swear that I'm ten seconds away from throttling her.

"I mean it, Elizabeth Hill. Shut your cute little pregnant trap."

We're in our old favorite haunt, Java The Hut, and I'm waiting for my caramel macchiato with a double shot of espresso while she waits for her mug of decaffeinated green tea.

Elizabeth holds her stomach, palms flat on her growing pouch, as she tries to subdue her laughter. "But your life is incredibly funny."

"My life is not a sitcom. My life is shit. I'm starting to hate my job. I have a black eye. My sister is barely speaking to me. I can't get laid to save my life. And the icing on the cake? The number one person that I need to steer clear of is now my freakin' landlord."

"He had some sort of fight with his brother."

"So?"

"I guess he needed another place to live, so he bought one." Elizabeth isn't laughing anymore, but it doesn't matter, because I can see it all in her eyes, that she is completely entertained by this twist of fate.

"Wait . . . do you think that he's going to actually live in the building too? What's he going to do. Kick out one of the tenants because—"

"What?"

"Wait he can't be."

"He can't be what?" she asks with a look of anxious glee.

"There's only one vacancy in my building that I know of. On my floor. Next door to Kyle. But he wouldn't."

Elizabeth takes a sip of her tea and smiles at me over the top of the mug. "Aah, but he would. He's a King."

I take a sip of my coffee like it's a shot of whiskey.

"So what you're saying is that you think it's totally possible that he bought my building and is moving in next door to me?"

"I'm afraid so. Hey, lift up your bandage so I can take a peek."

I lift up one side of my bandage for a few seconds then stick it back down.

"Is it presumptuous of me to say that he did this solely to get on my one last good nerve? I mean it can't be a coincidence. Didn't the dark knight tell you anything?"

"No, I only know about the dispute between the Kings, because I was eavesdropping on Roman's phone conversation with Camden. I didn't know anything about him buying your building."

"I'm never going home."

"What?" She giggles. "You have to. You live there. Let's order some croissants. I'm starving."

"It's cold in my house. My thermostat is broken. The super said the thing is busted, but that he'd need the landlord's purchase approval to install another one. The landlord never got back to him. Now I see why. He was too busy selling the damn building to a lunatic."

"Get an electric blanket and go home."

"If there were mice in my house I wouldn't go home."

"That's stupid too, and don't talk about mice when I'm hungry."

"You're afraid of mice as much as I am."

"Yes, but I'd hire an exterminator to get rid of them. I wouldn't just leave my home, crazy girl. I didn't realize that Cutter brought out this type of visceral reaction from you. What else happened when he came by your job that you're not telling me about?" She grins mischievously.

The best kiss of my life.

"You're getting some sick pleasure out of this which is very uncharacteristic of you, my *dearest* friend. That man of yours is rubbing off on you in all the wrong ways."

"What do you have against Cutter anyway? As you get to know him better, I think you'll begin to get a better understanding of who he is. He's really–"

"Let me stop you there." I throw up my hand in the formation of a stop sign. "I don't plan on *understanding* anything about Cutter King at all. My hope was that I wouldn't see the guy again until your wedding day or until the baby comes. Whichever comes first since you seem to keep changing your mind about when you're getting married."

"Blame Aunt Juliette. She keeps changing my mind for me."

"Guess it's all a moot point. I'm going to have to see him now. Doesn't mean that I have to like it though."

"But isn't that the real reason why you're so upset? You *do* like it?"

"Let's just talk about decorating my goddaughter or godson's room."

"Changing the subject on me?"

"I have a vision. Do you want to see what I have planned for the baby or not?"

She finally yields and pretends like she's zipping her lips with her fingers. Then she gets up to order us two croissants. While she's ordering I decide to pull out my pen and sketchpad. I like to make rough drawings of what I want a room to look like before I begin decorating it. Decorating rooms is just a hobby for me, but one that I take seriously if I'm going to do it right, and I can't wait to make Elizabeth's nursery a beautiful sanctuary for her and the baby.

She returns with the food and sits down. "Okay, I'm ready. Lay it on me."

"So I thought about going with a deep cherry wood crib, changing table, and dresser but selecting pure white bedding and window dressings."

"White?"

"I think the contrast will look beautiful and natural regardless of the sex of the baby. I'm going to do everything in organic or recycled fabrics and materials too. The bedding. The curtains. The flooring. It's going to look amazing and be chemical free for the baby."

"I'm sure I'll love everything you've got planned."

"You will." I smile. "And don't worry I'll make sure that you are involved in every part of the process. It will be fun for us to hang out and do this together. I feel like I haven't spent any quality time with you in eons."

"Agreed. Speaking of quality time, have you talked to Tiny lately?"

Tiny is one of our closest friends from college. She lived on our floor and is the third missing piece from our bestie trifecta.

"Not really. All the stuff going on at work has been kicking my ass lately. Last time we spoke was probably two weeks ago. I think she met a guy. I'm not sure. I was half listening and half arguing with a saleslady in the mall about a return when we were on the phone."

"Well at least she's alive and breathing. I haven't heard from her in a long time. So what's going on at work?"

"I'm sure that I've mentioned her before but there's this woman, Regan, who just won't leave me alone."

"Has she ever gone to drinks with us?"

"No, she doesn't really fraternize with coworkers. Not unless they're management. So anyway, if I didn't already know that she is strictly dickly, I would swear to you that she wants me in the biblical way. She's obsessed with me. Let me rephrase that. Obsessed with crushing me. And I can't for the life of me understand why. She's been at the company longer. Her sales territory is more established than mine. Her team makes more money than we do. And if the rumors are true, the head of our division is some old friend of her family's. So her job is secure. She'd damn near have to commit a felony to get fired. So why is she so worried about what I'm doing?"

Elizabeth sighs. "More pretty girl problems."

"What?"

"I call what you're going through pretty girl problems. You're just one of those women, Sloan. It's been like that since I've known you. It was probably that way before we met. You're gorgeous, you come from money, a famous parent, and you're good with people—especially men.

Women either love you or love to hate you. They're either in awe of you or they're intimidated by you. You're a threat to that Regan person for some reason that only her psychotherapist can probably explain. It's her problem. Not yours."

"Pretty girl problems huh? Well I think my butt is way too big and it's my parents who have the money, not me, but I get what you're saying."

"Perhaps another theory is that Regan is one of those women who believes that there can only be one female at your level. I mean I'm no expert on office politics, but I imagine that some women prefer to be the only ones in the room."

"You could be right. I swear to you that my team supervisor, another woman named Fern, likes to pit the two of us against each other. She masks it as two sales teams battling it out for bragging rights and bonuses, but I think that she may possibly be trying to weed one of us out."

"That really sucks."

"Yeah, it does. You don't know how lucky you are to be an entrepreneur and not have to worry about crap like this."

"I'm not sure that it has anything to do with luck. I made a conscious decision that I would work for myself when I was an undergrad because of this very thing. I hate office politics. I'd never be any good at it. You could try working for yourself too if you wanted to you know."

Elizabeth has always been a huge proponent of women starting their own businesses instead of working for the "patriarchy." I can't honestly say that I ever gave it any serious thought. I was just glad to get a job after graduation and prove to my family that I could do more than post Instagram photos."

"I can't sell Viagra independently like its Avon."

"Obviously you would do something else, Sloan."

"Eh, maybe."

I get our conversation back on track and start explaining my intentions for the nursery. I show her the sketch of a very basic floor plan, so that Elizabeth can visualize what the space will look like once I've worked my magic.

"Also I'm thinking about placing some built-in shelving here. Do you like that idea?"

She shakes her head with a mouth full of croissant. "Umm-hmm."

"You seem hungry."

"I am. This croissant isn't cutting it."

"You want real food?"

"Yep."

"Where do you want to go? It's on me."

"Maybe you could cook me a little something at your apartment?" She starts laughing hysterically. "I wonder if we'll see your new neighbor there."

I crumple up my napkin and throw it at her forehead.

That settles it.

Pregnant women *are* bitches.

SIXTEEN

SLOAN

I wouldn't describe myself as a terribly vain woman, but I definitely feel uncomfortable making sales calls with my face partially covered in medical gauze. I guess that's why for the first time ever, I feel a little unsure of myself when I press the elevator button to the office of my first appointment of the day, Dr. Aiden Clark. A man whom I've known through my work as a pharmaceutical sales rep for almost two years and one of my favorite clients.

Every time I present Dr. Clark with a new product from my company's generic brand of Viagra and why he should offer it to his patients, he gets on board. No questions asked. And while I know I do a pretty good job at selling, I'm sure my one hundred percent success rate with the good doctor has a lot to do with the fact that he's been patiently and politely asking me out for the last nine months.

"Good afternoon, Miss Pearson. Dr. Clark will be with you in a minute. He's just finishing up with a patient. He said you can wait in his office."

"Thanks, Paige."

Paige is the office manager for the practice and rarely says two words to me. From what Dr. Clark tells me, she's a huge basketball fan, which could probably be the issue between us. I think that she's one of those people who is dying to ask me about my father, but doesn't want to come off as star struck or something, so she says much of nothing instead.

"Can I get you anything?" she asks almost rhetorically. I cringe a bit, because her tone today is reminiscent of Regan's. Disinterested and dismissive.

"No, I'm fine. Thank you."

"I'm sure you know the way," she says while barely looking up from her computer. "Down the hall. Second door on your left."

"Of course. Thank you."

While I sit and wait for Dr. Clark, I get an unusual call from a blocked number, which reminds me to put my phone on vibrate. No calls during sales appointments. Then I slip it back in my handbag as soon as Clark enters the room.

"Well hello, Miss Pearson."

"Hi there, yourself."

Dr. Clark immediately looks at my eye and the bandages on my face and his face scrunches up.

"What happened to you?"

"Freak accident. I had a little disagreement with a concrete sidewalk."

"It's those heels you wear. They're too high."

He assumes I fell, so I just go with it.

"I thought about your many high heel warnings as I went tumbling to the ground, but then guess what I did the day after it happened?"

"You bought another pair of Manolo Blahniks?"

"This time it was Christian Louboutins." I laugh. "I bought them online."

He shakes his head.

"Tsk. Tsk. You really should wear flats more often. Heels are horrible for women's feet."

"Not my thing, Dr. Clark. Everyone's got their vices. Mine are lipsticks and high heels. Yours are?"

"I guess entertainment. I like to go to shows and ball games."

"Then you understand."

"Not exactly the same." He smiles. "The eye looks like it's healing pretty well, but I take it you have lots of abrasions under those bandages?"

"Pretty much. It could've been a lot worse though."

"A friend of mine from medical school is a great plastic surgeon. He has a six-month waiting list, but I could probably get you a consultation this week if you'd like. I think that you should definitely consider seeing someone, so that you won't scar permanently."

"Thanks, doc, but I'm betting that my mother has about three of the best surgeons on speed dial."

More like ten.

"No problem. The offer is always there if you need to take me up on it."

Dr. Clark smiles at me awkwardly. It's the kind of goofy smile he tends to give me right before he asks me out. He's done it enough times that I'm beginning to notice the signs. This time I decide to beat him to the punch and change the subject.

"So I've brought some great samples for you today. I told you about that new marketing push we've got going on, right? The product has awesome new packaging and information pamphlets I think you're going to like."

Dr. Clark looks somewhat disappointed by the new direction of the conversation but follows my lead.

"I'm all ears. Show me your goods."

I pull out some of my drug samples and marketing materials and spread them across Dr. Clark's desk. I make sure to point out the new question and answer section in the revised patient brochures. It was one of the things that he said he hoped would be updated in future versions of the pamphlets.

Dr. Clark is polite as he patiently goes through what I've brought, but I can tell he has something else on his mind. A date. I hate even thinking it, but I hope his desire to ask me out for what seems like the hundredth time won't distract him from making a commitment to order.

He's my biggest client. He has a large practice that spans three locations and a hospital throughout the city, and he also was listed as one of the Top Doc's in the annual Best Doctor's List in Philadelphia Magazine. In other words, he's a big deal in this town, and I need his business.

"So what do you think?" I ask.

"Well . . . I wasn't sure how to bring this up, but I already had a visit from your office."

"A visit?"

"Your coworker Regan."

What. The. Hell.

"I'm not sure I understand."

"I think it was a misunderstanding. She was following up on some old leads I think and called the office. Paige gave her the appointment. Paige doesn't really understand about how sales territories work in your company. I didn't know a thing about it until I checked my schedule at the last minute."

There is no way in hell that Regan was following up on an "old lead" that steered her directly to one of the best doctors in the city aka my client, but I don't want to drag Dr. Clark into our internal drama.

"So she showed you all of these materials already then?"

"Yes—at first I wasn't sure what was going on. I thought that maybe you had released me as a client."

"I would never do that, Dr. Clark. Not without telling you first."

"I should have realized that, Sloan, but even though we've known each for so long, I wasn't sure. I feel as if there's so much more to learn about you."

"I'm afraid that there's not much else to learn. I'm not that interesting."

"Actually you're one of the most confident, intelligent, and beautiful women I've ever had the pleasure of meeting. To say that you're interesting is probably an understatement. And don't worry. I told Regan that I'd get back to her. I didn't make any commitment one way or another."

"Thank you, doc."

Now I'm starting to feel badly that I've continually put the kibosh on any sort of romantic feelings for the doctor before giving him any sort of a real chance. On paper Dr. Clark is the ideal catch and meets all the requirements of my "perfect man" checklist.

He's an honest, attractive, successful, and most likely a one woman type of man. In other words, "a safe bet." Unlike another man I know, I doubt that he's left a lot of broken hearts in his wake. He seems to be too thoughtful and considerate to go around hurting women's feelings. In fact, he seems to embody most of the personality traits that I tragically run from in a man: respectful, kind, humble, trustworthy, and dependable.

Obviously, I realize that this is all kinds of fucked-up. But aren't we all essentially works in progress?

"So when did you decide that you were going to become a doctor?" I ask in an effort to make light conversation that doesn't make mention of anything romantic.

"I used to take care of all of the pets in our house when I

was a kid. Two cats, three dogs, a turtle and a parakeet. It was pretty clear early on that I'd be working in a helping profession. I also didn't mind school, and you have to really like to learn if you're going to get through medical school. It's grueling."

"So why urology?"

"You sure you want the real story?"

"Absolutely."

He gets comfortable and takes a seat on his rolling stool.

"It's actually kind of funny. When I was in high school I was in serious lust with this girl named Janet Jackson. No relation to the singer. She was a year older than me, and I thought she was the most beautiful girl I'd ever seen, but she'd always had a steady boyfriend until her senior year. When they broke up that's when I knew I'd been given my window of opportunity. I made sure to flirt with her extra hard that fall and lo and behold it worked. She finally started giving me the time of day.

"We went on a couple of dates and by the fifth one we had sex. Unprotected sex. She said she was on the pill, and I didn't want to risk missing my moment by telling her I needed to go by the store to pick up some condoms. I figured that most guys carried some with them."

"Was it your first time?"

"Not quite the first time but damn close. So needless to say I was on cloud nine. That was until a few days later. There was something strange going on with my penis."

"Ewww." I can already guess how this story ends.

"Yeah, it was gross. I didn't know much about the signs of gonorrhea at the time, so I literally thought my poor pecker was infected with a deadly disease. All the dripping. I was petrified. I was too frightened and embarrassed to tell my parents, so I broke down and begged my grandmother to take me to the hospital instead before my penis fell off. The two of us were close and she had been a nurse. She said she'd take a look at it first, before we committed to a long covert night in the ER."

I giggle. "Oh boy."

"Yeah, it's funny now, but I was horrified back then. My sweet old grandmother examined my penis closely for all of fifteen seconds, and then told me with great certainty that we'd be going to her family doctor and not the hospital, because all I had was a curable case of *the clap*. I was both relieved and mortified, and the experience stayed with me forever. I'd never forget about the day that I thought my most prized possession would fall off, which is why it ended up being a major influence on the specialty I ended up selecting during my residency."

"Dr. Clark—saving one penis, one day at a time," I say dramatically in my bad imitation of a commercial actor.

"That's me."

"That's a great story." I chuckle. "I guess the silver lining would be that you had your path figured out quite early in life. No stressing about what you were going to major in and all of that. Some of us aren't that lucky to have such definitive direction."

"You didn't have it figured out?"

"Well I didn't exactly dream of selling Viagra to guys like you for a living when I was growing up."

Clark laughs. "Guys like me?"

"Doctors I mean."

"So what did you dream of being when you were little?"

I think hard about it for a moment. I don't have a specific answer which is kind of sad.

"I guess . . . just happy."

"I suppose we all thought that would be easy enough when we were kids."

"My parents told me I could be anything I wanted.

Have anything I wanted. I even had the head start in life of being Dan Pearson's daughter. The problem is that you have to actually know what you want in order to go after it."

"I never thought about it like that, and that's so true, but guess what the cool thing is?"

"What?"

"It's never too late to figure it all out. I just read about a seventy-four-year-old woman who's in medical school in Texas. She's doing it for the simple fact that it was on her bucket list. You just have to write one. I imagine you could come up with a fantastic list."

Maybe Clark is right. It would be nice to be passionate about something and not constantly stressed out about a job that I'm beginning to dislike. Regardless of what this month's sales numbers say, I know that I'm good at my job, but somewhere along the way I've allowed it to define me. It's sort of like my badge of honor. I guess because my job is something that I've achieved all on my own with no help from my family connections, but does that mean that it's something I should be doing for the rest of my life? Is it my life's passion? Am I just settling?

Clark and I make polite conversation for a few more minutes, and then we finally talk about business. He makes the largest commitment he ever has to our full line of products. I'm so happy, and thinking ten steps ahead about my meeting with Mr. Stokes, that he catches me off guard with a question.

"So now that we've finalized the boring stuff, I was wondering if there's any chance that you'd like to go to a modern dance performance with me next Saturday night? Feel free to say no," he rushes to say. "But it's just that I have a pair of tickets unexpectedly. Really good seats at the Academy. I didn't want them to go to waste."

"Umm–well I'm not too sure about going out with my face like this."

A clear look of disappointment crosses his face, and now I start to feel like a piece of gum stuck on the bottom of his shoe. I went out for coffee with Elizabeth. Why couldn't I go out to a show with Clark.

"Oh . . . of course, Sloan. That was inconsiderate of me to even ask. I totally understand."

Yeah–he understands that I'm a bitch to the highest degree.

"Well–maybe we could play it by ear? If my bruising has faded a bit more by then, I'd love to go."

His face brightens.

"Then here's hoping that you heal quickly."

"Yes, here's hoping," I say half-heartedly.

When I leave the doc's office, he stays behind on a call, but Paige is leaning against the wall near the door examining her nails. She'd obviously been listening to our entire conversation, and at first, she doesn't say a word as we exchange cursory glances. I never saw it before, but only now do I realize what her real problem with me is. It's obvious. She has a thing for the doctor and now an even stronger dislike for me.

"The doctor is a good man," she finally says after cutting her eyes at me.

"I know that," I say defensively.

"I'm only saying that I've seen you on social media. I know what you're about. You two aren't a good match. You shouldn't lead him on."

"And what exactly is it that you think I'm about?" I take strong offense.

"You're the spoiled daughter of a pro athlete. A party girl. Doctor Clark is looking for forever, and I think you and I both know that you aren't a forever type of girl."

Her terribly candid comments remind me immediately of the look on Cutter's face when I unwittingly admitted that I was "just his type" because I don't believe in love.

I refuse to believe that both Cutter or Paige are right about me. I don't want to be *that* girl. The single chick who lives alone in a two bedroom with three cats, because she doesn't believe in Mr. Right but only in Mr. Right Now. I won't let it happen.

"I guess we'll see if I am a forever type of girl," I say rising to Paige's challenge.

I think my face might just miraculously heal by the night of the performance. I'm definitely going on that date.

"I suppose we will, Miss Pearson."

SEVENTEEN

SLOAN

Nude bodies are flying everywhere. Some muscular. Some lithe. Some ruggedly handsome. And some stunning. I'm not the biggest fan of professional dance performances, but I can see why some might be. Each dance is hauntingly beautiful. Each dancer interpreting the untold story of their dance with high leaps, strong kicks, and exquisite grace.

While the performers may not literally be in their birthday suits, they leap and glide across the stage in minimalist nude-colored outfits and tights giving the allusion of stark nakedness and delicate sensuality.

The clean-cut gentleman sitting next to me seems quite taken with the performance and occasionally glances at me in an attempt to gauge my reaction. Wondering if I am just as transfixed by the show as he is. I do my best to pretend as if I'm mesmerized by what I'm watching, but I've never been that big of a fan of professional dance. I'd rather "go" dancing. So I'm only somewhat entertained at best. The man by my side tonight is Dr. Aiden Clark.

"The dancers are really good, aren't they?" he whispers quietly in my ear. The doctor has a clean and practical scent. Reminiscent of clean sheets and Ivory Soap.

"Yes, doc." I smile in agreement, although I'm distracted by an incoming text from my sister. Our first communication since the incident outside of the restaurant.

Dawn: Just wanted you to know that your guard dog broke two of my boyfriend's ribs. Who was that guy!?

Me: Well hello to you too.

Dawn: I'm telling Dad you're hanging out with a criminal.

Me: Well, while you're doing that, you better mention how your boyfriend punched me in the eye.

Remember who the adult is, Sloan.

Me: Did he give you the money?

Dawn: I got it from Mom.

Me: And you're still dating him?

Dawn: Yep.

Me: Can you explain to me why you're still involved with someone who stole your money and assaulted your sister. Is he hitting you too? You can tell me, Dawn. I'll help you. I'll even keep it from Marsha if you want me to.

Dawn: He does not hurt me.

Me: Why haven't you posted on your Instagram lately? Does he tell you not to?

Dawn: What do you think I don't have a mind of my own? I have better things to do then play around online.

Me: You're sure he isn't abusive?

Dawn: I'm positive. Mainly because I don't say reckless things to him.

Me: So you're saying that it's MY fault I have a black eye?! 😡

No response.

I angrily stuff my phone back in my bag. I guess I'm not mature enough to be the bigger person, because she just pissed me off again, and I need to put her in a time out.

"Now I see why this show sells out every year," I continue talking to the doctor in the most pleasant tone I can muster.

"What did I tell you about speaking to me like we're on a work appointment?"

I turn and look at him. "You haven't really done much better. You've called me Miss Pearson at least twice tonight."

"I guess we're both a little stuck in work mode," he says making an obvious reference to me pulling my phone back out again to check if Dawn responded to my last message. "But I'm hoping we're both going to try really hard to change that, *Sloan*."

It's odd hearing Dr. Clark call me by my first name. It's even odder to watch him flirt with me. Openly. Obviously. Without the reservation and restraint he usually practices when we have sales appointments. He's always been so careful to keep it very professional between the two of us. Even when he's asked me out countless times, and I've rejected him countless more, he's handled it with grace. He's a gentleman through and through, and I've always appreciated that. That's why this new type of interaction between us outside of the workplace may take some getting used to.

"Well this performance is a nice way to start," I say. Sliding the phone back in my purse for good this time. "But there's no way I can call you by your first name after two years of calling you Dr. Clark or doc. It's just too weird. Maybe I'll just call you by your last name, and drop the doctor part?"

"So just *Clark*?" He considers it for a moment then grins. "I'd like that. No one else calls me that."

"Then Clark it is."

"I wasn't sure if I should mention it when I picked you up, but your face looks a lot better."

Since my face has almost finished scabbing over, I thought it would be safe to add a barrier layer of Aquaphor to the skin, then a little foundation on top of that. The scars and bruising are not completely camouflaged, but my cover-up job looks pretty damn good.

"Thanks. I'm just happy that my face feels a lot better. I'm pretty much off of all of the pain killers."

"Good." He leans farther over into my side. "Hey, since it's so early, are you up for grabbing a bite to eat after this?"

I really can smell the soap now, and it reminds me of my grandmother's bathroom. Talk about a turn off. Perhaps that's why my first instinct is to decline Clark's offer. It's total self-sabotage though. He's been a perfect gentleman, and any sane woman would want him (like Paige), but I realize that something's missing. I just don't feel an absolute pull to continue on with this date, even knowing that by ending it here would just be me repeating my past mistakes.

This is a pivotal moment.

I need to make a smart decision, and not an emotional one, or one driven by the need between my legs. I may be hard-headed, but I'm not stupid. I realize that the definition of crazy is doing the same thing over and over and expecting different results. So the smart decision to make would be to agree to the early dinner and see where this may go. So that's what I do. What could it hurt? Why am I overthinking this?

"Sure, let's do it."

When the first part of the performance concludes and the house lights turn on, it lets me know that it's finally time for the brief intermission I've been waiting for. I excuse myself to use the restroom while Clark uses his cell to check in with a patient who's been hospitalized. Some men experience adverse reactions to Viagra and end up with a hard-on for way longer than they bargained for. This particular patient has been erect for over six hours.

I definitely admire how dedicated Clark is to his patients. He doesn't just prescribe meds and send them on their merry way. He has a very holistic and hands on approach to his practice which I can appreciate. Not all urologists do. Another check in the "pro" column for him.

I stand in the longest women's restroom line ever for all of five minutes, before I decide that I'm simply going to use every one of my pelvic floor muscles to hold the urine inside of my body until the show is over. I've done it plenty of times at outdoor concerts and crappy bars, and I can do it here too, because there's no way on earth that I'm going to stand in a line of over twenty-five women to pee in a public bathroom. Especially when some of them are even giving the poor pregnant woman who's about seven people in front of me the side-eye for asking if she can jump ahead farther in line. Sheesh, women can be such bitches when they have to urinate.

"Excuse me, do you know how much longer the show will be?" I ask a plump, older woman, with butterscotch colored skin and a stark white bob standing in front of me. She actually reminds me of my grandma but with a much funkier aesthetic.

"Oh at least another forty-five minutes, honey."

"Really?" Is my reserved response, but internally I want to scream my head off. I didn't anticipate that this matinee would run this long, and that I would have to pee for the majority of it.

"Yes, this is one of the dance company's major performances of the year. They always put on such a lovely show when they come to the The Academy of Music. And to think they're going to do it all over again tonight. Isn't it spectacular so far? They work so hard."

"Phenomenal," I lie through my teeth.

Great, I'm going to have to either stand in this line now or wait to excuse myself during the show to go pee when there's no line. I'm leaning toward going after the show starts back up. Clark will probably think that I'm either terribly rude or that I have a bladder problem if I go with that strategy, but to hell with it. I'm not standing in this line.

"Enjoy the show," I say to the woman and the other line of waiting women as I leave to start making my way through the crowded vestibule to get back to my seat. But I'm halted dead in my tracks when not even a moment later I hear a familiar, gruff, voice behind me, and I literally almost wet myself.

"Princess."

I stop and turn my head around to find a man leaning against the bar who freakishly resembles the Marvel Comic character Thor. Larger than life. Sexy as hell. The only difference is he's holding a bottle of beer in his hand instead of a hammer.

All I can seem to do is silently gawk at him for a moment. Not just because he is probably one of the last people I'd expect to see today, but also because whenever Cutter King looks at me, the way he rakes his eyes up and down my entire body, makes me feel beautiful, dirty and disquieted all at the same time. I'm not entirely sure whether or not he's laughing at me or plotting to eat me alive.

"What are *you* doing here?" Is the first thing that flies out of mouth.

"Where do you want me to be?" The corners of his mouth turn up in amusement.

"I don't want you to be anywhere specifically," I respond flustered. "I just can't imagine that you paid good money to watch a modern dance performance in an upscale theatre like this."

It's like seeing a fish out of water.

A big, sexy, scary fish.

"The king is here enjoying the arts like everybody else. What kind of a fucking question is that?"

This man is nuts. Who talks about themselves in the third person like that? And this isn't the first time he's done it. It's always the king this and the king that. Give me a break. Not to mention that I seriously want to wash his mouth out with soap (although I have a potty mouth of my own to curb). Yet when Cutter uses foul language, his curse words come out coarse and buoyant, complements of the heavy bass in his voice as well as his thick Philadelphia accent. It travels through the vestibule garnering us unwanted attention. Probably because this is not the type of event where people commonly used profanity in everyday conversation.

"I didn't realize that you were into professional dance is all I'm saying," I say quietly. Doing my best to calm his savage beast and deflect any stares from strangers.

He rakes his eyes slowly up and down my entire body for another moment before he speaks again.

I internally yell at my traitorous ovaries.
They're quivering.
Then he licks the corner of his mouth seductively.
And the little traitors start to rattle.
"I'm into a lot of shit, princess. You don't even know the half of it."

EIGHTEEN

SLOAN

There's a raw energy that Cutter King exudes which I begrudgingly find intoxicating. It's bouncing off of him right now like gamma rays. Flirtatious, bright, and toxic. I felt it the moment we first locked eyes in Lotus. It pulls you in playfully but dominantly. Coaxing the average woman into a false sense of comfort as if he's totally harmless, but I'm not the average woman; and I know for a fact that using the words *Cutter* and *harmless* in the same sentence is a complete oxymoron.

I can tell that he's the type of guy that loves women and probably has since he came out of his mother's womb. You know the type. Men who know how to please us but also how to play us. Men who will quickly defend our honor but just as swiftly take advantage of our vulnerabilities. Men that know how to speak and understand our language, but tend to play deaf, dumb and blind when the time suits them. And then of course there's the fact that he's dangerous.

Literally dangerous.

I know this for sure about him. Not just because of the

urban tales I've heard about "the King brothers" from other people, or because he rescued me the other day after already being involved in some sort of other violent event, but because I've known men just like him my entire life and the signs are there.

For as long as I can remember, there were always people trying to insinuate their way into my father's life. Our lives. I think he permitted it because he came from humble beginnings and felt some guilt about his success as a professional basketball player. Therefore he allowed some people to sponge off of him financially while others were satisfied benefiting from his celebrity in other ways. In other words, my father would often be surrounded by men who were leeches, opportunists, and some who were simply menacing.

The dangerous ones were violent men, who often had prison records, and would convince my father to hire them as his *personal security*, but really, they were nothing more than glorified thugs. Vetting anyone and everyone who asked my father for an interview, a meeting, or a simple autograph. They'd bully overzealous fans or potential business partners, and would sleep with naïve women wanting entry into my father's inner circle.

Alongside my father, these men were some of my first examples of what men were like. Self-indulgent, overaggressive, uber alpha types who tended to attract drama anywhere they went. The conflicting part about them was that these same men were also good to me in many ways. Always protective of me, interested in my academic success, and often talking my dad into doing extracurricular activities with me when I honestly think he would have rather been sleeping, or drinking, or drugging. As I grew older, I remember developing innocent crushes on one or two of them, and ultimately as a teen ended up attracted to guys my age who were mini carbon copies of them. Men like Cutter.

Large in stature.

Gigantic personalities.

Strong alpha tendencies.

Dangerous as hell.

Total disappointments.

Big mistakes.

Despite my unorthodox upbringing, or perhaps because of it, I'm smarter now. I know that true love or healthy love, doesn't come easy, and doesn't come to most, and it certainly doesn't come wrapped in over six foot four inches of jean clad swagger.

I know better than to base a relationship on some sort of feral attraction. If something real is ever going to happen for me, I'm going to need more than that. Something like the man waiting to watch the second act with me in row seven, seat twelve.

"Okay, well, it was nice seeing you," I say blowing him off. "I need to head back to my seat now."

"Why are you rushing?" Cutter asks with a steel edge to his voice.

"Who says I'm rushing?"

"The smoke your heels are kicking up tells me something different."

"I'm not *rushing* anywhere. I just want to get back to my seat. The show's about to start."

"Anxious to sit back down next to the square you're here with, are you?"

"Stop talking like Yoda. You sound like a thirteen-year-old *Star Wars* nerd. And what exactly do you mean the *square* I'm here with? Of course any man who isn't huge, tatted, and scares people senseless for a living is a square to someone like you."

"You're awfully protective of what I'm assuming is just a first date and unfortunately for him the last."

"What do you mean the last?"

"He's not the right man for you. It wouldn't be fair for you to accept a second date. You'll just end up breaking his heart."

Why do people keep telling me that?

As if I need your seal of approval," I say impatiently. Dying to get back to my seat so that I can hold my pee in properly.

"What's wrong with you?" he asks. Cocking his head to the side.

"Nothing."

"Why do you keep looking anxiously toward the bathroom?"

"Because I have to go, okay?"

"So go." He laughs. "That's what intermission is for."

"There's no way I'm going to stand in that amusement-park-long line."

"You too good to wait in line with the other mere mortals?"

"Don't you have somebody's skull to go crack?"

"If you need me to defend your honor again tonight, I do."

"You're just not going to drop that ever are you."

"So you're telling me that you're going to sit for the rest of the show having to pee?" he asks in an amused laden voice.

"Sure am," I say matter of factly. "Haven't you ever held it until you arrived at a better destination?"

"Those are women's problems. Men can take a piss anywhere, and we do."

"Can we stop talking about peeing now? You're just making it worse."

"I hear they use a lot of water elements in the second act. Are you sure you can hold it as the waterfall prop *trickles* and *gushes* all over the stage?"

"What are you a comedian now?" I discreetly try crossing my legs to stop myself from urinating on myself. "I'll be fine. I have *amazing* muscle control," I counter suggestively, but even I have to laugh at myself. This guy brings out the dormant teenaged bitch in me.

"Now *that* I'd love to experience firsthand." He laughs.

"I bet you would," I mutter.

"And you'd love it," he counters. "Just like you loved that kiss I gave you. Tell the truth. You haven't stopped thinking about it, have you?"

"I'm done talking."

I turn and start briskly walking away hoping my bladder will feel better once I sit back down, and honestly, I need to get back to the only thing that will keep me from saying or doing anything else dumb with Cutter—and that's Clark.

"Stop," Cutter gruffly orders while reaching for my wrist. He pauses for a moment as our eyes lock together. "I know the management here. I can get you into one of the private restrooms. No need for you to hurt those precious muscles of yours for another half an hour."

Cutter rubs his thumb back and forth across the top of my hand while focusing his gaze on the part of my face where my bandages once were. It's a simple but disarming act that reeks of intimacy. A level of intimacy that we absolutely don't share. It's meant to rattle me, and to my chagrin it does, but I'll be damned if I'm going to allow him to see it. I'm sure this is one of his signature "moves" with the many women in and out of his bed.

I yank my hand purposely away from his hoping he won't notice how much his touch has affected me, but I can tell by the cocky look on his face that he knows. Another dangerous thing about him. He's the type of man that prob-ably always knows what a woman is thinking and feeling. He's definitely had a lot of experience at it. I just don't think he necessarily gives a damn.

"To pee or not to pee?" he asks facetiously.

I hesitate to respond for a moment, because I don't want to give him the satisfaction of a yes. Plus, I certainly don't want to have to owe him anything, even if it's just a thank you, but my bladder begs to differ. It's evident that I'm not going to make it even to the beginning of the second act. Honestly it was ridiculous of me to even try. I was just being a brat. So I reluctantly accept his offer. I'd be an idiot to say no. I check my watch, and see that I've got about seven more minutes before the show begins again. That's plenty of time for me to relieve myself and get back to Clark.

"Okay, Mr. Connected, let's go."

Cutter grins as if he's won some sort of contest between us and motions to hold his hand out. I hesitate and stare at his outstretched hand like it's a venomous viper. I take a look at it, then at him, and give him one of my "what the hell are you doing" looks.

"We have to go up a flight of steep steps over on the other side of the room, and your heels look kind of high," he offers as an explanation. "I think it would be best if you hold on."

I gawk at it a moment longer.

His enormous hand.

It's large and calloused. Tan and weathered. I imagine that it's very warm too. Maybe almost hot to the touch. I remember them being warm as he cradled me in his arms, and pulled me into his hard, stiff frame the other night.

I don't want to make a big deal out of his gesture, because the truth of the matter is that I am wearing five inch heels and it's definitely crowded in here. A little help up the stairs to this mysterious private bathroom won't kill me. At least I hope it won't.

Actually this is probably a really bad idea.

"Still waiting for your hand, princess."

Definitely bad.

Cutter looks especially hot tonight. He's a little underdressed for the venue in my opinion, but it almost doesn't matter. He's wearing the hell out of a pair of worn in, dark jeans with a cream cable knit turtle neck sweater which carefully hugs the slopes of his strong shoulder and pectoral muscles. It's a sweater that's meant to be touched. Worn by a man who's meant to be mounted and ridden. A man who's patiently holding out his palm for me to grab.

All the signs are painfully obvious.

Stay away, Sloan. Stay very far away.

I decide on a compromise. Instead of risking skin to skin contact, I grab the crook of his arm instead. That should be safer. Not really though. His bicep doesn't seem human to the touch, but instead feels like thousands of indestructible bands of steel underneath a warm skin-like surface.

I want to punch him in his brick hard arm when he snickers, as if he knows exactly why I've gone for the crease of his elbow instead of his hand, but I'd probably just end up breaking a finger.

"Your face looks a lot better."

"And I didn't even have to stay in bed for a week per your suggestion."

"I can think of much more pleasant things to keep you in bed for a week. So it's just as well."

I roll my eyes.

"How's your sister doing?"

"She's your typical self-centered seventeen-year-old."

"Which means she's fine."

"Exactly."

"Anything from the douchebag?"

"Not a peep. Just like I told you."

"Good. I'm glad that you're right for once. Well here we are, milady."

"Watched a little *Downton Abbey* with one of your minions last night?"

"Never heard of it." He laughs.

I don't even know why I'm surprised when we arrive to an inconspicuous door with no restroom markings and a silver-buttoned keypad that Cutter has the access code for. I'm pretty damn good at sales, but Cutter's got the type of personality that could sell ice to an Eskimo. I'm sure it didn't take much for him to gain private bathroom privileges here at The Academy of Music, especially if there was a woman involved. It's not a fancy bathroom by any means, but it's private, smells like vanilla and lavender, and it looks like no one has used it since the cleaning people last serviced it.

"Thank God!" I say unable to contain my excitement. "I guess your minions are good for something."

"I'll just be waiting out here."

The corner of Cutter's mouth turns up with smug satisfaction, but I choose to ignore it, because I've never been so happy in my life to pee. That is until he decides to hold a conversation with me. I can't even relieve myself in peace.

"So who exactly is the square?" he asks through the door.

"You mean my *date*?" I say while flushing the toilet.

"Yeah, him. Where'd you two meet? He seems like a step up from the last guy I saw you with."

"Has anyone ever told you that you're really rude?" I ask while washing my hands. Silently wondering what last guy he's referring to. I haven't been to the club in a while. "That's another one of those rhetorical questions by the way. And another thing, last time I checked, I don't think the two of us have the sort of relationship where we chitchat about each other's love lives."

I hear his muscular body thump as he leans against the door between us.

"I feel responsible for you now. So yeah, I think we have that kind of relationship."

"Responsible for me?"

"I saved your life. I feel a duty to make sure all my efforts weren't for naught."

"Seriously, though, have you been watching *Pride and Prejudice* during your down time? Using words like naught."

I rub my hands vigorously under the automatic dryer, so that the noise can drown out his over-inflated recollections of the other night. Although I don't think anything could stop this guy from talking.

"I don't mind a few English dramas here and there. My mother used to like them. Plus I've had a little spare time on my hands to watch them lately." He purposely raises his voice over the loud hum of the dryer. "Maybe you haven't heard but I've recently moved into a new place."

"The same place that you bought evidently."

"Oh, so you have heard?" He chuckles. "Nice to know you've been asking about me."

My phone starts to vibrate. Thank God, it's Elizabeth.

"You couldn't have had better timing," I say while refreshing my lip gloss.

"Hey, how are you feeling? You sound weird."

"I'm perfectly fine. I'm actually out."

Cutter knocks heavily on the door. "You all right in there?"

"Who was that?" Elizabeth asks.

"I'm fine," I answer Cutter through the door.

"The dangerous one." I huff in exasperation to Elizabeth.

"The dangerous one?"

"The *landlord*," I try whispering.

Any other time Elizabeth can practically read my mind or finish my sentences but not lately. Ever since she got herself knocked up we haven't been in sync. I blame it on her muddled baby brain.

"What–wait are you talking about Cutter?"

"Ding, ding, ding! We have a winner, winner, chicken dinner."

"You're with Cutter again? Where? It's too early for you to be at the club."

"I'm not at the club. Get this! I'm on a date," I say excitedly. "A real one."

"With Cutter King?" She practically screams with excitement through the phone. "I knew–"

"Quiet." I quickly cut her off. "Is the baby in your belly sucking all the common sense out of your brain? I'm not out with Cutter King."

"Oh, for a minute I thought the world had just shifted on its axis, because I could have sworn you told me that you had no interest in Mr. King," she replies saucily.

I place my hands under the dryer again hoping it will drown out the words I'm about to say, since the person I'm talking about happens to be on the other side of the door.

"I don't have any interest in freaking Cutter King for God's sake. I'm on a date with Doctor Clark. You've heard me mention him before, right? My favorite client."

"Sure, I remember the name. He's the guy that's been asking you out since forever and you keep putting him in the friend zone. Which is why I am now thoroughly confused. You're currently on a date with the good doctor, but Cutter is there?"

"I'm at The Academy Of Music, and it just so happens that Cutter's here too doing God knows what. I can't imagine that he actually spent good money to come dateless to an interpretative dance performance."

Hmm, now that I think about it, I don't know if Cutter is here stag or not. He could very well have a woman waiting patiently in her seat for his return just like Clark is waiting for me. In fact, the thought of him being here alone seems a little preposterous. He's probably never had a lonely moment in his life.

"What else would he be there for, Sloan? I really think you've got Cutter pegged all wrong. He's actually a–"

"Do I really?" I cut her off. "No offense, Bitsy, but your fiancé and his friends aren't what I'd call cultured. I mean they're practically . . . gangsters."

"Umm, offense frackin' taken. One of those gangsters you're talking about is the father of my child and my future husband."

"Sorry, prego, but I call them like I see 'em."

"You see *them* through very a very tainted lens, my dear friend."

There's a heavy knuckled rap at the bathroom door.

"Let's go," Cutter commands from the other side of the door. "Time's up."

I worry for a moment that he heard what I just said to Elizabeth, but honestly it serves his ass right if he did. All I did was speak the truth, and he shouldn't be eavesdropping anyway.

"Was that him again?"

"Be quiet, prego. I'll call and tell you about my date tomorrow." I try speaking quietly. "Pray for me. This is the first decent date that I've been on in a long time. Just when I was about to give up on men altogether and stick to battery operated devices, Clark asked me out one last time, and this time I saw the light and said yes."

"Are you enjoying the good doctor's company tonight?"

"If you want me to be honest, it's just all right. I feel like the girl whose big brother had to take her to the prom, because no one else asked her to go."

"So Clark is a dud."

"I didn't say that exactly. The date is okay so far. It just isn't fireworks and fireflies like your thing."

"That's why you should wait for them."

"Wait for what?"

"For your fireworks and fireflies."

Unfortunately I don't think those are in the cards for me.

"WELL I HAVE a great deal of respect for him, so I'm hoping that it will grow into something more. Until such time, it's not a crime to get laid. And if I have to, it's not like I've never faked an orgasm before. I'm an awesome faker."

"Sounds like a plan then." Her words full of disappointment with me. "Don't forget that we need to set a date to plan out the nursery. Oh, and make sure to tell Cutter that I said *hi*."

She's never going to drop this Cutter thing.

"Bye, Bitsy," I say dryly.

Another authoritative knock on the door startles me.

"I *said* let's go, princess."

Sheesh, he's bossy.

I examine myself closely in the mirror, tugging up on the band of my jumpsuit, making sure it's securely in place and that my strapless bra isn't showing. Then I check my fingernails for snags and double check my teeth in the mirror to make sure there's no lip gloss on them. I'm about to repeat my stalling ritual for a second time, just to get on Cutter's nerves a little bit, until I hear several clicks disengaging the bathroom door lock. I instinctually use all of my body weight to lean on the door and keep it shut.

"Step away from the door, Sloan," Cutter orders from the other side.

"Are you crazy? I'm still using the bathroom!" I protest. My heart racing from a mixture of fury and fear.

"No you aren't. You've washed your hands about five times and checked that lipstick of yours probably five more."

"Just wait a minute, I'm coming out right–"

Before I can finish my sentence, Cutter pushes his way inside of the bathroom. The weight of my body against the door is no match for the strength of his massive arms. He shuts the door behind him and stares at me with an intensity that makes me jittery, but I suppose that's the point.

The look he's giving me. It's kind of . . . wicked and so dirty that I can almost envision myself tied up and spread eagle across a bed, a table, or the hood of a car. I just get the feeling that he's into shit like that.

He moves slowly toward me like a predatory wolf, as I back up by mere millimeters into the corner away from him. I wouldn't say that I'm frightened of him, but it's just a natural reaction to move back when someone of his size and girth starts moving into your personal space. Plus there isn't much room to move in here.

Our bodies are flush against each other, and I instinctively swallow a breath when he raises one of his hands toward my face. That makes him crook a smile, as if he's enjoying how uncomfortable he's making me. He uses that same hand to firmly lift and hold my chin, and then he takes the pad of his thumb and slowly begins rubbing the velvet red lip gloss off of my bottom lip.

He does this silently.

While I gasp.

Then he repeats the same thing to the top one.

His lethal eyes laser focused on mine the entire time.

"You don't need to wear all this makeup," he growls. "You're fucking hotter without it. Now let's go."

NINETEEN

CUTTER

Every time I put eyes on Sloan Pearson, my dick gets instantly hard, without my brain's consent or permission. I'll admit that the head below my waist has a dirty little mind of its own. It's actually kind of funny in a metaphorical way if you think about it. Sloan makes a living selling drugs that help men get an erection, and all I have to do is look at her to achieve the same result.

Even though I've already committed every one of her curves to memory, when Sloan exits the bathroom she looks like a shiny, new toy to me. A toy I desperately want to play with. One that would distract me from all the other toys I should be playing with. A toy that I'd beat all the other kids asses on the playground to keep to myself.

Tonight she's wearing a simple black strapless jumpsuit that cinches her small waist but then drapes loosely down her long, lithe legs. It's tasteful, not tight and tacky, and expertly shows off her slim neckline and delicate collarbone. She's also wearing a pair of black strappy "fuck me" high heels on her feet, and her full lips are painted a glossy deep blood red.

Those lips.

It gives me the chills just imagining what those cherry colored lips would look like wrapped completely around my dick. Sucking the life out of it. Savoring the taste. I know what I'd do. What I'd like to do. And I'm confident that she'd enjoy that shit too. I'd slide my hand onto the crown of her head and grip her hair at the roots tightly.

Guiding her mouth down my dick.

Controlling each and every exquisite stroke.

And after that I'd get really fucking creative.

Unfortunately for me, my *wet* dream girl is dressed like this on the arm of someone else. *For* someone else. That's why I smeared that sexy cherry red lipstick off with my thumb. It was a small piece of her that I could take away from him tonight. I have to laugh at myself, because that was definitely some territorial caveman shit to do, which I don't have a rational explanation for doing other than it gave me complete fucking satisfaction. Maybe no man really knows the reasons why they preoccupy themselves over a woman, but I've been curious about Sloan from the moment we met.

If she were any other woman, I would have locked that bathroom door and been inside of her in less than fifteen seconds. Whether she was on a date or not, I wouldn't have given a fuck. Don't get me wrong, I only take what women are willing to give, but when a woman chooses to give herself to me, you won't find me asking a lot of questions about who's been there before or who might be waiting in the wings. I don't stay around long enough for any of that shit to ever matter.

Yet there's something inexplicable about Sloan which makes me want to slow down, take my time, and play with her. Like a cat toying with a mouse, I'm taking exquisite pleasure in the chase. Cornering her, then letting her scamper away–and starting all over again. It's been several months now since we met at the club for the first time, and I've enjoyed each and every one of our brief encounters. Of course I'm not sure that she would say the same. For some reason, I think she hates to see me coming.

I escort Sloan back down the stairs and into the vestibule. She doesn't grab my arm this time, but I make sure to initiate contact by placing my hand along the arch of her lower back as she makes her way down the steps. It's quieter now and most people have returned back to their seats, except for the few stragglers finishing up their drinks at the bar, as well as the last few women still waiting to use the bathroom.

"Thanks for the use of the facilities," she offers reluctantly.

It's obvious by the way she's avoiding direct eye contact with me that she's either affected or offended by me. I'm not entirely sure which one. Maybe it's the way I touched her lips without her permission, or maybe she's wondering whether or not I overheard her little phone conversation with Elizabeth while she was in the bathroom. Maybe it's both.

If she's wondering what I thought of what she said in there. I didn't like what little I heard. Sloan is not the type of woman who should have to force herself to date or fuck anyone, especially the suit that she's out with tonight. It screams of complacency, settling, and husband hunting. Traits that usually turn me immediately off, but I wish someone would tell my dick that, because *it's* still very much interested in one Sloan Pearson.

"You're welcome," I say as I reluctantly slide my hand away from her back. Raking my eyes across her bare shoulders and watching as small goose bumps appear. Goose bumps that I've put there.

So responsive.

Her eyes finally flick up to meet mine.

"Why . . . why are you looking at me like that?" she asks nervously. Unconsciously brushing two of her fingers over her lips.

Because I want to taste you, then bend you over, and taste you again.

"Like what." I feign ignorance.

"Never mind," she huffs. Her cheeks flushed.

Her phone rings. She mutters something about it being another pain-in-the-ass blocked call, then stashes it back in her purse. My inner alarm goes off.

"Do you get private calls a lot?"

"Not really, why?"

"When did the calls start?"

"It's not Damien."

"When did they start?"

"I'm not sure."

"If you start getting them every day will you tell me?"

"Sure, but—"

"And can I give you a piece of advice?" It's actually a rhetorical question, because I'm going to say what I have to say anyway.

"Advice about what?"

I stare quietly at her for a moment, swallowing a lump in my throat, because when those smudged red lips of hers finished mouthing the word what—I swear that my dick just jumped, and then blood rushed to my head.

Both of my heads.

"You said you were going to give me a piece of advice?" she repeats impatiently tapping her foot.

"Yes."

Dick. Still. Moving.

"Well, what is it?"

I do my best at discreetly adjusting myself.

"A woman like you doesn't have to work so hard."

"Work hard at what?" she asks as her eyes desperately attempt to look anywhere but at my hands.

"Searching for Mr. Right."

Her eyes pop back up.

"What gives you the idea that's what I'm doing?" she asks as if she's appalled by the question.

"Any idiot can see that's what you're doing. You're on a date with a man who is marginally attractive, who you have nothing in common with, and who is stupid enough to allow you to wander around the front lobby of this place unescorted looking like you do. You don't believe in love, but it looks to me like you believe in something much worse—mediocrity."

I can practically see the steam rising from her ears. She's pissed. I guess I have that effect on people (especially women) a lot, because I have basically zero filter. I just speak what's on my mind and deal with the consequences later. But I've found that life is so much simpler when you operate that way. There's no room for misunderstandings.

"He's . . . far from an idiot."

"But he *is* stupid." I grin. "Can we at least agree on that?"

"He's a wonderful man," she counters defensively. Almost angrily. Which in turn makes me pissed. Why is she defending this dude? She's fooling herself if she thinks that something between them can turn out any way but badly.

"That's the best you could come back with? That he's *wonderful?* Interesting how that's not exactly the person you were describing to Elizabeth when you were on the phone just now. What's so wonderful about planning on faking it in bed? As if you already know that the suit's dick will never be able to satisfy you. That's actually the saddest thing I think I've ever heard."

"Mind your business!" she admonishes me. "I knew you were eavesdropping."

"Just admit that the doctor is boring the fuck out of you."

"My date is not boring. He's normal. He doesn't live on the edge, bashing people's heads in for a living like some people," she snidely retorts. "He's a healer. You wouldn't understand a man like him."

Where does she get this shitty idea of who I am? And since when is handing out Viagra prescriptions considered God's work.

"I'm a successful and respected entrepreneur in this city. I don't bash people's heads in for a living."

"Now we both know that's a lie."

Okay, maybe it's a little bit of a lie.

"I *will* most certainly bash someone's head in if I have to or if I choose to. I think you can attest to how and when I choose to use my skills, since I just recently saved your ass– but it's not my daily grind. I think you underestimate my ability to talk people into anything. That's what the king gets paid the big bucks for. The power to persuasively fix any situation using my God given charm and wit."

I offer her one of my thousand-watt smiles. The smile that makes everyone feel safe but especially women. Like they should trust me. Like I'm their big brother, best friend, and boyfriend all rolled into one. The smile I flash the moment before I talk a woman right out of their panties and into my bed.

"Funny, I keep hearing about all of *the king's* so-called charisma, yet your charms don't seem to have any effect on me. I must be immune."

My body biologically responds to a challenge. It just does. Especially because it's coming from this woman. I have the strongest urge to pull her close and shove my tongue down her smart-ass little throat, but I compromise with my primitive desires and simply move in a little closer to her. Feeling exactly what I did the last time I was this close to her.

Heat.

Kinetic energy.

And pheromones bouncing off of her like a siren's call.

I've been strongly attracted to certain women before but *damn*. Whether she annoys me or amuses me, every time I'm within ten feet of this woman I have the deep desire to pound my chest, throw her over my shoulder, and club any man who dares to challenge me into a bloody pulp. And when her almond shaped eyes finally pop up to meet mine straight on, that's when I'm assured of something that I wasn't as nearly confident about a few days ago.

I see it.

Excitement, desire, and maybe a smidgeon of healthy fear. If I were a betting man I'd say that Sloan wants me badly, or at least she's mildly curious, but it scares the hell out of her.

As I move farther in, I place my palm on her chest above her breasts and get my confirmation. "Perhaps you're not as immune as you think. Your heart is telling me something different. It's racing."

She jumps back.

"No it isn't, and don't touch me."

I move only one final step forward, keeping my hands by my sides, and my lips very close to her earlobe.

"Don't worry, princess. The next time I touch you it will be because you either ask me politely or beg me angrily."

Panic settles into the corners of her eyes. She's going to run from me like her life depends on it. Sure enough when the houselights start to flicker to let us know the second part of the show is about to begin, she bolts for her seat without even as much as a goodbye.

"Excuse me," she says urgently to all of the spectators moving at a snail's pace down the aisle. "Excuse me, please."

I track her as she moves swiftly through the aisle. Mostly because I can't take my eyes off of her, and partly because I want to see more of the asswipe she's here with tonight. Usually Sloan meets her men at Lotus. The kind of men whose only concern is how fast they're going to make their first million during the day and how many women they can get to spread their legs at night. Never caring about the woman's pleasure. Barely even asking their names.

These are the kinds of douchebags I've watched Sloan talk to. Dance with. Flirt with. Complete wastes of her time, but easy enough for me to scare away. I've done it countless times unbeknownst to her, and even if she discovered what I was doing, I wouldn't care.

As soon as I spot her date again, I take a really good look at him and realize that this guy just may be different. He looks different. She didn't meet him at the club. In fact he doesn't look like he's been inside of a nightclub in years. Based on the soft look in his eyes when she sits back down, they may even have a history. I heard her mention a doctor on the phone with Elizabeth. Is he someone she works with or an old flame?

After I'm back in my seat, I can't help but keep my eye on her and her dry-as-toast date during the entire second half of the performance. Actually it's him I'm watching. He's definitely into her. I know the body language of my species well. His body is slightly leaning into hers, so that he can whisper some irrelevant shit to her throughout the performance. He's almost salivating at the mouth. He wants inside of her badly.

It makes me recall the kiss that Sloan and I shared. I wanted inside of her badly that day too. So the sight of this guy obviously feeling the same way about her is making my eye twitch which is always the precursor to an unpleasant interaction. I need to leave as soon as the show ends or something bad is bound to happen.

What am I doing? I'm losing my shit over a woman I've shared one kiss with. A woman who isn't mine. A woman that will never be mine.

"Who are you staring at?" my client asks with the loudest whisper ever.

"No one," I say grumpily. "Why aren't you watching the dancers?"

"Why aren't you?"

Because neither of us really wants to be here, but we have to be. My client, professional baseball star Roberto Mendez, and I are sitting in front of his club's general manager and wife per their invitation. Mendez was supposed to be here with a respectable woman on his arm since he and his wife broke up, but that's one of his issues— he doesn't do respectable. It's my job to make sure that he does.

Even though I've pulled back from my responsibilities at the club and the tapas lounge, it would have been totally unfair and unprofessional to abandon Mendez. Neither Camden nor Roman have any idea how to handle him and he pays us good money to make sure he's managed.

If I hadn't reeled him in tonight, he was going to bring a woman here, who if memory serves, has had the distinct pleasure of receiving a couple of my twenty-dollar bills inside the crotch of her panties at my favorite strip bar. So needless to say, I put the kibosh on Roberto's date plans and went with him instead at the last minute. Not my idea of a good time, but it's my job to babysit him and make sure that he and the general manager get the photo opportunity that the ball club's been wanting for the media. A shot that appears as if contract negotiations between Mendez and the ball club are moving forward like clockwork. Like they're homies hanging out, even though it's totally staged.

"Oh, now I see why you're looking over there." He smirks. "She's definitely one hot piece of–"

"Watch your mouth," I warn.

"She looks familiar."

"I said mind your business."

"Watch my mouth. Mind my business." Mendez starts cracking up. "You're mighty touchy about a woman who's here with somebody else. You losing your touch, King Cutty?"

I watch like a dickhead as the suit amateurishly puts his arm around the back of Sloan's chair. His fingers just inches away from her bare skin. I can't believe that old high school trick actually still works. Not only does she allow him to keep his arm there, but I'll be damned if . . . she actually leans into it.

Fuck me.

"Shhh!" The general manager's wife scolds the two of us from behind. "You both are being too loud."

My phone dings.

It's Roman.

Roman: You could have given me a heads up that DJ Khaled was spinning tonight. I thought he was coming next month.

Once a month I like to book a celebrity deejay for the club. I love music. In another life I would have been a musician, but sometimes you just have to play the hand the you've been dealt in life.

Me: This is what happens when you don't come to the club. You don't know what's going on. He's going out of the country on tour next month, so it was now or never.

I'm a little disappointed. I had to call in a lot of favors to get Khaled into Philadelphia this week, and I wanted to reap the fruits of my labor. It's been part of my long-term brand strategy to attract different clientele to the club certain nights, and tonight will be a big step toward that.

Roman: His management is looking specifically for you.

Me: The contract is in a file with his name on the desktop. The manager is looking for the side deal I cut with him to book the date. An extra $1000 on top of Khaled's price. The cash is in the safe.

Roman: Still, it would be better if you were here.

Me: Not coming.

"I swear I know her," Mendez says loudly in my ear.

The general manager's wife leans over to Mendez. "She's Dan Pearson's little girl. Now will you please be quiet."

"Not so little anymore," he says under his breath.

"Shut up," I whisper.

I take another long look at Sloan and for the first time in days, I ask myself what the hell it is that I think I'm trying to accomplish by bogarting my way into her life. What the hell is wrong with me all of a sudden?

She's the daughter of an NBA legend. She's been raised as a pampered princess her whole life. I don't care what she says about not wanting love, of course she's looking for the fairy tale. She wants a respectable corporate drone she can take home to mommy and daddy, marry, and have babies with. She doesn't want any parts of what I have to offer.

She wouldn't know what to do with a king like me.

TWENTY

SLOAN

Cutter King is a slumlord.

He's never here and he doesn't fix anything. Not only is my thermostat on the blink, but now I don't have any hot water. I can't even wash my hair, and I need to be showered, dressed, and at work by nine.

I suppose that's why he hasn't been around, not that I was looking for him, because I guess that's what slumlords do. They duck their tenants, so that they won't have to actually do anything that costs them money, time, or effort.

Thank God Kyle works from home. He has hot water and has graciously offered me the use of his bathroom. I pack up one of my reusable Whole Foods totes with toiletries and a towel and head down to his apartment. I knock on the door a few times, and when he doesn't answer I shoot him a quick text.

Me: I'm outside.

Kyle: Sorry, I'll be there in a second.

I lean against the door, my hands full of stuff, wrapped up in my fluffy robe when the door to 7B opens. The unit next door to Kyle's.

The hairs on my forearms rise and my nipples rise to attention.

Damn Benedict Arnolds.

"Morning, princess."

It was just a matter of time before we saw each other, and now I wish we hadn't, because my body is starting to crave what it can't have. This man gets better with time. Like a fine wine. Today he's wearing a pair of soft gray sweats which are slung low, showcasing the perfect V of abdominal muscles that point straight toward what looks like a large piece of morning wood. I can't imagine waking up to that every morning. Well, maybe I can. I'd never get anything done.

Focus on his face, Sloan.

Focus on his face.

"Landlord."

"Why are you at my neighbor's door in a state of undress?"

"Funny you should ask that, but I need to take a shower and lo and behold, I don't have any hot water. Do you know anything about that?"

"Did you report it to the super?"

"Of course I told him, but the landlord has to actually approve the work so that Pete can do his job."

Kyle finally opens the door with a messy head of hair looking like he just rolled out of bed. I know he says he works from home, but I've never really been sure about what he actually does. Something about networks and such.

"Sorry about that, gorgeous. I was on the can. You may want to watch a little TV or something before you go into the bathroom. Give the air freshener I sprayed a minute to do its job."

Good grief.

"Take a shower in here," Cutter offers. Actually it almost sounds like an order, not a suggestion.

"And who are you?" Kyle asks.

"I'm Cutter King, the new owner of this building, your next-door neighbor, and a friend of Miss Pearson's."

Kyle turns to me looking for confirmation.

"Yep, he's the new owner."

"Who you know and never mentioned?"

"Yes."

"That's interesting," he says giving Cutter another once-over.

"If you're tired of chitchatting out here in your pajamas, and you want to get to work sometime this year, I'd say it's time for you to come take that shower. I'll call Pete while you're getting ready."

Kyle looks back and forth between Cutter and I and much to my chagrin, I can tell that he already sees it. The pull between us. The fierce attraction.

"You know what, Sloan, I totally forgot about an appointment I have. The dentist. I'm actually going to have to hop in the shower right now to make it on time. So why don't you shower at Mr. King's here, and I'll catch up with you later."

He's totally lying.

"But Kyle–"

He grins mischievously. "Don't give me a hard time about it. You know how bad my molars are. I have to make this appointment or I'll keep putting it off. Go on now." He actually gives me a small push toward Cutter. "When you get off work tonight, I'm going to tell you about the brilliant thing my nephew did the other day. Little man called nine-one-one and nearly gave my sister a heart attack. They broke down the door to the house and everything."

"Ready or not," Cutter says.

I check the time on my phone. I've wasted ten valuable hair detangling minutes contemplating where I'm going to wash my private parts. It's not that serious. It's just a shower.

"Fine. Let's go."

One of things that helped me make a final decision about renting in this building was the fact that there are no two apartments in the building that look alike. Every unit has its own bit of individuality. Something special that makes it uniquely its own space. I've really never seen anything like it.

My apartment has these cool dark wooden beams running across the length of the ceiling. Kyle's has a cozy window nook where you can sit and drink coffee and read a book. And Cutter's has a large open face red brick wall in his living room. What he doesn't have much of is furniture or window treatments. It definitely looks like he just moved in.

"You know someone can see everything in here at night."

"Who can? We're on the seventh floor."

"What about the people in that building across from us. Right on the seventh floor, genius. They can look in here and see everything you're doing. You need some blinds or some curtains."

"I'm not modest. If they want to look they can look."

I roll my eyes.

"Forget I mentioned it. Just point me to the hot water."

"Right in here. How much time do you have to get ready?"

"Less than an hour. Why?"

"I'm calling Pete now. I'm not sure why some of the units have hot water and you don't, but he'll get to the bottom of it. It'll be repaired by the time you get home."

"Thanks, landlord."

My shower is heavenly and informative. There are

several brands of shampoo in Cutter's bathroom, no conditioner, only one brand of soap, and two washcloths. It makes me think that a woman has been in this shower lately. Of course I can't let that random thought go.

"Are either of these washcloths clean?" I yell through the door. Hoping he can hear what I'm saying.

He opens the door to the bathroom.

"Aah!" I quickly turn my body around with my back facing him. Although the doors to his shower are frosted, he can definitely see my silhouette through them. "Would you get out please."

"I couldn't understand what you were saying. It could have been important, so I came in."

"I asked if either of these washcloths were clean. I forgot mine."

"No, let me grab you a fresh one."

Figures.

"Here."

I crack open the door just enough to allow him to hand me the washcloth.

"And next time just ask what you really want to ask me. I'm an open book to you, darlin'."

"I don't know what you're talking about."

"I use two washcloths. One for my face and one for my body. I haven't had female company over at this place at all or at my old place in a long time."

"I wasn't asking you about any of that."

"You're a shit liar, darlin'. You were definitely asking that. See you in a few minutes."

After soaking my head under the showerhead to try my best to forget that I just freakin' embarrassed myself, I finish up and return to the living room squeaky clean and with my tote bag full of stuff. As I pass the open door to his bedroom,

I can see a part of a gun, a shoulder holster, and what looks like a cleaning kit on top of his dresser.

Totally reminds me of my youth.

I can't wait to get out of here.

"Thanks for the shower," I say as I hightail it to the door.

He stares quietly at me for a moment then growls out an order.

"Wait. Sit. Eat."

"I don't have time for breakfast. I have to go get dressed."

The food on the table looks delicious. There's hot bacon, scrambled eggs, bagels and butter, and a bowl of mixed fruit. I don't smell coffee, not everyone drinks it, but I see a few bottles of spring water over on the counter. But I'm literally standing in a pair of lacy underwear, a robe, and slippers. I'm not sure that I could manage to take two bites of what he's prepared sitting across from him in this.

"This looks great, Cutter, but I have to go."

"You've got ten minutes. Scrambled eggs are my specialty. Eat."

"I thought you said steak was."

He grins. "That too. I'm good at a lot of shit."

I bet, I think to myself.

"I bought a Keurig the other day. Shouldn't take long to set up. You want me to make you a cup of coffee?"

"I don't drink plain coffee."

"Coffee's coffee."

"Clearly you don't drink it."

He doesn't respond to that. I wonder why he even bothered to buy a Keurig machine if he doesn't drink coffee. Weirdo.

"So what kind of coffee do you drink then?"

"I like specialty espresso drinks. Like caramel macchiatos."

"Oh, fancy coffee."

I stare at the bacon. I haven't had a strip of that type of greasy goodness in months.

"Okay, maybe just a few bites."

The first bite is salty deliciousness and you can't eat bacon without eggs, so I take a nibble of them as well. He's right, they are good.

"What's in these?"

"If I told you, then I'd have to kill you." He grins.

"With the gun in your bedroom?"

"I'd prefer to fuck you to death."

"Seriously, do you have a permit for that thing?"

"Of course I do and that thing has a name."

"What?"

"My glock—his name is Benny."

"Do you wear Benny all the time?"

"Most of the time. When I'm in the club or when I'm working a fix. Why? Do guns bother you?"

"I just don't think they're necessary for city living. Do you know about the incident that happened with my father in 1999?"

"Absolutely, it was in all the papers."

"Do you really think that three people would have lost their lives in that nightclub that night if my father's security didn't have those guns on them?"

"They're security. It was their job to protect your father. From what I heard, your dad didn't have much of a choice. They were basically robbing him that night."

"He has a lot of money, Cutter, and not all of it was in his wallet that night. He should have just given them the money and left the club. End of story. No one would have been hurt."

"And then what do you think would have happened the next time he went out? Celebrities like your father are marks. Thugs like the guys that tried to rob him that night would have robbed him again and again and again. It would have never stopped."

"That would have been better than people losing their lives."

"I can't disagree with you there, but neither one of us were there. We don't know exactly what happened. Maybe your dad's people didn't have a choice. Either way you can rest assured that I don't go around shooting people at clubs. Even criminals. I carry my weapon for protection, and I've rarely had to use it."

"But you have used it?"

"Rarely."

"Uh, huh."

"Juice?" he offers with a saccharin smile.

"No, I'm good. I'll just drink a little water." I watch as he awkwardly maneuvers his legs from underneath the table to stand. "You know this dinette set is way too small for you. You need something bigger."

"It came with the apartment."

"Oh, I never saw her much. I wonder what happened to her."

"Don't know. Didn't ask."

Cutter stands behind me and leans over my shoulder placing a bottle of water in front of me. He smells delicious. Like bacon and leather and soap.

"So, tell me," his voice rumbles deeply with the sound of morning, "how did your date end the other night with the suit?"

"Wonderfully."

Actually it ended without fanfare. Not even a kiss good night. Clark and I ended our date, like we end our sales calls, with a cordial goodbye.

"Did you end up having to fake it?"

He sits back down at the table and looks at me straight on.

"I don't put out on the first date," I say resolutely.

"Really?" He raises an eyebrow. "So it *was* the first date."

"Yes, if you must know, it *was* the first date. A very nice first date."

"But it was the last one, princess."

"What makes you so sure? I think my guy may have something to say about that."

"Your *guy?*" he asks incredulously and then one of his eyelids starts to jump. "Trust me when I say that after I get inside of you, that there'll be no second date. Now pass me an everything bagel, and when you're done eating, I'll drop you off at work."

TWENTY-ONE

CUTTER

I'm completely mind fucked.

The moment Sloan stepped out of my bathroom, fresh faced, no makeup, and with her hair pulled back from her face, I had a moment of recognition.

A realization.

A revelation.

It. Is. Her.

How could I have been so stupid not to have realized all these months that they were one in the same. The pretty girl who stopped me cold in my tracks when I was just a kid sneaking into the stadium is the same stunning woman who is stopping me dead in them today.

It explains so much.

It explains everything.

The attraction. The incredible pull I have to fix her every problem. The desire to be the source of all of her laughter. I don't need a psychology degree to understand that I've been unconsciously tapping into some childhood fantasy shit.

Me: You'll never believe this.

Camden: So you're speaking to me now?

Me: You're the only one who will understand. So for now, yes.

Camden: What is it?

Me: Sloan is the girl from the stadium.

Camden: The girl you trolled every high school in Philly to find?

Me: Yes.

Camden: The glamazon is THAT girl.

Me: YES!

Camden: Well fuck me.

Me: Exactly.

Camden: Is that why you bought her shitty ass building? I heard that's where you're living now.

Me: I didn't know it was her when I bought it.

Camden: Well God help her now that you've put these two puzzle pieces together. She's never going to get rid of you.

Me: It all makes sense now.

Camden: What does?

Me: My fixation with her. It's not me falling in love or anything as ridiculous as that.

Camden: Yeah, then what is it?

Me: An unfulfilled childhood crush. You know that's some powerful shit.

Camden: And now that you know this, Dr. Phil, are you over her?

Me: Once we sleep together, and it ruins the "fantasy" of the perfect fourteen-year-old her,

it will be done. Then I can get back to life as usual.

Camden: The titty bar.

Me: Exactly.

Camden: Good luck with that rewarding relationship goal.

Me: Thanks, asshole.

There's a long pause while Camden continues to type. I can see the dots moving.

Camden: Roman and I decided not to take on any new clients until you come back.

Me: Your choice.

Camden: I'm focusing on the tapas lounge and he's handling the club. Jade is helping with both.

Me: I figured.

Most of our private clients cannot actually pay us to fix their problems using money from their corporate accounts. They'd have to cut us a check, and checks leave paper trails. Trails that have to be explained. Most of our clients decide to pay us privately. Off the books.

On the flip side, if we accepted payment strictly as consultants, it would raise red flags with the IRS. That's why we own the restaurant and the club. To wash the money. But they are still legit businesses that have to be run. Businesses that have to be successful in order to continue washing the money. It isn't as easy as Joseph used to make it look. That's what I'm hoping my brother and Roman are getting a glimpse of. Just how much work it takes to keep everything we're doing squeaky clean and functional.

Camden: How much more time are you going to need before the three of us sit down and figure this out like rational human beings.

Me: Since when are you rational?
Camden: When, Cut.
Me: Don't know.
Camden: Fine.

∼

THE MAJORITY of my day has been spent getting to know Pete the superintendent. The first thing on my to-do list was for me to call him and introduce myself as the new owner of the building. I had a feeling that he was used to the previous owner's lack of attention, so I had to explain that it was a new day and things were going to be a lot different.

His first assignment was to see what was going on in Sloan's apartment. I told him I wanted the hot water running and the thermostat replaced by lunchtime. Unfortunately it wasn't as easy of a fix as I'd hoped. Thanks to the neglect of the previous owner, there's a bigger overall pipe problem in the building, so my little glamazon is going to have to go without hot water and dependable heat for a few more days. She's going to just love that shit.

Now I'm meeting with Johnson for a burger and an update. When Sloan was showering at my house, her phone rang and another blocked caller popped up on her caller ID. There's no way that she should be getting that many blocked calls. Something in my gut tells me that it's the kid.

"Thanks for buying me dinner, boss. I've been strapped for cash lately."

"What are you doing with all the money I pay you?"

"I have a sick grandmom at home."

"Really, Johnson?"

"I'm serious. She raised me since I was six years old. I

take care of her now. Medicine is expensive. I was thinking about moving the two of us to Canada, so we could get some of their free healthcare and maybe some cheaper drugs."

"Why don't I find you a permanent position with benefits once you're done with this assignment."

"Really? That would be great, boss. What would I do?"

"Let's talk about why you're here first. The kid. Was he the one hired for the mailroom position?"

"Yes, it has been confirmed. One Damien Hardwick was definitely hired for your girl's building. My connection was able to pull his HR file. How do you want to handle it?"

As I consider what I'm going to do about the little woman beater, I'm distracted by the lilt of a familiar voice. A voice that belongs to a pair of beautiful almond eyes, long muscular legs, an apple shaped ass, and tits that sit round and high. A voice that immediately makes blood rush to my dick. And when I see where it's coming from, every muscle in my body tenses.

Sloan is sitting at the hotel bar having a glass of red wine and chatting it up with a suit. And not just any suit, but the same doctor from The Academy of Music.

A second date.

Damn her.

Even with a purple fucking eye and scars on the side of her face, she's drop dead fucking gorgeous. What isn't so attractive is that she's smiling and flirting with the square as if he's the most interesting man in the room. In a second, I think she's actually going to bat her eyelashes at him. What the fuck?

I laugh a little at myself. Just a minute ago I thought I had her figured out. I was so confident that my interest in Sloan was just a momentary diversion. Nothing serious. Just a passing fancy. Like watching high quality porn. Intoxicating, addictive, but at some point, you've got to let it go for real life and real sex with real women. The kind of women that don't have a pretentious bone in their bodies. The kind who don't hold degrees from fancy schools and would suffocate in a corporate environment. The kind of women who aren't the subjects of my deluded childhood fantasies of the perfect girl. The kind of women who are nothing like Sloan.

But as I watch her sitting here. Laughing. Sparkling.

All of that shit goes right out the window.

Sloan is this wild intriguing mixture of things. As soon as she enters a room she commands everyone's attention, although I don't think she's the attention seeking type. She was raised in a high rent downtown district, attended prestigious private schools including an Ivy League college, and holds down a demanding sales job. Even though she's the daughter of one of the NBA's legendary bad boys, which means she's basically Philadelphia royalty, I rarely see her use her daddy's legacy as currency. I respect that.

She's strong willed, silver tongued, and fiercely independent yet the flip side of all of her great traits is that she repeatedly picks the wrong men. None of them can handle her, but I think that's the point. She doesn't really want a man to handle her. A man like me.

"Princess," I greet her crossly. Still pissed about her black eye and especially pissed that she's out on a second date with said black eye.

"Cutter." She almost smirks. No doubt happy with herself that she's proven me wrong.

"We keep popping up at the same places I see."

"I've been going to this pub for years."

"That's interesting, so have I."

"Funny how our lives keep revolving and intertwining with each other."

More than she realizes.

"Is this a friend of yours?" The suit asks while assessing me in the way that men do when they're sizing up another man. Chest out. Voice dropping one octave lower. Looks like he's on date number two, and he already thinks she's his property. Asshole.

"Cat got your tongue, princess? Answer the man."

Sloan shifts in her seat. I take pleasure in the fact that on occasion I can make her feel quite uncomfortable. I'm not sure if it's what I say, how I say it, or the fact that I'm saying anything to her at all, but I definitely take a sick pleasure in making her squirm. It's just a prelude to all the many other ways I'd like to see her squirm.

Under me.

On top of me.

"He's a friend of a friend." She refers to me dismissively. Then she takes a long, drawn out sip of her wine and gives me a hard glare from head to toe behind the glass. "And my landlord."

"I'm Doctor Aiden Clark. Sloan's . . . date."

He makes sure to exaggerate the doctor part of his name as he offers his hand for a handshake. I paste on a fake smile and accept it reluctantly.

"Cutter King."

"Is my hot water back on, Mr. King?" Sloan asks. Eyes sparkling like she's winning some sort of battle of wills between us.

But I make sure to look both at her and the doctor when I say, "The problem is bigger than Pete or I had anticipated. Your water will be off for another day or so, but no worries, you can take your showers at my place again."

I move closer to her stool.

Almost touching her knees.

Staring directly at her bruised eye, then her lips, then

her breasts. Sensing how her breathing is becoming more erratic, my dick inadvertently responds.

Hardening.

Extending.

Straining against the zipper of my jeans. Completely ignoring everyone around us especially the suited stranger with his chest poked out.

"Your washcloth is right where you left it. Next to mine."

I'm loving how she's looking at me right now. Angry. Passionate. Those eyes. Even with one bruised, Sloan's eyes are sexy as fuck. They're almond shaped with irises the color of topaz, framed by long black lashes that flutter when she's frazzled or angry or both.

She turns quickly to the doctor to talk her way out of this.

"He lives on my floor. We have mutual friends. He offered me the use of his shower, so I could go to work."

"Don't forget breakfast," I add. "You like a good piece of bacon."

"I didn't ask you to make that!"

"Yet you ate every morsel."

The doctor quietly nods at her explanation, but he doesn't look like he understands. In fact the poor sap looks like he's going to be sick.

"I get it. He's your neighbor and you needed to shower. No explanation necessary, Sloan."

She looks back at me with a venomous glare.

"Don't let us keep you from your evening, Mr. King. I'm sure you don't want to keep your dinner companion waiting."

I don't miss how Sloan attempts to inconspicuously look behind and around me, as if she's looking for someone I may be here with. It's cute. Jealousy suits her.

"Clark and I would like to finish our meal–"

"Actually, Sloan–" He throws a few bills on the bar top. "I have to head out. Sorry about this, but I need to check on one of my patients. He's having some trouble adjusting to a dosage increase."

Sloan motions to stand, but I quickly grab onto her wrist to stop her from going after him, because for a minute it looked like she was about to. I know she's probably angry with my behavior tonight, but Doctor Clark would just be another mistake like all the other mistakes she's made with men in the past. Once again, I'm actually doing her a big favor.

I'll just put it on her tab.

"Of course, Clark. Your patients come first. I'll call you later," she says way too cheerily. My guess is that it's totally for my benefit. She doesn't give two shits about this guy or she would have left with him. Plain and simple.

"Nice guy you were about to spread your legs for."

"So what if I was? Are you my daddy now?"

"I'll spank you like your daddy if that's what you're into," I tease, but the sexy visual of my hand across Sloan's perfect ass is only teasing one person right now and that's me.

Sloan pivots slightly on her stool, so that she's directly face-to-face with me, leans casually back on the bar top, and spreads her amazingly long, jean clad legs far apart. Even with clothes covering that piece of the promised land between her legs, my mouth still begins to water.

"I'm into *all* of that shit, Cutter King, but you'll *never* get to know. And that's what the real problem is isn't it? You've never met a woman who didn't think you were adorable, or hysterical, or who didn't want to immediately drop to her knees and suck you off, have you? Someone who's absolutely, unequivocally, *not* interested in you."

That mouth.

The fire in her eyes.

This woman's going to be the death of me.

If this is what *not interested* looks like, I can only imagine what *interested* does. "You think you that you don't like someone like me, but all this fire you're spitting at me, is nothing but pent up need."

"Puh-lease."

"You're absolutely right about one thing, princess, I've never met a woman who didn't want to perform that very specific act you just described on me. An act that you've clearly been thinking about doing to me for a very long time. I bet you're good at that shit too."

The lines around her mouth contort into the cutest little puke face.

"Don't flatter yourself. You haven't even been a fleeting thought."

She's saying one thing, but her body language is saying another. And now she's just given me the worst thing you can offer a King. Possibility. When there's even the slightest chance for me to get what I want, I'm like a dog with a bone. I won't fucking let go.

And I want her.

I bend over and position my mouth closely to her ear. Her first instinct is to pull away, but there's nowhere for her to go. I can see the goose bumps rise on the back of her neck and forearms. I'm not sure if they're there due to fear or desire, but either way I'm good with it.

"Not even one fleeting thought?" I taunt.

She's silent but smiling as she nods her head to dramatically to make her point.

"Nope."

"Did you take an Uber here?" I ask.

"Why? Are you offering me a ride home since you scared my date away?"

One corner of Sloan's pretty mouth turns up when she asks her question. If I didn't know better, I'd almost think she was flirting with me.

"Let's not pretend that was some sort of date. At best you were just trying to prove some point to me, and at worst he was just another suit you were going to use as a bed warmer to give the old vibrator a break. You don't go on dates. You don't believe in love. Remember?"

Her mouth drops in shock for only a moment, and then she presses her lips together tightly in anger. She's definitely about to rip me a new one when we're interrupted by Johnson. Hell, I forgot he was here.

"Sorry to interrupt, boss, but it's Granny. I've got to get home and help her get ready for bed."

"No problem, just send me the file and I'll take it from there. I'll put the payment in your account tomorrow. Thanks for everything."

"Thank you, boss."

Johnson doesn't move as he stares at Sloan for a moment waiting for an introduction. He obviously knows that this is the woman we're working to protect, and he wants to say hi.

"Oh sorry. Johnson, this is Miss Pearson. Sloan, this is Johnson."

"Nice to meet you."

"Same to you. Hey, do you need a ride home, Johnson? Seems like your boss here is in the mood for giving out rides."

I give Johnson a quick look that he knows very well. It means to scram. Then before she can say anything else to him, I lean over and cradle the right side of her face with my hand. Gripping the base of her neck with my fingers and using my thumb to touch her lips.

Her mouth parts for me as I gingerly use my thumb to rub the coral colored lipstick off of her lips. I'm almost tempted to slide my thumb inside of her mouth, wondering if she'd suck it or more likely try to bite it off, but this isn't the place for that.

"Let's go home, princess," I growl. My dick brick hard from our minimal contact. "I'm definitely giving out rides tonight, but the only passenger will be you."

~

TWENTY-TWO

SLOAN

I'm not exactly sure how I ended up here. I shouldn't even be talking to this man, but there's something about the way Cutter words things which makes him a powerfully persuasive man. Now I think I'm starting to see what everyone's talking about. He's the ultimate negotiator.

He makes a convincing argument about it making more sense for me to take a hot shower at his house. So I do. Changing into a pair of clean black leggings and a Nirvana sweatshirt. Then all of a sudden, he whips up a delicious ribeye steak while we watch a comedy special on Netflix. One of his favorites. Then after dinner we have a glass of wine and watch the first episode of *Downton Abbey*. My favorite. And now he's pulled out a deck of Uno cards. My favorite card game and evidently his too.

"Let's play for something," he suggests.

"For fun?"

"No. Kings don't play for fun. Let's raise the stakes."

"I thought I made it clear in the car that I'm *not* riding you."

He laughs. "We don't have to raise them that high. How about the person who wins the hand can ask the other a question. A question that has to be answered honestly."

"There's nothing that I want to know about you," I lie.

"Really? Because there's so much about you that I want to know."

"Then I guess you'll have to win your hands, but I have to warn you, I'm a master Uno player."

"We'll see."

I've been beating people in my family at Uno since I was twelve years old, so I win the first hand in about five minutes. The first question belongs to me.

"All right," he says with a flirty smile. "Ask your question."

"Why did you really buy this building?"

"You owe me a debt, and I'm here to collect."

I raise my eyebrow at that then shuffle the cards. Dealing each of us seven cards. After a longer game than the last, Cutter finally wins. The second question belongs to him.

"Have you ever seriously considered sleeping with me?"

"You're getting right to it, aren't you?"

"Answer honestly," he singsongs.

"Maybe."

"That's honest?"

"Ok fine . . . yes."

"So why are you fighting it when you and I both already know that it's going to be amazing between us."

"That's two questions." I laugh. "You'll need to win another hand if you want an answer to that."

"I love it when you laugh."

There's an awkward moment of silence between us, because I don't know what to say in response to that. Thank you? I take a sip of wine instead. He poured me a nice glass of pinot noir to go with dinner.

"Why did you go out with the doctor tonight?" he asks me with a serious look on his face. His earlier playfulness gone. "You think that's going to keep me away?"

"That's a third question," I say nervously.

"The game is fucking over."

All of a sudden Cutter moves his chair back. The sound the legs make scraping against the floor startles me. He stands up and begins to circle me slowly. Stopping directly behind me.

I sit stock still.

Concentrating on my breath.

A thick heavy silence fills the air.

He slides his palm onto the back of my head. Gripping my hair at the base of my scalp. He pulls my head to the side, grazing his mouth against the side of my neck.

"Stand up," he orders.

I try to pretend as if I'm unaffected by what he's doing by taking another sip of my wine, setting the glass down, and then slowly coming to a full stand. Still with my back to him.

"Were you trying to teach me a lesson tonight?"

I don't answer. Savoring the prickly feeling of his five o'clock shadow against my skin as he speaks.

"I know that I said I wouldn't touch you until you asked me nicely or begged me angrily, but as you can see that's shot to hell."

He waits for me to respond, but I say nothing.

"What, no clever come back this time?"

"What do you want me to say?"

"I don't want you to say any fucking thing. I want to make you scream."

"I'm not a screamer."

"I don't believe that for one second, and I hope that waiting to make the first move has been as painful for you as it has been for me," he says gruffly near my ear.

He uses his other hand to trace a path from my clavicle down the center of my chest, past my navel, and straight inside of my leggings to my clit."

My knees buckle, and I fall back against him.

His aggressive touch was unexpected.

And my body very much likes it.

"That's a good girl," he practically purrs. "Lean completely on me and spread your legs wider for your king."

Cutter releases the hand that was in my hair and slides it around the base of my throat. Holding me in place against him as his other hand continues its carnal exploration of me.

It feels just as exquisite as I hoped, or rather that I fantasized, submission to Cutter would. Another strange feeling of dichotomy. I love how he is making my body feel, and I hate that I love it.

"You're still way up in your head when the only thing that should be doing the thinking for you," he pats me gently, "is this pussy."

Then he slides one of his thick fingers inside of me.

And then another.

And then he takes his time stroking me with his fingers over and over while praising me for my obedience.

"You're a very good girl, princess. Now spread just a little wider, and I'll give you one more finger if you do what you're told."

"Shut up," I say because my inner feminist is both turned on and offended by how he's talking to me.

This is so confusing.

He lightly chuckles by my ear, pulls out his fingers, and then playful slaps me on the ass. The grip around my neck gets just a bit tighter when he does it. I gasp not exactly for air, because I can breathe just fine, but mainly out of surprise.

"If you want to continue to play you're going to have to be a bit more polite." He slaps me again on my butt. This time a little harder. It stings in a good way if that makes any sense. "Do we understand each other?"

"We do."

"That's fucking fantastic. So you want to try this again?"

"Yes."

"Good."

His free hand goes immediately back in between my legs. This time gently rubbing my clit and then pinching it with his thumb and pointer fingers. Over and over he continues this type of erotic massage until I'm so slippery, that he uses the juices leaking out of me to slide his fingers back inside of me.

Back where they belong.

And I pant in pure bliss again.

His other hand releases my neck and begins to playfully pinch and roll one of my nipples. I think his majesty is about to discover my weakness. I love nipple play.

The feeling is so exquisite that I raise both of my arms behind me and reach around Cutter's neck. It's hard because he's so tall, but he bends over a little more to give me what I want.

"I think my princess likes her tits to be touched. I wonder what you'd do once my mouth is on them."

"Probably whatever you wanted," I pant.

I can feel him smiling behind me.

"I can't imagine it would be that easy. Nothing about you is easy, Sloan. That's why I'm going to fuck you hard. Just the way you deserve. The way you'll like it."

His fingers pick up speed and the nerve endings in my

body feel as if they're highly sensitive to sight, sound and touch. As if all they need is just one more piece of sensory input to send them into a state of high alert.

Then all of a sudden, he stops.

Saying nothing but licks his fingers the entire time.

"What are you doing?" My question ends up sounding more like a plea.

"What do u want from me, Sloan?"

"I want you to finish what you started."

"Then you'll have to ask nicely."

"You mean you want me to beg."

"Begging is nice too. Whatever works for you."

He walks away while I contemplate how on earth I'm going to do something I never in do in bed with a man and that's beg. I watch him move toward a large black duffel near the door. He opens it and pulls out another smaller black bag. He places our dinner dishes in the sink. Wipes the table. Then puts the bag on top of the dinette and begins pulling items out one by one.

I'm kind of astounded that he's choosing this particular moment to unpack his shit. Not after doing what we just did. I continue to stand in the middle of his living room like an idiot not knowing exactly what to do or what he's thinking until I notice the items he's lining up across the table.

A pink one.

A silver one.

A blue one.

A plastic one.

A metal one.

A large one.

A tiny one.

Vibrators of all shapes and sizes in plastic packaging.

After placing the last one on the table, he stands up and

pulls his sweater over his head. I swallow with great diffi-culty as I watch the muscles in his arms contract and flex as he tosses it on the floor. He's beautiful.

His brief striptease reveals several beautiful tattoos that adorn his arms and back. Each is its own distinct pattern of swirled black ink highlighted by reds and blues. The artist captured Cutter's spirit expertly. His ink is beautiful and playful just like he is. He unties and kicks off his boots. Each making a thunderous clunk as they land against the wall. Adding to the building tension between us.

He watches me closely as he lines up each toy. I'm uncomfortable. Not because I've never owned a vibrator before, but because I've never used one in front of or with a man. Just alone. The guys I've been with in the past have never been this . . . creative.

My eyes continue to land on the purple vibrator with what looks like a collection of loose pearls inside the casing. It's pretty in a freaky sort of way.

"I guess purple it is."

My head pops up.

"What?"

He grabs some clean paper towels and alcohol out of the same small duffel, then takes the purple vibe out of the packaging and begins cleaning it.

"When this one is turned on, it not only vibrates but it simulates the movement of a penis. The pearls massage the inside of your pussy as it moves. You'll like this one."

Next Cutter takes two pieces of long rope out of the bag. There's a stainless-steel rack that hangs above the island in his kitchen for pots and pans. He ties the two pieces of rope onto the rack which is easy enough since there are no pans hanging from it. He only has two pans, and he used them to cook dinner.

He walks over toward me, his bare feet thumping across the floor, and whisks me up in his arms.

"Cutter!"

"Lift your arms."

He sits me on the island and lifts my sweatshirt above my head, making sure not to disturb any of my remaining scars or my eye. He throws it on the floor with the rest of his things.

Now I'm left with a bra and a pair of leggings on. Sitting on top of a man's cold kitchen countertop. Relinquishing control bit by bit. It makes me anxious and totally uncomfortable yet mysteriously aroused.

He kisses the inside of my left wrist before he ties it to one of the hanging ropes. Pulling on the other side of it to keep my arm raised and secure. He does the same to the other. I try moving my arms just to test the strength of the overhang. It's pretty damn strong. I can't move my arms and the rack isn't moving.

He reaches back into his ominous black bag and grabs a pair of scissors. I inhale sharply as he carefully slides the blades across the top of my breasts, then down my side, then he snips.

Cutting my bra open on one side. Then the other. Then continuing to snip until there are literally pieces of my bra all over the counter and my breasts are exposed.

He bends down and places his mouth around one of my nipples and sucks. My back arches in pure carnal delight. I want to give more of myself to him. I wish he'd take more.

I almost mouth the words but there's still something holding me back. Like he said, I'm still inside of my head. I can't totally allow myself to just be in the moment. I don't trust him. I don't trust myself.

He moves to the other breast. This time his teeth lightly graze my nipple. And I cry out. The crotch of my leggings are soaked. I almost don't want him to touch me there, because I'm so embarrassed by my response to him. I'm not sure that I've ever been this wet in my life.

"I smell you, princess."

Then he starts to slide my leggings and panties off. After he pulls them off, tossing them aside with the other clothes, he touches my clit with just one finger.

"You're soaked."

He walks away and back to the table. Picking up the ominous looking purple vibrator, and I shiver inside. I'm not going to be able to handle it. I ache so much between my legs already.

"Open your knees."

I don't open them.

"Trust between us is paramount if we're going to have fun playing. Now open up."

I spread my legs as best I can. It feels good. The cold granite feels like a cooling balm on my aching pussy.

"Kiss me, Sloan."

He leans over and puts his mouth on mine. Sliding his tongue inside where he meets my willing tongue. He tastes sweet, like the semi-sugary aftertaste of a mint, and we begin a slow exploration of each other's mouths. My arms swaying but basically immobile as we kiss each other passionately.

We continue like this for a few more moments before he starts to slide the vibrator inside of me. Inch by inch it feels enormous. Probably because I haven't had sex in a really long time, and additionally because there is no forgiving bend in a piece of motorized plastic.

I moan as I feel the ripple of the pearls sliding against my walls as it burrows its way inside of me. Midway in, Cutter stops.

I don't feel discomfort, but I do feel very full.

I hear the sounds of heavy breaths in the room.

They belong to me.

He steps back and stares at me. No doubt to admire his handiwork. My arms tied above my head in ropes. My legs splayed open with a purple vibrator halfway inside of me. My cheeks flushed. Nipples hard. Pupils dilated. Waiting for me to give him the words.

"Finish it," I finally say.

He walks back between my legs and leans over with his mouth by my ear.

"I told you all I want to hear are screams."

Then he turns the knob on the vibrator all the way up.

My core contracts violently and immediately I explode.

The howl of my orgasm is so boisterous that he silences it by shoving his tongue down my throat. I arch my back and yank at the ropes, but they don't budge. The feeling of being constricted of movement and flooded with release is euphoric. I see flashes of light behind the lids of my eyes as I float in orgasmic bliss.

When Cutter turns the vibrator completely off my heart is still racing.

"You are so fucking beautiful when you come. I need to taste you."

He gently slides the vibrator out, drops to his knees, slides my ass forward and begins to devour my pussy. Hungrily he strokes the inside of me with his tongue. Lapping up every bit of my release. And the hunger in me begins to coil once again. This time it winds slower than the last time. Making me feel all the more desperate to reach climax.

I want to grab his head or slap him in the face, but I forget that I can't. How clever of him. My arms are tied.

"Please," I beg.

Crying out breathlessly as one lone tear starts to fall

from my eye. I've never been a crier, but now I'm seriously starting to consider that it's because I've never been fucked properly before.

Because this is certainly a feeling that makes me want to wail.

TWENTY-THREE

CUTTER

I'm starting to understand why some of the women in the club have nicknamed me The Viking or even why Sloan calls me a caveman. I fucking feel like one.

Primitive.

Primal.

Possessive.

Her plea for release turns a switch on inside of me that I didn't know was there. I want to drive my dick so deep inside of her that I will not be able to figure out where I begin and where she ends.

If this is how Camden feels about Jade, now I'm starting to truly understand the change in him. There's no denying that this is some different shit. There's no better sound on earth than the cry Sloan just made when she came for me. That shit is addictive. I can only imagine what it will be like once I get inside of her.

I pull the purple pussy eater (my nickname for this particular vibe) out of her, toss it aside, and lean in. It's time to clean her up and I snarl like a dog when she tries to close her legs together. I bite the inside of her knee to let her know that I'm not playing.

"Spread 'em," are the only words I need to say to remind her who's in charge.

It's only natural that she tries to fight this. She's on full display for me. In my kitchen. Tits up high. Legs spread wide. Skin flushed with a mixture of satiety and need. This is hard for her. Relinquishing control. Trusting me to give her what she needs. That's why I'm taking this particular fix very seriously.

I look in between her legs for a moment before I taste. Admiring the view. She is beautiful like I knew she'd be. I kiss the top of her mound. Then inhale. I smell a faint mixture of jasmine and musk. When I remember that her arms have been hanging for a while, I realize that I'm not going to be able to take my time with her like I want. I'm going to have to speed things up before she loses all feeling in her fingertips.

I slide my hands under her ass and dive in. Hungrily eating out her pussy like it's the first time and the last. She tastes sweet and salty like caramel corn. I could stay in between her creamy legs forever, but her body is swaying with need and I know that I'm going have to give her what she wants fairly soon. She's tugging against the ropes. Arching her back to try and give me even more access. Another orgasm is building inside of her and it's building fast.

She's holding her breath.

She's about to blow.

"Come for me, baby."

And this time she doesn't scream. This time it's her body that's violent. Her body seems to bow as her body contracts in orgasm. Her ass lifts up high as she simultaneously squeezes my head together with her thighs. Pulling on the ropes hard. Eyes shut tightly. It's the most beautiful sight I've ever seen and it's scaring the shit out of me, because I know without a doubt that if I can, if she lets me, I want to make her feel like this every single night.

I start to massage her thighs and press light kisses along her hips and stomach to bring her down. I start to work my way up her body and make sure to spend extra time at her breasts. She seems to like that a lot. As her breathing continues to slow down, I start kissing and massaging her arms, and then untying them from the rack.

"Wrap them around me."

I pick her up off the counter. Her arms around my neck. Her legs around my waist and I take her to the bedroom. I sit her gently down on my new cherry wood, four-poster bed, the only new thing I've ordered since moving here.

"Sit and watch," I tell her.

I take off my pants, and then my boxers, and watch her eyes grow with desire as my dick juts to life. I stand in my full glory while she stares back at me.

"What do you want?" I ask her while I stroke myself as she watches.

"I want you," she says.

"Where do you want me."

"Inside of me," she answers softly as I stroke harder.

"How do you want me," I demand to know.

Her eyes lower, so I lift her chin up with my hands.

"How do you want me," I repeat.

"From the back."

Interesting choice.

I move to the bed, pick her up, and flip her over.

I surprise her by starting to eat her again from behind. It wasn't the plan, but I couldn't help myself. She tastes so damn good. I stop myself in between laps to smack her ass for good measure which makes her sopping wet. This is exactly what I need so that I don't hurt her as she gets adjusted to my size. When I think she's ready, I roll on a condom and get on my knees behind her and push in the tip.

Fuck me, it feels good already.

I try to restrain myself, because this isn't about my horny ass. This is all about Sloan and her pleasure. Plus I don't want to fuck around and scare her off. Now that I've gotten inside of her pussy once, I'll be damned if I'm not coming back for seconds. I push in a little farther and watch her body for a reaction. She's not moving much, so I must be a little snug for her.

"Is my dick too big for this pussy?"

Immediately I feel more slip inside of her.

It's obvious that she likes it when I talk dirty.

"Do you want this dick inside of you?"

"Yes."

"Then act like it."

She starts to work her hips more. Moving them back as I slide in forward. My stroke getting deeper and faster. I think I made a mistake getting her going, because I'm literally going to come in two seconds if I don't slow down.

I decide to sit up and lean back on my heels. Bringing Sloan in sort of a sitting reverse cowgirl position. It gives her more control as to how fast she will work me inside of her. It feels phenomenal. She continues working her pussy down farther until I'm almost totally inside of her. My eyes are practically rolling up inside of my head. I could die now and be totally fine with it. It's ecstasy.

She's soaking wet now and she starts bouncing her ass up and down on me. Really getting into it. I hold onto her tits from behind and play with them as she continues to bounce and rock on top of me. Working herself into a frenzy.

I burrow my head into her shoulder. Squeezing my eyes tightly shut. She's fucking the shit out of me, and I'm about to blow.

"Sloan!" I growl.

"Can you handle this pussy like a man?" she throws back my words at me. Turning me completely on. "Do you like fucking me?"

"Dammit, yes!" I yell as she simultaneously yells a few expletives of her own as I drive myself as far inside of her as I can and we climax together.

Sloan falls back against me. Shuddering. I'm kissing her neck, her shoulders and her back reverently. I am completely in awe of this woman. I've had plenty of good sex before, but this was something else. She turns around and there's a huge smile on her face. A smile that I proudly put there. The same smile I'd like to see tomorrow night and the next and the next.

"I thought you didn't put out on the first date," I say in jest. Kissing her nose.

She rolls her eyes and smiles. "That was fantastic, your majesty."

"I know," I say in earnest as I toss the used condom in the trashcan with one shot. "I knew it would be. I was born to command your every orgasm."

She pushes me down on the bed. Kissing my chest. Then farther down my body. Tracing my abdominal muscles with her tongue until she gets to my promised land. I thought she may be exhausted by our session, but it looks like we're just getting started. Aren't I the lucky one.

"Let's play another game," she says as she starts to suck

the life out of my cock. "If I can't make you come in under three minutes with just my mouth, then you get to ask me another question."

Fuck me.

"I think I like this game."

~

TWENTY-FOUR

SLOAN

Elizabeth is in my bedroom stretching her back, while I sit at my French inspired vanity desk, humming to a Bruno Mars tune.

"Look over my sketches while you stretch, Bitsy. You have to learn how to multitask now that you're going to be a mother. Let me know if there's anything you want to add to the design."

"You're humming," she says with laughter in her voice.

"So what?"

"You never hum."

"I like this song," I say defensively. Already aware of what she's implying. "A lot."

I continue to carefully apply my overpriced serum and cream to my face making sure not to miss any part of my face or neck. The scrapes on my face are healing nicely, and I swear it's partly due to the fact that my skin is absorbing a coat of silky seaweed magic.

I've been back in my apartment for a couple of days now. My hot water is working fine and my thermostat was replaced. With no excuse to come over and use his shower anymore, tonight I'm meeting Cutter at the tapas lounge per his request aka command for dinner. This is the third night in a row we've met to eat.

These are not dates.

I repeat these are not dates.

These are dick appointments.

We eat a good meal. We laugh a little bit. We exchange war stories. He tells me about how badly his brother and Roman are treating him in the business. I tell him how hard Regan is trying to shit on me at work or how much my little sister drives me crazy. And then we go to his apartment or mine (mostly his) and bang each other's brains out.

It's been incredible.

It's been educational.

It's been addictive.

Tonight I decide to go with an overpriced pair of high-waist, skinny jeans that fit my curves like a glove and make my legs appear even longer because I always like to play up my best asset. On top I wear a one-shouldered, blush colored blouse which cinches at the waist. And to top every-thing off, I accessorize with a pair of open-toed, black stilettos along with a pair of simple silver hoop earrings and a few Alex and Ani bangles on my wrist. My overpriced outfit is simple but classy. Figure flattering but not over the top.

"These sketches look great, Sloan. You did a lot more to them since we met at Java. Honestly, I forgot that you could draw like this. You're a great artist."

"Thanks, prego. You want me to give you a quick massage. You look like you're struggling over there."

"No, finish up what you're doing. You're putting a lot of effort in to your appearance tonight." She smiles. "Must be important."

"I'm just happy that my scars are fading and my eye is only a little pink. I feel human again."

"I don't think that's the only thing making you feel human again."

"It's not what you think."

"If you're meeting Cutter again tonight than it's exactly what I think. You're excited."

"Oh hush."

I've been growing out my pixie haircut and decide to wear my newly blunt cut hair down, sleek, and parted on the side so that some of it covers one of my eyes in a very old Hollywood glamour type way. I apply a neutral rose shadow to my eyes, cheeks, and lips but make sure to offset it with a bold swipe of black eyeliner across my top lids.

"This doesn't match," I say out loud while staring at myself in the full-length mirror on my closet door.

"What doesn't match?"

"My hair and my outfit."

"What are you talking about? You look great as usual."

"I'm going to change."

"I'm telling you, you look fine."

I stare at myself for another moment.

"No, it doesn't match."

I go back into the closet and pull out my favorite dress. It's a wine colored, bodycon dress that pulls me tight in all the right places. The dress has a long slit up the left thigh and shows off my legs in a way that my high-waist jeans never could.

"That's your "fuck 'em girl" dress."

"Mind your business."

"He's going to love it."

"It's not for him, Bitsy."

Lies. Lies. Lies.

Once I'm satisfied with what I see in the mirror, I open

my laptop and login to my work dashboard. I want to take a quick look at my sales figures. Thanks to Clark's order and orders from two other new clients that my team worked hard to woo, my numbers are up, and that puts a smile on my face.

"My numbers are up."

"Excellent. Do you think you'll beat Regan's team?"

"It's possible but unfortunately this month's win may be at the expense of losing my best client. I've called Clark several times since our date to apologize for how our evening ended, but he's been "too busy" to take any of my calls and hasn't returned a one."

"Maybe it's that Paige woman not delivering your messages. If she has a thing for the man, I wouldn't put it past her to try something like that."

"I don't know. She's never done that before. She may be a bitch, but she's professional. Plus I have his personal cell number now. He hasn't returned those calls either. I'm not sure how I'm going to book a sales appointment with a doctor who refuses to talk with me. I think that I have to accept the fact that I may have lost his business because of one bad date."

"That's what you're calling it? A bad date?"

"What would you call it?"

"Cutter practically peed all over the man that night, and I'm sure the hardest part of that for the good doctor to swallow is that you let him."

~

I'M early but the tapas lounge is already packed. I've eaten here several times before but never on a Saturday. The hostess is adding a couple to the waitlist, so I look around to see if Cutter's arrived yet while I wait my turn.

"Do you have a reservation, miss?"

"Well, I'm not sure. I'm meeting one of the owners here. Mr. King."

The hostess's eyes enlarge.

"Which Mr. King?"

"Cutter King."

"Umm, he's not here," she stutters and practically chokes on her own tongue. "Let me check with my manager to see if he's on his way."

"Thanks."

A portly woman who's dressed in all black and has her hair shaved on one side and long on the other approaches me with the waitress lagging behind her.

"Hi, Ms. Pearson. I'm Joan, the manager here. Let me show you to your table. Mr. King will be here shortly."

She knows my name in advance. He gets cool points for that.

"Thank you."

I might be a little paranoid, but I swear that every employee in this place is watching me walk toward my booth. Maybe it's because I'm being escorted to it like I'm the Queen of England.

"Can I get you anything while you wait, Ms. Pearson?"

"I'll take a glass of your house Cabernet."

"Coming right up."

Soon there's a low hum in the room. That's how I know when he's arrived. I've seen this before. Everyone notices Cutter when he enters a room. He's hard to miss and difficult to turn away from.

As usual he looks amazing. His hair is freshly shorn but he's letting his beard grow out, and he's wearing a gray henley that hugs his every curve with a pair of worn in jeans.

When he spots me across the room, his face lights up,

and in turn mine does the same. Before he can make it over to me, Joan stops him and whispers something in his ear. His face frowns for a moment but quickly changes back to a pleasant one the moment he slides in next to me in the booth.

"Princess."

"Landlord."

"I love this dress."

I smile inside thinking back to my conversation with Bitsy earlier. I totally lied to her. I did wear it for him. I'm glad that he likes it.

"Thank you."

"I can't wait to get you out of it."

I blush from the comment. Now that I know that he can back up every dirty thing he's ever said to me, I tend to blush more often.

"You know most people sit across from each other when they sit in a booth for dinner."

He wraps his arm around my shoulder basically caging me in the booth, takes a sip of my wine, then offers me a sip as well. I drink.

"I haven't seen you in twenty-four hours. Won't be inside of you for a few more. I'm sitting next to you. Need to be near you."

God, his voice is deep and rougher than usual. Like sandpaper. As if he's had a rough night of drinking or something.

"Give me my kiss."

He leans over before I can say anything in response and kisses me softly with just a little bit of tongue. It's not as intense as some of our other "private" kisses, but it's tender and it still lights a fire inside of me.

"You smell like jasmine."

"It's my—"

Before I can finish my sentence he discreetly slides his hand inside of the slit of my dress. His mouth turning completely up once he realizes that I'm not wearing any underwear.

"You're going to be the death of me," he says gruffly.

"Am I?" I tease.

He gently rubs my clit as a punishment.

"You want me to make you come in this booth?"

"No," I whisper.

"You sure?" He continues stroking me as I grow slicker.

"Stop it," I say half-heartedly.

"I'm hungry tonight." He grins as he pulls his hand away. "I'm going to order all of my favorites. Anything in particular you want?"

"No," I say trying to calm myself down. "I'm good with whatever."

Cutter raises his arm, waves his pointer finger, and all of a sudden, a server arrives to our table with a menu and another glass of wine. Of course he winks at her. That seems to be his usual greeting to humans of the female persuasion.

"Thank you, darlin'."

"Do you want the usual, Cutter?"

"Actually I'm a little hungrier than normal. I want the chef special."

"Awesome."

"How's your brother doing?"

"Thanks for asking and for everything," she says thankfully. "He's doing a lot better. The doctors finally figured out what was wrong with him. It's an ulcer."

"At his age?"

"I know, right? But stress and stomach ailments run in the family."

"Well then I will, I mean *Camden* will, keep a close eye

on you. Make sure you're not over scheduled. You need your rest."

A look passes over the waitress's face that is a mixture of worry and adoration.

"Everything is fine as is. Please don't go changing anything around for my benefit."

"As long as your happy."

"I am, thank you." She turns to me. "Did you decide on what you want to order, miss?"

"Just double my order, darlin'," he tells her.

"Gotcha."

After Cutter's biggest fan leaves to place our order we continue our conversation.

"I'm curious. Do you even know her name?"

"What makes you think that I don't?"

"You called her darlin' about a hundred different times. Thought maybe you forgot her name."

"Her name is Hazel August. She's been a waitress here for a little over a year. Her brother has been in and out of the hospital over the last six months, and the doctors weren't sure what was wrong with him, because he didn't have health insurance and the hospital would only do a limited series of tests. Once she hit her year anniversary of working here, I made sure to get her a family insurance plan which allowed her to add her brother."

I'm stunned.

"That was really . . . nice of you."

"Nice, maybe. Smart, yes. It's not good business to have a lot of employee turnover, and a decent benefits package is the key to keeping people around these days. Hazel's a good worker."

"Sounds expensive."

"Worth every penny."

There's a lull in our conversation, which I'm learning is

something that tends to happen between us, because Cutter likes to watch me. Honestly, I think he likes to watch all women. He's a very visual person, and he seems to be quite taken with the woman's form. He has the ability to make any woman feel like she's the most beautiful woman in the room. Almost. I know better though.

"You seem really good at what you do. The club. This restaurant. I know you told me you were having a difference of opinion with your brother and Roman, but it seems like you miss it and they miss you."

"I definitely miss it. The club, the restaurant, and even our building are not just investments for me. They are businesses that I care about. If I'm going to be a part of it, I want to see it grow. Flourish."

"Is that why we came here for dinner? So you could check on things."

"You caught me."

"Is that what Joan was talking about with you when you came in?"

"Yeah, the staff seems to be having a few personality clashes with Camden. He's not the easiest guy to work for. He spends most of his time on a computer not with people."

"So you're not going to come back to work?"

"My brother and Roman take for granted that I will run the club and the restaurant when all they're concerned about are the pain in the ass fixes that they keep booking. So no, I'm not coming back."

"Sounds like you don't really like the fixes anymore."

"I'm good at them though."

"You're probably good at a lot of things. That doesn't mean that you're supposed to do them all."

"I don't know if I would feel comfortable with my brother going into a fix without me having his back. My dad died when we were eleven. My mom died when we were in high school. We practically raised each other."

"But isn't that what he did to you? I thought you said he left you hanging with a client."

"Not exactly," he snaps.

I may have hit a really sore spot.

"We can change the subject," I say.

"I didn't say we had to change the subject. I just . . . I don't know. I know he didn't mean to leave me swinging like that. It's just that he was distracted."

"With?"

"His lady."

"Oh, Jade. I've met her."

He looks like he doesn't want to talk about this anymore.

"Hey, what do I know," I say trying to calm the waters. "I don't know what to do about my seventeen-year-old sister."

Hazel brings out several different appetizers for us to nosh on. The chicken skewers, stuffed shrimp, and Kobe cheesesteak egg rolls look particularly amazing.

"Your situation is much more complicated than mine," I continue.

Cutter turns to me and slides an egg roll in my mouth with his fingers.

"Bite."

It's delicious.

"They're good, right?" he asks excitedly. "I hired a new chef a couple of months ago."

"Too good."

"Nothing is ever too good," he says with an intensity which I'm finding makes me hot. "You either love it or you don't. I just happen to *love* it."

Don't let him inside your heart, Sloan. You know better. This isn't real. This is a dick appointment.

"Do you think you'll ever move back into your house?" I

ask trying to change the flow and direction of the conversation.

"No."

"No?"

"It was time for me to go. I just needed a reason to do it. Cam and Jade should have a place for themselves."

"Oh, I thought–"

I stop myself before I say something stupid.

"You thought what?"

"Never mind."

"You thought what?"

"I just . . . I heard that you and your brother share women sometimes."

"Where did you hear that?"

"Just around."

I play around with some of the food on my plate. I had no intentions of ever bringing his reputation up with him because this is not a relationship, but it's been in the back of my mind for a little while. Sitting there. Like a little sleeping bear waiting to be poked.

"Look at me, Sloan." His face serious. "I've done a lot of things in the past with and without my brother that have nothing to do with what we're doing now. The only woman I'm interested in is sitting right at this table."

"Oh, well, I wasn't sure. It's not like we discussed how whatever *this* is, is going to work."

"I think *this* is working just fine, and even though we're not a couple, I hope you understand that at least for me what we're doing is exclusive. I'm not sleeping with anyone else and I hope that you aren't either, or that guy is going to have a lot of trouble eating without his teeth."

I laugh.

"You're nuts."

"There it is," he says.

"There what is?"

"The light in your eyes. It's back. Just like I remembered."

My cell phone rings just as my heart flutters.

Dammit, it's Fern.

"Excuse me for a minute," I say to Cutter. "Hello?"

"Sloan."

"Yes, Fern."

"I'm sending my final list for the training and you're not on it."

I hold my ear down, so I can hear, and try to speak clearly but quietly in the phone. "I meant to come see you the other day."

"But you didn't, and I'm not handing in my stuff late because you're procrastinating."

"So what do you want me to do? It's after work hours."

"Do whatever you want to do, but give me a yes or no. If you want to go, you need to fill out the application and the waiver and email it to me by tonight. If not, just say so."

Cutter is staring down my throat, trying to listen to my conversation, probably because I look so distressed.

He mouths the words, "What's wrong?"

I shake my head and tell him to give me a second.

"It's a yes," I tell Fern. "I'll fill it out and send it to you tonight."

"Before eleven please."

"Absolutely. Thanks, Fern."

I hang up the phone and take a sip of wine.

"Who was that?"

"My supervisor."

"What did she want? You don't look happy about it."

"There's a sales training course that all the managers take. Three-month course. Lots of my Saturdays. A lot of seminars and webinars."

"Why did you agree to it."

"All the managers take it."

"But?"

"But . . . I just don't know if I'm in love with my job anymore."

"I can understand that. Will they offer the training again?"

"It's only once a year."

"So, see how you feel next year about it. Don't commit today because that Fern person put you under a little pressure."

"Maybe."

It's nice to talk about my job pressures with someone that is going through a little job dissatisfaction of his own.

"Can I tell you a funny story?"

"Sure."

"The two of us met a long time ago."

"We did?"

"I was sixteen years old. Camden and I were sneaking into Soldier's Center to watch your father's first playoff game, and you were there."

"Really?"

"We literally bumped into each other when I was being chased by security."

A lightbulb goes off in my head.

I remember that boy.

Wow, it was Cutter.

I grip his forearm. "I remember that."

"Of course you do. How could you forget someone like me? Even as a kid, the king was unforgettable," he jokes.

At least I hope he's joking.

"My dad's friends kind of blocked you from talking to me that day. Not that they needed to. I wasn't going to talk to you anyway. I could tell you were too much for me even then."

"Am I too much when I'm inside of you, princess? When you're riding me on that down feather couch of yours or when I tied you spread eagle to my bed? Was I too much then?"

His eyebrows wiggle.

"Not at all, your majesty," I say like he's being tiresome.

Then I pop an egg roll in my mouth to keep from laughing out loud.

"Let's go home and make sure." He looks across the room to find Hazel. "Check please, darlin'! I've got a point to prove tonight."

<<<<>>>>

SLOAN

I give my body a long stretch as I wake up yet again in Cutter's bed with a deep ache in muscles that I hadn't realized existed. And when the reason for that soreness registers in my still waking brain, I end up with the broadest smile on my face. Something I've been doing more often than not when the two of us are together.

I spent half of my night gorging myself on caramel corn and laughing my head off at some of Cutter's stories. He's had a colorful life for someone so young, and he's definitely met a lot of interesting people in his line of work. In other words, his majesty likes to name drop, and suffice it to say that some of the world's hottest singers and actors are freakin' deviants who probably owe their careers to him.

I also spent the better half of the night with my ankles tied to Cutter's four-poster bed begging for him to stop, then begging for him to never stop. He is a very creative lover that gets some sort of sadistic satisfaction out of watching me come . . . and come . . . and come.

As I open my eyes while recollecting one of those

yummier moments, I wake to find that Cutter is sitting on the bed staring right at me.

"Morning," he says in the deep authoritarian voice I've begun to get used to.

"Morning." He looks like he has a lot on his mind. "You all right?"

"I'm good. You want breakfast?"

"Do I smell bacon?"

"You do."

"Then I want breakfast."

"That's my girl."

He bends down and kisses me tenderly on one of my exposed nipples and then my mouth. It's one of the sweetest kisses he's ever given me, but I feel like something's off with him.

"Go grab a shower, and I'll get your eggs started."

I grab his wrist when he turns to walk away.

"What's wrong, Cutter?"

He sighs for a moment.

"A while ago I discovered that I may have another brother."

"Another King brother walks this earth? I don't think there's room on the planet for another one of you."

His mouth turns up into a small grin. "Probably not."

"So, what's bothering you? That seems like good news."

"I think he's had a hard life. If what I heard is true, I think he's been in jail for a long time."

"Oh."

He notices my reaction.

"I'm not judging him at all. I realize that people make mistakes or get bad breaks in life. Hell, a quarter of the guys I grew up with have done some time. I just feel fucked-up that I have a brother out there who's had a tough go of it."

"And you haven't?" I question. I think Cutter and Camden had a really rough start too.

"Not like him. I've at least always had Cam by my side."

"Have you two worked out your differences yet?"

"We will."

"What's his name? Your other brother."

"Stone."

"What made you think about him today?"

"Not sure."

He rubs the inside of my wrist with his thumb. Then lifts it to his mouth and places a small kiss on it. "This would be the perfect place for your first tattoo."

"Yeah? What should I get?"

Cutter pulls back the covers and slides his hand in between my legs where he finds me already wet and waiting. I've been wet since he said good morning.

"A small crown so you can remember who your king is."

I spread my legs wider.

"Maybe you should remind me right now."

I FEEL like I am in the middle of a Disney movie. Squirrels are scampering by me happily, the birds seem to be chirping louder, and I feel like everyone I'm passing by on the sidewalk is about to break out into song at any moment.

I enjoyed myself so much last night and this morning that I should be totally wiped, but actually I feel better than I have in a long time. That is until I hit the lobby and realize that for the first time in my career, I've forgotten to handle my business. I failed to email my advanced sales training program application to Fern.

Shit.

"Morning, Sloan." Gidget greets me eagerly as soon as I pass through the glass doors.

"Morning, Gidget."

"Can I talk to you for a minute in your office?"

I don't see Fern anywhere in the vicinity, so I might have a few minutes before our inevitable confrontation.

"Sure, sweetie. Come on."

"So, I've never told you how I ended up with the company, but I'm sure you're aware that I didn't get this job the old-fashioned way."

I never asked, but it was pretty obvious by Gidget's age and lack of work experience that she didn't get her job on her own. Pharmaceutical companies typically don't hire brand-new receptionists because there is more involved to the job than just answering phones. They like someone who is more experienced working in a medical environment. Someone familiar with medical terms and the names of drugs. But I never cared—to me Gidget's a natural and a quick learner.

"We all have our connections, Gidget, and we shouldn't be afraid to use them. No judgment here."

That's ironic coming from me.

"Well—Mr. Stokes is actually my mother's half-brother."

"So, he's your uncle?"

"Yep."

"Umm wow, Gidget."

"I know. I know. Uncle John and I made a deal that we wouldn't tell anyone in the office for the obvious reasons, and it really hasn't been that difficult to hide, because it's not like we're super close."

"So then why are you telling me now?"

The reason can't be good.

"Sometimes he has conversations when I'm around as if I'm not in the room, like he always has since I was small. I overheard that one of your clients called the office and asked to be transferred to Regan's team. A big client."

Clark.

"I know exactly who you're talking about."

"Anyway, Uncle John evidently had a conversation with this doctor and didn't like what he heard. Then I saw him and Fern with their heads together this morning. I think something is going down. I just don't know what it is. I could be making way more out of this than it is, but if your job is in jeopardy, I just wanted to give you a heads up. You're the coolest person that works here, and I don't want to see you blindsided."

Regan's already managed to do that.

Twice.

"Thanks, Gidget. I appreciate it. I realize that you didn't have to tell me anything. Mr. Stokes is your family after all."

"You're welcome. We girls have to stick together."

THE FIRST THING I do when Gidget closes the door to my office is call Clark to settle this once and for all. He doesn't take any of my calls and now he asks to be reassigned? What a coward.

"Morning, Paige, its Sloan Pearson."

"Morning."

"I'm calling for Doctor Clark again. Is he available?"

"He's with a patient."

"When does his schedule free up?"

"It doesn't. Today he's booked."

"Listen, Paige, I know how you feel about me. You've made that quite clear, but Dr. Clark and I need to settle some business. So, I need you to find a time slot in his schedule for me to talk to him. Please."

"I give him all of your messages."

"So then, what do you suggest?" I ask with frustration.

"I don't know what you did to make him so upset with you, but you should probably start with apologizing."

Before I can respond to that, Clark interrupts and asks Paige who she's talking to. When she tells him it's me, he grabs the phone.

"Morning, Miss Pearson. How can I help you?"

So we're back to formalities.

"Morning, Dr. Clark. I've been trying to get a hold of you for a while. Glad to finally get you on the line. How are things?"

"I've been tied up with work. What can I do for you?"

Clark is being extremely rigid and cold with me. I've never seen this side of him, and I don't think I deserve it.

"We've been friends for a long time now, Clark, and I think—"

"Let me stop you there. We were never friends, Ms. Pearson. I think you know that. Do you think someone like me needed to order from a brand-new sales rep like you?"

"What the hell does that mean?"

"Transfer the call to my office, Paige." After a moment, he picks up the line in his office. "It means that I was putting the work in. I was taking it slow. Building trust. Treating you like a lady. But it became pretty obvious to me that night, that you don't respond to that sort of approach."

"Clark—"

"I felt like I was an intruder on my own date the way you were looking at him!"

"So this is why you moved your business to Regan without even consulting me?!"

"Yes."

"I didn't realize our work relationship was contingent upon or rather a precursor to us having a romantic relationship. Must you date everyone you do business with, *Harvey Weinstein?* Are you going to make Regan date you too?"

Silence

"Wait . . . are you dating her already?"

"I don't appreciate that Weinstein crack, Sloan. I'm not a predator. It's just that Regan and I discovered that we have a lot more in common than I originally thought. It's not so *difficult* with her."

Jackass.

"So you discovered all of this about each other in a matter of days."

"I didn't pursue her earlier, because I thought you and I might work out, but now–"

"All righty then." I clap once to myself. "Thank you for this."

"For what?"

"You've taught me a huge lesson. There are way more dangerous men out there than the ones I've known. It's the ones you don't see coming that are the worst, and I definitely didn't see your assholery coming, Dr. Clark."

"Look–"

"You have a nice life."

~

MY DISNEY KIND of day was quickly disintegrating into a horribly written suspense thriller. Gidget was right about Fern and Mr. Stokes putting their heads together about something in regard to me, but it had nothing to do with Clark and where his allegiances lie.

It was something altogether worse.

I'm invited to the company conference room via messenger and around the table are Mr. Stokes, Fern, one of the human resources managers, and the spawn of the devil himself–Damien.

"Have a seat, Sloan."

The human resources manager takes the lead.

"So we've called this meeting to address some charges made by Mr. Damien Hardwick."

What the hell?

"You work here?" I ask incredulously.

"You can speak directly with me, Miss Pearson. My name is Mrs. Rickard, and I specialize in mediating corporate conflict and resolutions. I'm here to address the charges that Mr. Hardwick has made against you."

My stomach drops.

Blindsided again.

"I'm not sure what's going on here, but whatever this is doesn't seem like normal procedure. I should have received formal notification from my supervisor." I glare at Fern. "As well as by HR that there were any kind of accusations being made against me before you called this meeting."

"This is not a formal meeting, Miss Pearson," the Rickard lady says in a very calming voice. "This is all very informal. We're hoping to simply mediate and negotiate a positive outcome for both parties. That's all we want, so we can all go about the business of doing our jobs."

"I'm sorry, but what does Mr. Hardwick do for the company?"

"I work in the mailroom as you well know, Miss Pearson," the kid interjects, and I swear I didn't know he knew how to speak the King's English a few weeks ago. Or dress in normal clothes. He's wearing a crisp, white oxford shirt with a pair of clean khakis and cheap dress shoes. Looking as American as apple pie.

"Speak only to me, Mr. Hardwick," the mediator responds. "So we're here, because Mr. Hardwick said that you may have misconstrued something that he said to you as a romantic overture and then told someone close to you about it. A man who ended up assaulting him."

"This is absolutely surreal."

"We understand that in today's climate, many things a man may say to a woman could be misinterpreted, but we want you to understand that we take this type of thing seriously here. We want you both to feel that your workplace is a safe space. Just like this room right now is a safe space to tell us everything that happened."

"I don't need a safe space. His story is a complete lie."

"I'd rather not say that anyone's lying, Miss Pearson. The way I like to reframe things is that people often see the same set of facts through a different lens."

"The lens of a liar. This boy is my kid sister's boyfriend. He's lying to get back at me for an incident that happened between the three of us. An incident he caused."

"Is that true, Mr. Hardwick? Are you dating Miss Pearson's sister?"

"I've never met Miss Pearson's sister."

Oh. My. God.

He actually said that with a straight face.

"Listen to me." I stand up angrily. "This kid is a pathological liar. He is dating my sister. He physically assaulted me. And I think he's been crank calling me for weeks."

"When did he assault you?" Mr. Stokes chimes in.

"The black eye and bandages on my face that I've been sporting for weeks. He did that!" I point to him.

"Please calm down, Miss Pearson," the mediator requests.

"Why didn't you report it with HR?" Fern interjects.

"He didn't work here when it happened. At least I don't think he did," I say.

Damien dramatically stands and lifts his shirt showing

the black and blue marks of what I believe are his ribs healing.

"The only one who's been assaulted in this room is me, and I don't feel safe in this environment anymore," he says putting on the act of a lifetime. "I was attacked by Miss Pearson's boyfriend for something that I didn't do."

Everyone's eyes turn to me.

"I'm afraid we have footage to back up what Mr. Hardwick is saying, Miss Pearson. The man who visited you a while back, a Mr. Cutter King, is seen on tape threatening and physically assaulting Mr. Hardwick in the mailroom area. Punching him in the very area that is bruised. Grabbing his throat."

"Is there audio of that footage?"

If Cutter did approach Damien here, he would have definitely said something about Dawn in his threat. I can't believe that he hasn't mentioned a word of this, and I've been sleeping in his bed for days.

"I'm afraid it's only video footage like most CCTV's."

"I'm sorry if you thought I was making some sort of pass at you, Miss Pearson. That was not my intention. I tried explaining that to your boyfriend, but he tried to choke me, and then he promised that he'd return to finish the job if I didn't leave you alone. I just got this job, and I really like it so far, but now I'm afraid to come to work. Could you talk to him?"

Holy shit and the Golden Globe for best actor goes to . .
.

I throw up my hands.

"Do I need to get a lawyer?"

Fern and Mr. Stokes give each other some sort of look.

"Thank you for meeting with us, Mr. Hardwick," the mediator says. "Your supervisor and the HR department will get back to you about this matter. In the meantime, please report to work at eight tomorrow."

"As long as this situation is handled I have no problem coming to work."

Unbelievable.

"Don't forget about that statutory charge, you prick," I say as he walks out. "You fucked with the wrong girl."

While Damien doesn't verbally respond I watch as he balls a tight fist on his way out the door. Once the door is shut, Mr. Stokes speaks to me.

"We're not idiots, Sloan. We know something doesn't smell quite right with this guy's story, but he does have footage of your guest threatening and assaulting him on the property. He could sue us."

"That's why I asked if I needed to get a lawyer," I say.

"Here's the thing," he continues. "You didn't sign up for the managerial training course, your numbers are lower than any other team in the company, and you just lost your best client to Regan Pullson. We're starting to wonder if this is where you really want to be."

They're trying to push me out. I don't even like this stinking job anymore and they want to push me out.

"I'll let you know who my lawyer is in a day or so."

Then I stand up to put on my coat.

"Wait, Sloan," Fern speaks. "Is this really how you want to handle this? You'll never get another pharmaceutical gig if you're at the center of a lawsuit. The pool of associates is small. Managers even smaller. Trust me, you'll want to handle this quietly."

"You mean you want me to resign."

"The boy has evidence on you."

"Not on me. Someone else."

"The man threatened him in your name. A lawyer will

use that in court. A lawyer can say that you asked him to do it or hired him to do it."

"I thought there wasn't any audio. How would you know he did it in my name?"

"Hardwick thinks you sent this man downstairs to hurt him."

"I didn't even know he worked here!"

"But you do know him?"

"How many times do I have to tell you? Yes! I told you he's my sister's boyfriend."

"And that's probably all true, Miss Pearson," the mediator jumps back in. "But it almost doesn't even matter. You two have a connection. You and the man in question have a connection. An assault did occur on tape. The common denominator is you.

"This coupled with the fact that your performance here is at best lackluster, we thought it'd be in your best interest to offer you a nice package and a stellar reference so that you can move on."

The soft and sweet "let's work this out" mediator has all of a sudden disappeared. Now she's playing hardball.

"Are you a lawyer, Mrs. Rickard?"

"I am a mediator."

"With a law degree?"

"Yes, if you want to be technical about it. I am a lawyer."

"Then the next time we all speak, I'll be back with mine."

~

TWENTY-SIX

SLOAN

My parents are an American success story. My father comes from humble beginnings in rural Virginia, and became a popular championship point guard for the basketball team at a university in Kentucky. He met my mother there while they were both students. She was a beautiful, tall, thin golden goddess on campus. Long legs, long wavy blond hair, ice blue eyes and very popular across campus. She had dreams of becoming a professional model and definitely had the looks to actually make it happen, but her relationship with my father got in the way of that.

My father is also a beautiful man, and looking back at old photographs of him, I realize just how handsome he was in his prime. He was a tall, muscular man, with closely shorn black hair, beautiful chestnut colored skin, and a killer smile. My mom fell hard for him in college, then followed him to the city of his first professional basketball team, married him, and then quickly became pregnant with me.

While she didn't become the catwalk superstar she dreamt of, she ended up carving out a respectable career for herself as an agent. She ran the "parts" division (hand models, foot models, hair models) of one of the largest modeling agencies on the East Coast for many years, but has now settled into a life of service. Raising money for a variety of worthy charities important to residents and many politicians of Philadelphia. Much like Elizabeth's Aunt Juliette does for autism.

While my parents have a lot of faults, I've always been grateful for how hard they both worked and the life of privilege that it afforded me. Yet unlike many of my contemporaries, I've always been adamant about forging my own path. I never wanted to be like some of the girls I grew up with.

Some of them ended up fulfilling the path of our social circle by marrying well, popping out a couple of kids, and continuing the circle again. Some are strung out on pills. Some are sleeping around with half of Hollywood. Some are drunk at the ripe old age of twenty-six. Many ended up trying to salvage whatever fame they were desperately trying to hold onto by starring in low budget, low class, reality shows.

But I was so supposed to be different. Special. Better.
Yet am I?

I ended up in pharmaceutical sales, because a professor I almost slept with at Penn advised me to try it. He said I *looked the part,* and that I'd probably have a very good run at convincing middle-aged doctors, like Clark, to purchase drugs from me.

I was appalled and disgusted by the professor's comments at first, but I knew that in his own twisted way he actually meant well. I was barely holding my head above water in his class, but he knew that what I lacked in actual comprehension of the subject matter, I made up for in determination to pass the class. Come hell or come high water I was going to succeed in this world. On my own. And have a good-ass damn time while doing it.

Yet here I am.

Swimming in a murky reality of my own.

And I'm not having a good time at all.

My best client, the one I was so proud of, never respected me. He just wanted me on his arm and in his bed. The job that I thought I'd earned, the one that defined me, turned out to be something I fell into and then something I forced. It wasn't really ever a natural fit, and now I'm being squeezed out. The boy that I thought was too dumb for my sister turned out to be a freakin' criminal mastermind that I totally underestimated. He's been one step ahead of me at every turn planning my demise.

I thought I was right about all of these things, but I was mistaken. Pitifully mistaken. And so, the one thing I thought that I may have originally gotten wrong, the man who happens to be the common denominator in all of this, ended up being the one thing I had always been right about.

He has been my biggest mistake of them all.

I'VE BECOME A SQUATTER and a recluse.

I haven't gone to work.

I haven't checked my cell phone.

I haven't showered.

I haven't moved.

It's been three days, and I've been staying at my parent's home on the mainline, because I've been too much of a chickenshit to go back to my apartment. It wouldn't be good for me to go back home.

If I see Cutter, I'll run to him.

I'll tell him about how horribly Clark treated me. I'll tell him all about the web of lies that demon Damien has caused. I'll tell him about the plot to get rid of me at work. I'll tell him all of this, because I'll know he'll try to fix it. He'll try to avenge me. He'll try to protect me. And then he'll try to fuck me senseless, and I'll let him.

I'll let him because I miss him like crazy. I'll let him because I crave him like crack. I crave him, because he's the only man to make my body and my heart come alive simultaneously.

And then I'll curse him out.

Because at the end of the day, Cutter is the cause of all of this.

No client. No job. No sister. No home.

I should have known better.

The only way this thing was ever going to end was badly.

MY MOTHER DOESN'T BELIEVE in stewing in your own juices for too long, so by day three she's had enough of my wallowing.

"That's it, Sloan. If you don't take a shower that sweatshirt of yours is going to walk on its own back to Penn."

"I'm exhausted, Mom."

"From what? If you want your job back you're going to have to fight for it."

I haven't told her everything. In fact, I've probably lied about mostly everything including why my face looks like this. If I told her the truth about Damien, she'd go straight to Marsha, and it wouldn't be for the right reasons.

My mother looks for any reason to throw Marsha's bad parenting into her face, because out of all of my father's women, she hates Marsha the most. Dawn's mom is the only one that had a baby. Daily "in your face" proof of my father's infidelity. All the other women failed their paternity tests, so my mother can pretend that they were simply lying "gold diggers" looking for an easy payday. She can't do that with Marsha.

"That's just it. I don't know if I want it back."

"What would you do?"

"I don't know."

"What are your hobbies?"

"I don't really have any."

"Is there a social issue you're passionate about?"

"Not really."

She walks around my room as I look for something in my old dresser drawers that I could possibly wear. She happens to stumble upon an old sketch book of mine from high school and starts flipping through the pages. I used to carry that thing with me every day.

"Mom, you should really switch this furniture out. It looks exactly like ten years ago."

"I don't come in here that much, so it doesn't bother me. It's still your room."

She stops on one particular page of the book. A sketch I made of our attic before it was renovated. I used to love playing up there as a kid with my dolls.

"Well you should update it, so it aesthetically goes with the rest of the house."

I hit the jackpot and find an old Daughtry hoodie and a pair of jeans that still fit in one of the drawers.

"Remember when I loved *American Idol*, Mom?"

"Maybe that's it, Sloan," she says ignoring my question.

"What?"

"You can decorate homes for a living? Maybe even commercial spaces. Didn't you tell me that you were helping out with Elizabeth's nursery?"

"Yeah, but I'd never charge her for that. I'm the godmother."

"I know, but you could absolutely charge other people."

"I don't know, Mom." I'm unconvinced.

"You have a certain sense of style. A certain eye for pieces. People will pay for that. It took my friend Margie three years to decide on curtains for her living room. Three years! She would have gladly paid for you to have made the decision for her."

"Well, I guess that's an idea. That just seems like a very hard career to get off of the ground."

"I can think of seven people off of the top of my head who I could refer you to. Do a good job and word of mouth will spread. In the meantime, I don't mind giving you a little allowance to cover your bills for a while."

We all have our connections and we shouldn't be afraid to use them.

I remember the words I said to Gidget.

"I'll think about it, Mom."

"Good. Now that I've solved all of your problems, you can get dressed, so we can grab something to eat. I need a salad in my life."

I laugh.

The first laugh I've had in three days.

"Okay, give me thirty minutes."

My mother looks impeccably put together as usual. Her freshly dyed blond waves are perfectly coiffed, and she's wearing a pair of fashionable jeans, blouse, and pumps on her slender frame that most women her age couldn't possibly pull off.

"I thought we were getting a salad?"

"We are."

"I'm in a hoodie and you're in . . . that."

"My plan was to stop at Saks Fifth Avenue and grab you

something else to wear. Wouldn't that make you feel better? Shopping always cheered you up when you were a horrible teenager, I mean a little girl."

I roll my eyes. I forgot to mention that my mother thinks she's a comedian.

"Forget it. I'll go in this."

"You sure? I'm buying."

"It's only been three days that I haven't been to work not three years. I have my own money, Mom. If I wanted to buy an outfit I would."

"Okay, okay. You're so touchy."

We arrive at Sambuca's. One of my mom's favorite Northern Italian restaurants. A small, laid back place with friendly staff where they serve really fresh salads and seafood. Back when my parents pretended that they were actually still a couple, we used to rent out the entire restaurant and come for her birthday every year. Now my parents live very separate lives.

"Where's Dad?"

"I think he's still in Boston?"

"What's he doing there?"

"He said it was a recruiting trip, but you know how that is. He probably has some pretty young thing up there."

Since retiring from the NBA, my father has worked in various coaching positions for one of the local universities.

"Can I ask you something?"

"Sure."

"Were you ever happy with Daddy?"

"Definitely."

"Was it ever hard being married to someone like him? The life you had? All those scandals. The violence. The hanger ons?"

"Why would you ask about that?"

"I just know someone a lot like him."

"A ball player?"

"No."

"Hmm, well my life with your father was a whirlwind. He was my first love, and it was exciting and even magical at times. I'm sorry if our life was hard on you, but we both did the best we could. Like all men, your father has his weaknesses. He's terribly insecure, so he uses women to validate himself. I thought he'd grow out of it, but he never did.

"He also feels guilty about his success. Most of the guys he grew up with are out of work, in jail, or are barely scraping by. So that's why he would hire all those guys that were security. They needed the work, and he needed them. They meant well, but they didn't really know what they were doing. So they made a couple of mistakes that resulted in a lot of people paying a high price including your father. This life isn't easy."

"So why are you and Dad still together?"

"It's complicated, Sloan. People aren't perfect. Love is hard. Nobody ever tells you that."

TWENTY-SEVEN

CUTTER

It's day three and I've had just about all I can take. The only reason why I haven't ripped this entire city fucking apart, is because Elizabeth sent me a text letting me know that Sloan is alive and breathing.

I use my key and enter the carriage house hoping I'll find Camden. He's never where he's supposed to be, but hopefully he's home with his head buried in a computer this time. I need his help.

"Cam!"

"Back here."

"Where's Jade?"

"Welcome home, dickwad. She's at the restaurant. What the hell is wrong with you?"

"I need an address for Dan Pearson."

"Sloan's father?"

"Yeah. It's not listed."

"Well, yeah. He probably pays a lot of money to hide that information from the average crazy Joe." He gives me the side-eye.

"I need to find her."

"Is she in trouble?"

"I don't know. She hasn't been home in days. This isn't like her."

"This isn't *like* her? Now you're an expert on the glamazon?"

"We've been spending some time together. A lot of time. So no, this isn't like her."

"Did you talk to Elizabeth about it?"

"Yes, she heard from her, but she claims she doesn't know where she is. A boldface lie, and I can't even grill her about it, because she's all pregnant and that wouldn't be polite."

Camden chuckles and continues scrolling through a web page.

"So the glamazon's fine then."

"Until I put my eyeballs on her myself she's not fine."

"This is messy, Cut." He looks back up at me. "You're getting real messy. This is her parent's home you're trying to just stroll up to, and you seem real emotional now. Maybe you should wait until you calm down. Both you and I know all about your itchy trigger finger."

I squint my eyes at him. I know Camden like I know myself. He knows more than he's saying. He's being way too argumentative.

"What do you know? Any other time you would have given me the ride over there yourself. Why are you trying to stop me from handling this?"

"I'm just saying, Cut."

"You're saying what?"

"Roman is pissed at you."

"I don't give a shit about Roman right now!"

"He told you to leave the kid to him for exactly this reason. He could tell without any confirmation from me that you were catching feelings for Sloan eons ago and now look. You've made a mess."

That's what's going on.

"Did that Damien fucker touch Sloan?"

"Nothing like that. I would have told you that."

"The sister?"

"No."

"Then what?!"

Camden sighs.

"Sloan's job has you on tape. Yanking the boy's throat. Tapping his ribs a little with your fists. They're blaming the glamazon for it all. They don't want to prosecute because they don't want the press. They just want her to leave quickly and quietly. Hoping that she'll take her "drama" aka *you* with her. The kid set her up lovely. Made it look like she asked you to do that shit to him."

I scrub my face a couple times out of frustration. This is a clusterfuck. I should have never gone there. I should have gotten the security footage. I shouldn't have kept her in the dark about it either. She wasn't prepared. She must be furious. There's so much shit I should have done differently. No wonder she hates me.

"I'm going to kill him."

"One of the best handlers in the game can't convince a twenty-one-year-old loser to fall back? You could only be this sloppy because of a woman. You see what I'm talking about, little brother? It happens to the best of us. Love can cause you to make mistakes, but it's also a hell of a motivator to get you to fix them. Banging on her door and demanding that she talk to you won't work. Do what you do best and fix this shit. Make this right. That will bring your girl home, Cut. That's *if* she's your girl."

~

"I'D HOPED to never see you again, Cutter King."

I look around the office at all of Newman's achievements. Graduate of Penn State. Graduate of Temple Law. City of Philadelphia Man Of The Year. District Attorney Of Philadelphia Plaque. Pictures of his kids on his desk. A girl and a boy. He could have lost it all if it weren't for me. All of this is worth way more than the money he paid. Even more than the information that he gave us about Stone. If you think about it, a man would pay almost any price to protect everything he holds dear. Everything he loves.

"How have you been faring, Newman?"

"I've been good. Got myself busy with work. Going to Paris next year with the family. I'm getting my shit together, King."

"Glad to hear it."

"I'm not sure what you said to my brother-in-law to keep him quiet about being shoved into the trunk of a car, but he hasn't said a word."

I don't know what Roman did to fix that situation, but I suppose everyone has their price or their secrets. I'm hoping that's the case. That's why I'm here.

"So, what brings you to my office?"

"I need your help."

"My help?" he asks as if he has no intentions of going down that road with me.

"Remember I told you that you owed me one for putting your ass up those couple of nights. Wifey thought you were away. That was extra."

He bows his head.

"Yes, now I remember. Tell me what you need."

∼

TWENTY-EIGHT

From: Dawn Pearson
To: Sloan Pearson
Re: Where are you?

Dear Sloan,
    I'm writing this in case you are checking your emails, because clearly you aren't picking up your cell phone or your landline. I thought about having my mom call you. Thought you may be avoiding my calls, but it's okay if you are. It might be better that I'm writing this anyway.

I've been really angry and really sad for a long time, and you've been one of the only people in my life who put up with me. So thank you. You were right about, Damien. He wasn't very nice to me. He had all these thoughts about what a good girlfriend was, and when I didn't live up to them, he said mean things. Nasty things. Things that made me really sad. Things that made me not want to do anything but go to school and sleep.

It doesn't matter now. He's decided that I'm too immature for him and has started seeing another girl that he met at a bar I think. So it's over, and I just wanted to tell you that we were done, and that I'm sorry he hit you, and that I'm **really, really** sorry that I didn't say so.

Your sister,
Dawn

P.S. THAT CRIMINAL (LOL!) is looking for you. You better go home. He's actually a nice guy once you talk to him.

TWENTY-NINE

SLOAN

After reading her email, I end up talking with my sister for close to forty minutes on the phone about all types of things. The prom. Her grades. Marsha. Our dad. Us. It was cathartic and frankly the best conversation we've ever had. If I was a crier, I would have shed a tear or two. Dawn and I will never be the same. I feel it in my bones that we're going to have a closer relationship now, and I know that's primarily due to the P.S. mentioned in the letter.

Him.

I've never spent as much time as I have today thinking about what to wear. In the past, I've always considered what I was in the mood to wear. What cuts look best on me. What pants would make my ass not look so big. What color would complement my coloring. But today all I care about is who I'm dressing for.

Him.

I decided to take my mother up on her offer of a shopping spree and look for the perfect dress. It takes me an hour and four stores to find it. Upon first sight, it doesn't look like much. A simple strapless dress. Short. Purple. But on me it looks like a garment made with my exact measurements and motive in mind. Fits like a glove.

When I arrive to Lotus, the air is heavy with sweat and seduction, but I know that he isn't here yet. I can just feel that there's something missing, because whenever Cutter is around he takes up the entire space.

I notice Marco tending the main bar as usual and ask him for a glass of shiraz. Not just because I want a drink, but because this is the best seat in the house. There's no way Cutter can miss me when he comes in. No matter what entrance.

How do I know he's coming? Cutter has spies everywhere. Someone in this club is going to tell him that I'm here, and if I know him like I think I do, he'll come looking for me immediately.

"You look especially gorgeous tonight, Sloan," Marco says.

"Thank you." I smile.

Marco and I continue making small talk about his new car, club gossip, and how Elizabeth is feeling now that she's in the second trimester of her pregnancy. We're deep in our conversation when a man approaches me who I've never seen before. He's a bit overdressed for the temperature of the club, it gets really hot in here, but that's probably because it's his first time and he doesn't know any better.

He slides an American Express card across the counter to start a tab and asks Marco for a whiskey neat. While he waits for his drink to be prepared, he strikes up a conversation with me.

"Is it always like this in here?"

"Pretty much. Is this your first time?"

"How did you know?"

"You have on way too many clothes. It gets really hot in here."

"You'd think they'd have a better air system," he says. "That's my line of work by the way. That's the only reason why I have an opinion."

"Oh, gotcha."

"Just out of curiosity are you seeing anyone?"

I smile as I consider the question. "I am."

And that's when I feel it. The buzz in the air that alerts me to his presence. The king is definitely in the building. *That didn't take long.* I turn my head immediately in his direction while the man I'm next to is still talking about something. I'm not sure what. It doesn't matter, because my entire reason for being here just walked through the door.

I can see the top of his head as he moves with large confident strides through the crowd and across the room. I'm a little disappointed that he's not looking at me, but surveying the entire crowd instead as he moves. I wonder if he sees me. I wonder if he's even looking for me.

My question is quickly answered when all of a sudden, his eyes find mine. He stops directly in from of me and holds me in place with his eyes. He doesn't say one word, but just all of a sudden bends down and slides one of his hands in my hair, behind my ear, and plants a kiss on my lips that makes me weak with need.

It's a powerful kiss. A kiss that is trying to communicate a million things. Telling me in more ways than one that Cutter missed me. That he wants me. That he's mad at me. That he's relieved to see me. I can feel every single thing he's trying to say. I don't need the words. I hope my kiss is saying them too.

Fireworks and fireflies.

When he pulls back from me, I notice that the man I was talking to hasn't left my side and is in fact watching us.

"Thanks for keeping my girl company, Midland. I appreciate it. Your next round is on me."

"No problem, Cut. She was easy to find like you said she'd be. The most beautiful woman in the room."

"You know him?" I say.

"I know a lot of people."

"You had him keep an eye on me?"

"I had him keep you company until I got here. That's all."

"I think he was testing me. He asked me if I was available."

Cutters rakes his eyes up and down my entire body, as if he's doing an inventory check. Making sure all the parts are present and working.

"And what did you say?"

"What do you think I said?"

"The right answer would have been hell no."

"I wouldn't speak that rudely to a stranger like some people I know."

He grabs one of my hands and lifts my wrist to his mouth.

"Don't ever do that shit again, princess. I worried like crazy about you. This was some mean shit you did to me. If Cam hadn't talked me off the ledge, your mother and I would not have had a good first meeting."

"What were you planning?" I giggle just imagining what he had in mind.

"I was going to camp out on your front lawn, and if that didn't work I would have used a pocket knife to pick the lock."

"Yes, that would not have gone over well. How did you know I was even there?"

"Now what kind of fixer would I be if I didn't know how to find people? Plus, I went to every place I thought you could be. That was the only place left."

"Did you go to my job?" Worried that he may have put himself in harm's way.

"I did."

"You shouldn't have done that. I should have called you earlier to tell you, but Damien–"

"Maybe we should go home and talk about this."

"No, I want to talk about it now. I need to tell you why I've been tripping out for the last few days. A lot of crap happened in the last seventy-two hours, and I mistakingly blamed most of it on you."

"I already know about everything that happened. Damien set us up. Your job asked you to leave. That Regan bitch stole your client. I went to your job, so I could have a meeting with Mr. Stokes about it all. Thanks to a little information that an old client gave me, he and I were able to have a long conversation about how I could help him with a problem that he's having at home."

"What kind of problem?"

"That's confidential, babe, but he was so grateful for my assistance, that he said he'd be happy if you'd stay with the company. He even said that he had some ideas about expanding your territory to help make up for the loss of the doctor's business.

"You blamed me for everything, because it was my fault. All of it. That kid knew I was going to flip when I found out he worked in your building. He baited me. And I know I could have handled things differently when you were out with the doctor. I was just so angry. You looked like you were having such a good time with him. I was jealous as fuck. Apparently I'm a bit of an asshole when I'm jealous, Princess."

"Shhh, you talk too much," I say pulling him closer to me. "This is a club not a therapy session."

He bends down and kisses me again. This time the kiss

is slower. Sexier. Not as desperate. I run my hand across the top of his head, and down his neck, doing my own sort of exploratory check.

He groans in my mouth. "Let's go home, baby."

"Not until you dance with me," I say.

"I'll dance with you at home all night if you want. We can dance naked. We can dance while we eat bacon. We can dance while we watch *Downton Abbey*."

I laugh at him.

"Sounds like a good idea, doesn't it?" He smiles brightly.

"I want to dance with you here. Where everyone can see that the king is taken."

He holds me around my waist and leans his forehead against mine.

"Is he?"

"If he wants to be."

"He does."

"Then he should dance with me."

There's a reason why the club is one of Cutter's favorite businesses to manage. It's obvious that he loves music, and he's a terrific dancer, which is sometimes difficult when you're as tall and muscularly built as he is. I could stay in his arms all night.

"You're a great dancer. Why didn't I know this about you?"

"I never dance in public."

"Why?"

"It ruins the persona. I'm supposed to be a charismatic tough guy in here."

"That's not your persona."

"Then I'm in big trouble."

"You're the good guy in the white hat. The friend who protects. The brother who worries. The boss who cares. The lover who—"

"The lover who what?"

We're swaying and grinding against each other's bodies closer now. I can feel how stiff Cutter is through his jeans. It reminds me of all that I've been missing this time we've been apart.

"You see what you do to me, princess?"

"I can feel it," I say seductively.

"This dress is sexy as fuck. You should be wearing it while tied up somewhere in my house. Dress up to your waist. Wall against your face."

His words make my core clench.

"I wore it for you, so you better like it."

"Is purple your favorite color? First the vibrator, now the dress."

I wrap my arms around his neck as we continue to dance. Rocking our hips back and forth against each other. This probably isn't the best idea, because I'm not wearing any panties, and I'm getting wetter by the minute.

"Purple is the color of royalty, and since I belong to the king, I thought it only fitting that I wear his royal colors."

A wicked grin spreads across Cutter's face.

"Can we go home yet, because you're talking all types of sexy shit that's going to get you into a lot of trouble in this club. I'm not adverse to spreading you out on that bar top and licking you clean for the entire club to see."

"You'd never do that!"

"I'm into a lot of shit, princess. You still don't know the half of it."

THIRTY

SLOAN

"Your place or mine?"

"Yours. I haven't been in my house in days, and it probably stinks to high heaven. I think I left old food in the kitchen trashcan."

"Mine it is."

When we arrive in front of Cutter's door, Kyle peeks his head out of his apartment.

"You brought our girl back?"

Cutter nods. "Yep."

"Sweet. I guess I'll see you when you come up for air then?" he says to me.

"Okay," I say a little surprised by their friendly exchange with each other. "We'll catch up tomorrow."

"I'll get the brie and crackers, you bring the prosecco."

"Deal."

"When did you two become so chummy?" I ask Cutter after Kyle shuts his door.

"I went around and met all of the tenants. I had to get a detailed list of repairs for Pete to start working on. We talked for a few. He's not so bad."

After we walk inside of the apartment, Cutter shuts the door with his foot and his hands immediately begin ripping off his clothes.

"I'm jumping in the shower," he announces grumpily.

"Um, okay."

I'm a little disappointed. I thought he was ripping off his clothes, and then he was going to rip off mine. I guess there's plenty of time for that though. It's not like I was off to war. It's only been a few days.

"Maybe I should grab a couple of things from my place?"

"I washed all the clothes you left over here. You don't need to go over there if you don't feel like it."

"It's literally ten steps away. I'll be right back."

"Okay. Take my key to let yourself back in."

My apartment ends up not being as bad as I thought it'd be. In fact it looks a little cleaner than I remembered. The trash is empty with a fresh liner in the can. My floors look swept. My mail is neatly stacked on my counter. My bed is made. Clothes that I'm sure were on the floor have been folded neatly at the end of it. There could only be one person who would break into my apartment and leave it better than when they entered. This man is so good to me.

"Did you go into my apartment while I was gone?" I ask when I return.

"Maybe."

Cutter walks out of the bathroom looking like one of those hot Instagram models. The ones who flash their abs, and their tats, holding a cute dog or cooking half naked in the kitchen. The only thing he's wearing are a pair of loose, navy blue sweats. No shirt. No shoes. I can still see a few water droplets on his back, and it's taking every ounce of self-control I have not to go lick them off.

"Either you did or you didn't."

"I did if you think it looks wonderful, and I didn't if you're mad I went in without your permission."

"Then you did. Thank you. I appreciate you taking care of it while I was . . . getting my head together."

"No thanks necessary. I needed something to keep myself busy anyway since someone wanted to take herself off the grid for a while."

I notice a new piece of furniture in the living room.

"When did you get this love seat thingy?"

I don't like it.

"Two days ago. It was sitting in the basement of the carriage house, so I brought it over."

"It's too small for you just like everything else in here."

"Yeah, well, shopping for furniture isn't my thing. I'll figure it out later."

He goes to the kitchen sink and starts rinsing a couple of dishes.

"So . . . uh I guess I'll take a shower. It was a little sweaty in Lotus."

"Okay, I'll pick out a movie."

What in the ham sandwich is going on with him? We were all hot and heavy at the club, and now that we're home he's cooled off considerably. Did he change his mind about me between there and here? Is he angry that I'm going to hang out with Kyle tomorrow?

When I finish my shower, one of my favorite comedies, *Bridesmaids*, is cued up and there is an assortment of salty snacks on the two little TV tables he has set up.

"Great," I say hopping up on the love seat next to him. Deciding I'll just make the best of the night. "I love this movie."

"Yeah, it's a funny one."

"So what did you decide about your brother?"

"Which one?"

"Actually, both."

"I went to talk to Camden when I was looking for you. I think we understand each other better now. My expectations of him have always been super high, because he's my older brother and he's always put me first. But now that he and Jade are together, I have to understand that sometimes she'll come first."

"True but you had some fair complaints."

"I did but he admitted that he was wrong, and that's all I really needed. Awareness. Respect. We're considering having me manage the secondary businesses myself, and he and Roman focus on the fixes. Me and Benny would only have to come in when needed."

I roll my eyes.

Him and his gun.

"And what about Stone?"

"We're going to look for him together."

"The information you got didn't tell you the name of the prison where he's being held?"

"Yeah but he's out."

"Well I think that's a good idea you going to look for him."

"Not sure what we'll find when we find him, but willing to try."

I lean back on the end of the couch, and Cutter pulls my legs up on his lap and starts to give me a foot massage. He has the oddest, almost constipated look on his face and after watching the first fifteen minutes of the movie in silence, I've had enough.

"What's wrong, Cutter? Are you nervous about meeting Stone?"

"No."

"Are you mad that I made plans with Kyle? I thought you liked him."

"I said he was okay, not that I liked him."

"So you're mad?"

"No, Sloan. I'm fine if you want to hang out with him. He's your friend."

"Then what is it? We haven't seen each other in days, you were all over me in the club, and now you're giving me foot rubs while we watch movies with a scowl on your face. What's up."

He stops rubbing my feet and looks me in the eyes.

"Do you believe in love, Sloan?"

"I think we've had this conversation before."

"Is the answer the same?"

"No." I swing my legs down off of his lap and climb over to straddle his lap. "No, my answer is not the same."

"So what's changed in a matter of days?"

"Everything's changed. A man that I'm crazy about did everything within his power to make me happy. You got my crappy job back, which I'm not going back to by the way. You performed a miracle by not only talking to Dawn but impressing her, and if you think I don't know that Damien was heavily persuaded to dump Dawn, you're delusional. He would have stayed with her just to get under my skin for the next ten years if he could have.

"I know you're behind it. I don't know what you did, and I don't need to know. What's important is that I realize that you did it for me. So I'm thinking that you might have done of all of that because you either have too much time on your hands or what's more likely– you're falling for me."

I start to run my fingers across his chest. Tracing one of his intricate warrior tats. It's one of my favorites. He grabs my right hand and kisses the inside of my wrist. One of his favorite spots on me.

"I can't think when you touch me like this. We're having a serious conversation. Something I don't do often. So pay attention."

"I'm sorry," I say in a cutesy voice. "What else did you want to say."

"I'm saying that the plan was to fuck the fantasy of you out of my head and go back to my old life of titty bars and one-night stands."

"Yuck, that sounds like a crappy plan. I don't like that plan," I say as I start to kiss his chest lightly. Ignoring his requests to "pay attention."

"Obviously it didn't work. It completely backfired. I was fooling myself. I only wanted more of you after we slept together, and I want even more now."

"You could try again."

"Try what?"

I start to feel him stiffly poking through his pants.

"Try fucking the fantasy of me out of you. We could keep trying until it sticks," I tease as I start to gyrate on his lap like a stripper.

He places his hands on my hips to still them.

"You're not playing fair."

"I play to win, your majesty."

"Our relationship is not just about sex anymore. You know that, right?"

"Is that what's wrong with you? You don't think we're on the same page? We are, my sensitive little caveman. It was never just about sex between us. I was just too stubborn to see it."

I push myself off of his lap, stand up, and push my sweats down to the floor. Stepping out of them one by one. Then I pull my sweatshirt over my head and toss that aside as well.

A smile finally spreads across my brooding Viking's face.

"Purple underwear?"

"Do you like them?"

"I do."

My new favorite thing (Cutter's dick) angrily bounces up and down as he frees himself of his sweats and boxers. Sometimes I wonder how that thing fits inside of me. Yet it always seems to work out.

"Grab the condom off of the counter over there, and come sit back down on your king," Cutter orders as he hungrily licks the corner of his lip. "And keep the panties on."

"Well how's that going to work?"

After Cutter rolls the condom on, I spread and straddle my legs across his lap. He slides the crotch of my panties to the side and pulls on the back of them so that they ride up the crack of my ass.

"Sit. Down."

He holds on the back of my panties like the reins of a saddle. Guiding me farther and farther down his cock. Until I'm so deeply seated that I'm perfectly full.

"Now move," he orders by my ear. Holding his makeshift "reins" with one hand and wrapping the other around my throat.

I start lowering my hips down on his cock, taking light gasps as my body becomes once again accustomed to his girth. I missed this so much. This is how it always should be. I start to pick up momentum, bouncing and winding my hips, as he meets me stroke for stroke. The sensation of the fabric between my butt cheeks, his hand around my throat, and the feeling of him inside of me are quickly building a tightness in my core that's building and building.

My eyes close shut from the pure pleasure.

"Look at me," he demands gruffly.

I pop my eyes back open.

"I am," I whimper.

"I love you, princess. You belong to me now."

He pulls the reins tighter.

Fuck.

I can't even say it back. I can't say shit. I fall forward. My hands holding onto the top of his head as I continue to wind and bounce. I feel like there's a runaway train inside of me. It's almost like an out of body experience. I'm coming and it's going to be hard.

"That's my girl," he growls in my ear. "Work that pussy for your king."

His dirty words push me over the edge.

And I claw at his entire head while I free fall in orgasmic bliss.

After he thrusts up a couple of more times inside of me, he finds his own release, spewing a few intelligible profanities. I love that I can make him feel as out of control as he makes me.

As we hold onto each other, breathing heavily, we both start laughing.

"I think we might end up killing each other before this is over," I say panting.

"And what a sweet death it would be."

He kisses me softly against my neck.

"I love you too, Cutter."

"Good that would have been real embarrassing if you didn't say it back."

I laugh again.

"Did I tell you that I'm going to be an interior decorator?"

"No, baby, I was too busy fucking your brains out."

"Well I am, and after Bitsy's nursery, my next project is going to be this apartment."

"How much is that going to cost me?"

"I don't know if I should charge you. I mean I do owe you a huge debt for fixing my life, don't I?

"No, princess."

He wraps his hands around one of my breasts and slides the other in my hair at the base of my neck.

"I'm happy to say that your debt is paid in full."

Cutter was the wild, badass, King brother who fell hard for the glamazon, but STONE is a tough, brooding, felon who is new to the family.

He's determined to get what he thinks he's owed by any means necessary, but will it be at the expense of the innocent Ariana?

"Stone is hands down my favorite King brother."
-Amazon Reviewer

Grab this intense King romance now.

DOWNLOAD BROKEN INSTANTLY
Also Available On Audio

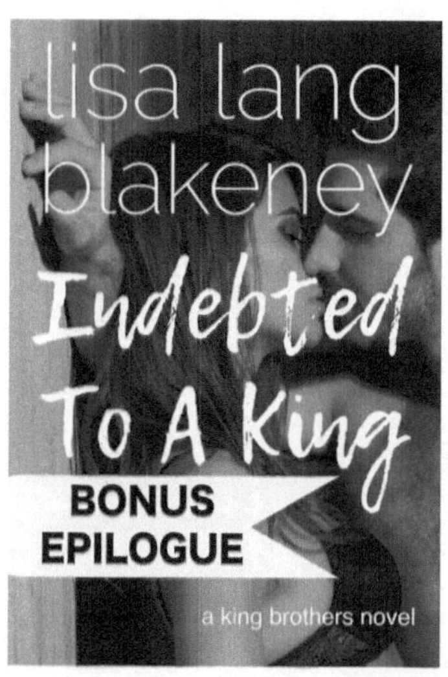

INDEBTED BONUS EPILOGUE

Sometimes you don't want a story to end, and I definitely felt that way about Cutter and Sloan. I wrote an extended chapter, long after the book was completed, which continues their story. It contains a "bareback" love scene.

CLICK THIS LINK TO DOWNLOAD IT INSTANTLY

WHERE YOU CAN FIND ME

1. I have a VIP mailing list. I only send free books, new release, sale or special giveaway information to this group. No spam. You can join here: http://LisaLangBlakeney.com/VIP .

2. I have a private Fan & Readers Group also known as my "Ninjas" a.k.a. "Alpha Romance Warriors" where I share all things new going on, teasers, yummy pics, and just chit chat. It's a closed group for ages 18+ and over, and what we post won't show on your public feed: https://www.facebook.com/groups/romanceninjas/

3. I have a special ARC team. If you enjoy my books and would like a free advanced reader copy of my next book in exchange for an honest review on release day, then feel free to apply. There are only a certain number of slots and participation is strictly enforced, but I'd love to have you:) To apply, please go here: http://lisalangblakeney.com/arc-reviewers/

ACKNOWLEDGMENTS

This is my sixth novel, and I think I'm finally starting to carve out a "process". Part of which includes NOT cooking on heavy writing days or release week, and asking the folks on my virtual team the same questions ten times in a row. (lol!)

That's why I need to thank in no certain order:
The love of my life, Deric; my loving & understanding daughters (the A team); my awesome mother-in-law, Noemi; as well as my supportive besties: Erica, Tracy, Vicki, Donna, Robin, Kelly, Stacey, and Kelly J.

Thank you to my editor who works hella fast and calms me down, Marla Esposito; my readers group leader, Johnnie-Marie Howard; the woman who straight up has my back, Lauren Valderrama; and all of the amazing authors and bloggers I have met at live book signings this year.

A HUGE thank you to all of my amazing Ninja Alpha

Romance Warriors and my bomb ass Street Ninjas. You ladies are (as usual) amazeballs!

*Special shout out to the super ninja who named Sloan's nemesis (Regan) **Gayle Fulawka**. Thanks so much!

Finally, I want to thank every single reader who has taken a chance on me and my alphas. You all are awesome! Please keep reading. My alphas demand it!

Love Y'all,
-Lisa

ABOUT THE AUTHOR

Lisa Lang Blakeney is an international bestselling author of contemporary romance sold in more than 28 countries. Worried that her fellow PTO moms might disapprove, she wrote and published her steamy debut novel Masterson under a different title and pen name in August of 2015.

Thanks to strong reader support of her alpha male character, Roman Masterson, she was encouraged to continue with the series and published the entire Masterson Trilogy the following year. She hasn't looked back since and continues to write novels featuring strong alpha men and the smart women they seek to claim.

A romance junkie for sure, you can find Lisa watching a romantic comedy, reading a romance novel, or writing one of her own most days of the week. If she's not doing that, she's outside in the garden tending to her roses.

Lisa is the wife of one alpha (whom she met in college), mother to four girls, and two labradoodles. Get news on releases, sales and giveaways when you become one of Lisa's VIP readers at : http://LisaLangBlakeney.com/VIP

www.ingramcontent.com/pod-product-compliance
Lightning Source LLC
Chambersburg PA
CBHW051646180726
48284CB00006B/1880